MW00488149

# SPARTANBURG

## RICHARD FLEMING

LifeRich
PUBLISHING

Copyright © 2019 Richard Fleming.

All rights reserved. No part of this book may be used or reproduced by any means, graphic, electronic, or mechanical, including photocopying, recording, taping or by any information storage retrieval system without the written permission of the author except in the case of brief quotations embodied in critical articles and reviews.

This novel is a work of fiction. However, several names, descriptions, entities, and incidents included in the story are based on the lives of real people.

LifeRich Publishing is a registered trademark of The Reader's Digest Association, Inc.

LifeRich Publishing books may be ordered through booksellers or by contacting:

LifeRich Publishing
1663 Liberty Drive
Bloomington, IN 47403
www.liferichpublishing.com
1 (888) 238-8637

Because of the dynamic nature of the Internet, any web addresses or links contained in this book may have changed since publication and may no longer be valid. The views expressed in this work are solely those of the author and do not necessarily reflect the views of the publisher, and the publisher hereby disclaims any responsibility for them.

Any people depicted in stock imagery provided by Getty Images are models, and such images are being used for illustrative purposes only.
Certain stock imagery © Getty Images.

ISBN: 978-1-4897-2165-5 (sc)
ISBN: 978-1-4897-2164-8 (e)

Library of Congress Control Number: 2019934116

Print information available on the last page.

LifeRich Publishing rev. date: 03/13/2019

# CONTENTS

# ONE

# A Chill

"A man is following me," muttered Abigail Marie Potter, aloud but to herself. "A Nigra man, I'm sure." She glanced behind where she had been slowly walking, convinced that someone had slipped out of sight and among the trees.

The sky was a dull gray, boring, she thought, after such a bright and beautiful day. It was hot, and the air, still and humid, hung around her like an old worn out nightgown. She was not feeling good, it being "that time of the month," and she had skipped the Sunday evening church service that she regularly attended. Instead, she had gone to the general store up the road to pick up some medicine, some Lydia E. Pinkham's Vegetable Compound, which a doctor had once suggested. However, she had more faith in the other item, a large bottle of Rousseau's laudanum.

Abigail had long suffered from the side effects of her monthly period, and even at this young age she had become somewhat addicted to the laudanum compound. Of course the mixture also contained a good measure of alcohol, which as a good church member she abhorred.

"It's just medicine," she protested to her husband Jacob, for he had objected vigorously when he learned she was taking the laudanum mixture. Now she had to hide it from him, but tonight he was gone on a trip to Hendersonville up in North Carolina, so it was no problem.

The store was nearly a half-mile from Abigail's home, a sturdy two-story farmhouse with three white columns on the front porch. The eighty acre farm in back of the house and other out buildings had been

1

given to Jacob Potter by his father, Tom, as a wedding present and the newly weds had moved there just after the new year. The street in front of the house was sparsely populated, lying just below the tracks of the Southern Railway, which ran from east to west toward Spartanburg. There were numerous places where the woods crowded the roadway on both sides.

Abigail stopped for a moment, the scared feeling beginning to arise in the pit of her stomach. She looked back to her right where she thought she detected the rustling of leaves, then pivoted until she had turned a complete circle. Although she saw nothing, she was even more convinced that someone was there. She began walking again, increasing her pace. It wasn't a matter of outrunning the trouble, rather just a hope she could reach a safe haven before her pursuer made his move.

The safe haven was not too much farther, but she began to worry about that. Her husband was not home, and it wouldn't be safe inside if the man were in there with her. She wondered if she might not be better to go on past and try to reach the Foster's place that was not far beyond her house. Of course, that house was set back from the street and at the end of a long, wooded path. Besides, the Fosters might well be at church. Her own house was the best choice.

It was not far now, and she quickened her pace once again. The woods on her right ended and the grassy expanse of her lawn appeared. It was nearly dark as she turned up the cobblestone path that led to her front porch. She hazarded a quick glance back up the road but she could see no one there.

"He's in those woods," Abigail shouted, although there was no one at her house to hear. Bounding up the steps and onto the porch, she began to open the front door, which was unlocked. This brought her to a stop.

"What if he beat me here," she thought, "and what if he is already inside?" Her fears paralyzed her for a moment, and she could not move. She felt the sweat on her brow, and violently wiped it off, not sure about what to do next. Maybe it would still be best to try to get to the Foster house.

That notion had been rejected once before, and she rejected it again. Pushing the door open, she rushed inside, turning to throw the dead bolt after slamming the door shut. She leaned back against the door, breathing heavily. She shook her head, as if to clear her mind, and the silver brooch, holding her tresses together in the back, flew off. The sound of it hitting the floor startled her. She imagined the noise was coming from the next room. Then she wondered if it was someone on the porch.

Abigail stood for a moment in the entrance hall, peering cautiously into the parlor, which was just ahead. Her eye fell on the telephone attached to the wall to the left of the doorway to the parlor. Jacob had insisted that they have one of the new telephones, and they were both proud of the fact that they had one of the few phones in the neighborhood. She could call someone for help, but who could it be? There was a telephone at the store, which also served as a post office, and it was the closest. She could ask the operator to send the police, but from where? The Spartanburg police might not come. Her home was outside the city. The sheriff would respond, but it would take him too long. There was a town marshal in Glendale, but he barely had his feet on the right side of the law. Jake said he was lazy to boot.

Abigail saw the brooch on the floor, and stooped to pick it up, struck suddenly by some clarity of thought. The back door needed to be locked. She could not remember if she had locked it earlier, but this would be the most logical place for the man to try to come in. She glanced at the steps just inside the parlor to her left. There were three steps, then a landing where the staircase took a right turn and thirteen more steps to reach the second floor. Yes, it might be strange that she knew exactly how many steps there were, but she did. Maybe the safest thing was to just go up there and barricade herself in the bedroom she shared with her husband.

Despite being quite faint just a moment earlier, Abigail, feeling better, was filled with an infusion of strength and resolve. She lunged forward, still clutching the bag with the medicine and her displaced brooch. It was dark in the house, but she had no difficulty crossing the parlor, through the dining room and into the kitchen where she placed the bag and the brooch on the table. Hurrying to the door that led onto the back porch, she was dismayed to find it unlocked. She closed the latch and stepped back, deciding quickly to not go out onto the porch.

"Oh, Lord," she cried aloud. "He could be in here already."

She ran back through the kitchen, but stopped just before entering the dining room. She remembered her need for what was in the medicine bag, and grabbed it from the table when another thought hit her.

"A knife, a knife," she said. "I need to get a knife."

She went to the counter, and opened a drawer and picked up a butcher knife. She held it in her right hand with the eight-inch blade pointing forward. Clutching the bag of medicines in her other hand, she ran back through the dining room and parlor without looking to either side. Flying up the stairs, she entered the bedroom and shut the door. There was no lock, but without hesitation, she began dragging furniture to place against the door. The dresser was too heavy for her to move, so Abigail took out each of the four drawers, pulled the heavy piece to the door and pushed it tightly against the frame. She replaced the drawers, then sat down on the bed, breathing heavily.

"It's the best I can do," she said, as if someone were there to hear her. "I don't suppose it'll hold him though, it he's determined to have me."

Another thought came to her suddenly. "Where is Sally, I wonder? Could he have done away with her?" Sally was her little black Scotch terrier, who usually was quick to greet her when she came into the house. The thought concerned her greatly for a bit, but she put it away.

Sinking back on the bed, Abigail was suddenly overcome by fatigue. She tried hard to remain alert, listening for sounds that would betray her stalker. Mysterious creaking sounds were not strangers to the house, but she was sure that she heard someone on the stairs. Then nothing came of it. Her attention to that perceived danger began to dissipate as the severe cramping returned to her belly and her lower regions. A wave of nausea nearly overwhelmed her, then died away.

"Oh God, it hurts," she cried, tears forming and leaking down her cheeks. "My medicine, my medicine."

Panic stricken, she began searching for the bag of medicines, frightened at first that she might have left it somewhere downstairs.

Then she recalled having brought it with her, and she was greatly relieved when she saw the bag resting partly under the cedar chest at the end of the bed.

"Thank you, God," she said, lifting the bottle of laudanum from the bag. Ignoring the bad taste, she took two large gulps of the liquid she had come to love. It would help her sleep, but she also knew it would make her drunk. The only thing that mattered to her now was to get relief from the pain, and to try to sleep. After a visit to the closet where the chamber pot was kept, she fell into the bed, not even bothering to pull the covers down. Sleep came very soon.

# TWO

# An Innocent Abroad

It was later in the morning than Will Fair had intended to arise. He was expected at a new job in Wellford that day, and it meant he had to catch a train. His wife, Rosa, had tried to wake him earlier but he had gone back to sleep. He wasn't looking forward to facing her either. She had been all over him when he had come home the night before, and he was sure more of the same awaited him now.

"Are you up yet, you lazy dog," came the call from the kitchen. "You ain't goin' to make that train if you don't hurry."

Rosa wasn't really his wife, at least not in the legal sense, for they had never gone through with getting a license and paying the fees. He had been with her for 14 years, and he sometimes wondered why. She had been quite pretty back in the early days, but that was some hundred pounds ago. She didn't do much anymore to try to look good, but he supposed he was part of the problem himself, for he failed to pay her much attention. That, and the four kids they had together had cooled their ardor considerably. She was a good cook, though, he had to admit that, and it was easier to just stay with her.

He had beaten her once, when her nagging had driven him to distraction, but he had felt very bad about that and it hadn't happened again. Some of his friends insisted that wives had to be beaten now and then to keep them in their place. He supposed they were right, but he just didn't feel good about it. He had been unfaithful a few times, of course, but he reckoned that he had been a decent mate, all considered.

He was out of bed and pulling on his pants when Rosa came into the bedroom.

"This is what happens when you stay out drinkin' all night," she complained as she tossed him a clean undershirt. "You ain't good for nuthin' the next day."

Will was seized with a sudden desire to kiss her. He could never have explained why, but he grabbed her and pulled her tight against him. She struggled and shook her head, preventing him from kissing her on the mouth. She wrested an arm free and pounded him on the chest, pushing away at the same time. He laughed and let her go.

"Why are you tryin' to kiss me, Will Fair? You was out screwin' some floozy last night I imagine, so don't be tryin' it with me."

"You're wrong about that, Rosa. I was just out with some of the guys on the old ball team."

"Ball team, hell. You ain't played no ball in years."

"Well, we don't play no more, but we like to git together and go over the old times." They'd had a good team once, one of the best colored teams anywhere around. It was true that he had spent some time with his baseball friends, but he knew Rosa was not to be convinced. Of course, it wasn't all he had been doing last night.

"Yeah, you're still playin' all right, but it's with them young gals you're playin'. How can you do that and face the preacher down at the church every Sunday?"

"'Cause I ain't doin' nothin' wrong. The preacher was there himself, you can ask him anytime."

"You gotta take the boy down to the mill before you go off on the train," she said, changing the subject.

The boy she mentioned was their 14 year-old son, whose name was Tom. "What you talkin' about woman? I got no time to take him anywhere."

"Well, I ain't talkin' about the Glendale Mill, I mean Thompson's Mill down at the creek."

"That ain't no real mill, not much more'n an old blacksmith shop."

"Don't matter 'bout that. Old man Thompson said he'd pay Tom one whole dollar for comin' there today and doin' some cleanup work. We need that money."

"Can't disagree with that none," said Will. "But why's he need me to take him there? He knows the way."

"Cause I don't want Thompson to take advantage of Tom. If you're there with him, the man will know he has to be fair."

Will couldn't really see the logic in that, but he was tired of arguing, knowing it wouldn't make any difference anyway. He sat down to put on his shoes. "Got anything to eat?" he asked Rosa.

"I can cook you some eggs, but I ain't got no meat. I could fix you a lard sandwich."

"That'll do, I reckon," said Will, though he was thinking that a nice pork chop would have been quite fine.

"Why did you have to come?" asked Tom later as they made their way to Thompson's place. "I know what to do." The boy was already taller than his mother and gaining rapidly on his dad. He was becoming a bit difficult to handle, but his father looked on him now with pride.

"Cause your mama wanted me to," answered Will, with a laugh.

"That ain't no good reason," argued Tom.

"It's good enough, Tom. You'll learn that when you get older."

They soon arrived at Thompson's and the proprietor greeted them with a sneer. "'Bout time you got here," he said to Tom.

"Treat the boy right now, George," said Will, "or you'll answer to me." Thompson had a reputation of working his help hard, and sometimes forgetting what he promised to pay.

"You kin take him home with you right now, if you feel that way," snarled Thompson.

"That ain't necessary," said Will. "He'll do the work right fine. Just remember what I said." With that, Will Fair hurried away, worried now that he would miss the train that would take him to Spartanburg and connect to the one to Wellford.

He was right to be worried, because by the time he was in sight of the White Stone station, he could see the train pulling out. "Damn," he cried out, "I've missed it."

A local farmer, named J. H. Pickens, was passing on the other side, and he noted the look of dismay on Will's face. He turned back to see the departing train, and nodded to Fair, but said nothing. Will acknowledged the nod with one of his own, but did not speak. He hurried on past the train depot, and turned in at the house of a friend, Nathan Black. Nathan was on the front porch speaking with another of Fair's good friends, Will Glenn.

"Hello boys," was the greeting by Will Fair as he climbed the first steps up to the porch. Nathan Black stood up from the old worn-out sofa that sat under the front window.

"What you doin' here Will Fair? Thought you was s'posed to be on that train." Nathan turned to Glenn, who was standing in front of an old wooden ice box, one of its doors hanging by one hinge. "I think he missed it."

"Reckon I missed it all right, Nathan," agreed Fair. " You ain't soundin' too sorry for me neither."

"Don't reckon so," laughed Black. "I told you to get home early last night."

"Wasn't that. I had to take my boy over to Thompson's."

"Well, I'd be glad to offer you a cup of coffee—might ease your pain."

"I need to get to Wellford. No time for no coffee."

"You can still catch the electric car over to Glendale," suggested Will Glenn, wanting to be helpful. "That'd git you up to Spartanburg."

"You're right, Will," said Fair. "Might still get the train over to Wellford. But I'd better hurry. No time to talk with you gents."

Fair jumped down from the stairs and set off with determination along the street, heading for the road up to Glendale. He felt the urgency now, and he alternated between a slow trot and a fast walk. As he neared the lane that led to the Foster house, he saw the young woman coming down the wooded path to the street. He'd seen her before, and knew she was the wife of Jacob Potter, a farmer he had worked for a time or two.

"Now that's a fine lookin' woman," he muttered to himself. "Mighty fine."

———◆———

Abigail Potter had awakened with a dry mouth and a bad headache. The first thing she saw was the half-empty laudanum bottle sitting on the cedar chest. The cap was not visible and that concerned her. She was still in her clothes from the night before, and was surprised to realize that she had never been under the covers all night. She sat up and while turning to put her feet on the floor she noticed the dresser still pushed up against the bedroom door.

"What?" she started to ask, and as her head cleared she began to remember something of what had happened the night before. "Oh, the man! He was here in the house." She stood now and walked over to the window that stood on the west side of the room. She pulled the curtain back and peeked cautiously at the yard below. There was nothing unusual to see.

As she turned back toward the room her eyes focused on the bed where she noticed a spot that could only be blood. She assumed that her flow was starting, which usually brought some relief, although just now the cramping had started again. She walked to the cedar chest and picked up the bottle of laudanum. She took one swig, and raised the bottle to take another, then thought better of it. Although realizing that she should get something to eat, the idea of fixing something right now was not appealing.

"I must get out of these clothes," she said aloud, and then remembered that the dresser needed to be moved back. She had best do that before putting on fresh clothes, she thought. It was a matter of reversing what she had done the night before, but she found it more difficult this morning, when the adrenaline rush had dissipated.

In a few minutes Abigail had restored the room to its usual order, and placed the laudanum bottle in a spot where her husband was unlikely to check, then put on a colorful cotton dress. She had decided to visit the Foster's, where she knew there would be fresh coffee and probably some kind of sweet roll.

The 200-yard walk to the Foster's house was pleasant, even though the cool morning had already been replaced by the usual heat of a South Carolina summer day. She stopped a moment on the path that led up to the house, enjoying the colorful flowers that Mary Foster was so good at nurturing. Smiling, and feeling much better, Abigail strode quickly to the door and knocked.

It wasn't long until the door opened and Abigail was face to face with young Ruth Foster, the family's only daughter.

"Hello Mrs. Potter," she said pleasantly. "Won't you come in?"

"Thank you, Ruth," answered Abigail. "Wow, something smells awfully good."

"Momma's makin' cinnamon rolls," explained Ruth. "You're just in time to have one."

"Who is it, Ruthie?" came the call from the kitchen.

"It's Mrs. Potter, Momma."

"Well, have her come in," replied Mary.

"I'm already in, Mary," laughed Abigail. "Ruth is very polite."

"That's good. Come on back, I'm in the kitchen."

"Yes, I know. The smell is wonderful."

Mary Foster had placed a big platter of cinnamon rolls on the small kitchen table, along with three plates. The rolls were steaming, and as Ruth and Abigail watched, Mary drizzled some white frosting over each of the rolls.

"Ruth, why don't you get us each a glass of water," suggested her mother. "Could I interest you in a cup of coffee, Abigail?"

"You sure could," was the reply. "I was thinkin' about your good coffee all the way over here."

"What brings you out on this Monday morning?" asked Mary.

"I had a pretty bad night, and needed somebody to cheer me up. My husband's gone to Hendersonville."

"Oh, well I'm glad you think that I might be good at that," said Mary with a smile. "What is bothering you?"

"Well, first of all, it's that time of the month again," replied Abigail with a sigh, looking down at the sweet roll on her plate and cutting off a small piece with her fork.

"Ah," groaned Mary sympathetically, glancing at her daughter and wondering if this discussion might better be avoided. Young Ruth had taken a renewed interest in the conversation, staring at Abigail to see if her condition might be noticeable. "Have things started yet?" continued Mary.

"A little, but I'm still terribly uncomfortable." Abigail smiled at Ruth, hoping to take the edge off what the girl might be thinking. "But that's not all that happened," she blurted. "A man was following me."

This announcement caused Mary to spill the coffee she was pouring. "What?" she cried. "Are you sure? Who was it?"

"It was a Nigra man," said Abigail, suddenly more sure of herself. "He followed me back from the store and I'm sure he got in the house, too."

"My goodness," exclaimed Mary Foster. "He was in the house with you?"

"I think so," said Abigail. "I locked myself in my bedroom upstairs, and I guess he gave up."

"This is awful," asserted Mary. "Did you let anyone know? The police?"

"I didn't know what to do, and I was feeling faint, besides."

"You should have come here instead of going home."

"I thought about that, but decided he might catch me before I could get there."

"You poor child," said Mary. "When will Mr. Potter be home?"

"This afternoon some time."

"Well then, you best just stay with us 'til he gets back." Mary nodded to Ruth and pointed to the little bedroom off to the side. "Get a blanket, and we'll let Mrs. Potter rest there on the bed for a time."

Ruth jumped up to comply with her mother's command, but Abigail protested. "Oh, no," she pleaded. "Don't do that. I need to get back home."

"But aren't you afraid?" asked Mary, who was feeling a bit uneasy herself.

"Yes, but I don't want Jacob to know about it. I don't think the man is anywhere around now anyway."

"Would you recognize him if you saw him again?"

"I don't know," answered Abigail, who couldn't bring any image of a black man to mind. "I didn't get a good look at him at all."

The pendulum clock on the mantle above the fireplace in the front room began to strike. At the tenth stroke, Abigail arose from her chair, still finishing the last piece of cinnamon roll. "I must go home now," she announced. "Thank you so much for the food and the conversation. I'm feeling a bit better now."

"I hate for you to go over there by yourself," said Mary. "Ruthie could come with you if you like."

"No, but thank you very much. I'm sure I will be all right now." Abigail took hold of both of Mary Foster's hands and squeezed them tightly. "And please, will you not tell Mr. Potter about this?"

"Of course not," Mary assured her as they walked to the front door.

"Thank you again," said Abigail, as she eased down the porch stairs and onto the flower and bush-lined path.

"You're welcome, honey," replied Mary, shaking her head as she watched her young neighbor move down the lane.

———•———

Vergie Moore and her friend Annie Clowney were strolling up the road, headed for the post office. Annie, whose brother was off at far away Howard University, had written him a letter and they were on the way to post it. Vergie was quite impressed by her friend, for Vergie, and most of those close to her, did not know how to read or write. Most people, Vergie believed, would have expected her to be the smart one rather than Annie, who was timid and shy, and rarely had anything to say. But Annie's family was different. They had moved here from Memphis a couple of years ago, and Annie's father did some preaching at the local colored church.

"There's the Foster house," Vergie pointed out to Annie as they approached. "I've been a maid there a few times." Vergie earned a meager living as a maid, trying to support her small son. She'd had a husband, but he left her more than a year ago, and she had taken to spending time with the Clowney family. In fact, Annie's mother often offered to keep the little boy, which was a big help. He was there now, even though Vergie was not working on this particular day.

As the two women watched, they noted that a man was passing by the path up to the Foster house, just before a young woman appeared where the wooded lane joined the main road.

"Who is that?" asked Annie, observing as the woman in question stooped to tie her shoe.

"You mean the man up ahead? I can't tell from the back, he's too far ahead." Vergie did think he looked familiar, though, and after a minute she made a guess. "He did look a bit like Will Fair, you know, who lives up the street from your house."

"No," said Annie, meekly. "I mean the woman there by the side of the road."

"I think she lives in the next house up the road there," replied Vergie. "I don't rightly know her name though. I think they just moved in there right after the new year."

Abigail Potter had not seen the two young women but she was quite aware of the presence of the Negro man who was moving quickly up the road toward her home. She stopped and pretended to tie her shoe, although her real reason was to allow the man to get on ahead of her. Her fears from the night before returned, and she thought hard about returning to the Foster house. She remained where she was until Will Fair reached her place, and watched as he went on past. The road made a slight turn to the left and Will was no longer in view. She decided to go home, and she hurried out into the street.

As she neared the path up to her porch, Abigail was dismayed at being unable to see any sign of the man who had passed by earlier. She could see part way up the road, and she thought he should be visible if he was still on the road. Her head was pounding and she was feeling faint, troubled by the idea that he could have turned aside into the woods and come back to her house. Rushing up the walkway and onto the porch, Abigail quickly unlocked the front door, and relocked it once inside. She moved immediately through the house and through the coatroom to the back door.

In her haste and confusion, Abigail unlocked the door, thinking she was locking it. She stood with her back against it, trying to gather her thoughts.

The coatroom was actually a rather cozy little room. On one side there was a small handled water pump that emptied into a porcelain sink with a drainpipe that went down through the floor and into a spillway below. On the opposite wall stood a small dresser with a mirror above it. As she took steps back toward the kitchen, Abigail saw her reflection in the mirror.

"My hair is an awful mess," she said, and she went to the dresser where a brush and comb rested on a colorful doily carefully centered. She picked up the brush and began to stroke her hair, and as she did so, her little dog, Sally, appeared, jumping up on her leg and begging for attention.

In normal circumstances, Abigail would have stopped to play with the dog, but now she did nothing to acknowledge Sally's presence. She continued to brush her hair. Then she looked down. She saw two human feet.

"Oh, God!"

# THREE

# Flight

John Suber was coming out of the general store and post office when Will Fair appeared. "Why hello, Will," Suber called, cheerily.

"Hello yourself," answered Will, who was a bit out of breath.

"You 'pears to be in a big hurry, and worn out to boot," observed John. "What's goin' on man?"

"Headed to Glendale," said Will, dropping down on a bench that sat in front of the store. "Gotta catch the electric car."

Suber took a drink of Hires Root Beer, then handed the bottle to Fair. "Here, Will, have a drink of this here root beer. It's mighty tasty."

Fair started to refuse his friend, conscious of his need to hurry on, but didn't. Root beer wasn't a usual drink for him, yet he was thirsty and was surprised at how good it tasted. "Thank you my friend," he said with feeling as he gave the bottle back to Suber.

"Why don't you just set a spell," suggested Suber. "I'd even let ya have another drink if you treat me right."

"Can't do it, John," sighed Will. "I've got to catch that car and there ain't no time to stay here and chat with you, much as I'd like it." He jumped to his feet and after waving to his friend, he moved on down the road, breaking into a fast trot. After a half mile, he reached the intersection with Glendale-White Stone road, which angled off to the north and across the railroad tracks before turning slightly to the northwest. As he came to this curve he heard a loud noise behind him.

He knew immediately what it was and he moved instinctively off the road to his right.

The Glendale-White Stone road was little more than a two-lane path with a grassy median. As he turned back, Will could see the creator of the noise coming at him at what seemed like breakneck speed and being chased by a rising dust cloud that hung in the air for a great distance behind.

"By God, that's an Overland roadster," Will exclaimed aloud, his eyes twinkling with pleasure. Automobiles were becoming much more numerous on the streets and roads of Spartanburg County, and Will regarded himself as somewhat of an expert in recognizing the different brands. He knew he would probably never own one, or even learn to drive, but he often dreamed about what it would be like to be behind the wheel. Just a few days ago he had gone into the showroom at Nesbitt's car company on Broad Street in Spartanburg to look at some of the new cars. Although he couldn't read much, he saw that one of those roadsters would cost more than $1000. Still, he enjoyed looking until one of the salesmen saw him and chased him out.

"Git outta here you damned nigger," the man had yelled. "You ain't never gonna be able to afford one of these."

Will had left in a hurry, but was quite sure the experience was worth being yelled at.

He turned his head away now from the boiling dust as the car sped by him. The driver, wearing a long duster and a white cap with a dark bill, did not acknowledge the pedestrian, his eyes focused on the dip in the road as it ran down to the narrow bridge ahead that carried the road over the little stream called Richland Creek. Will Fair watched as the vehicle disappeared from view then reappeared and swayed around a slight curve. He removed his hat and shook off the dust, and after brushing as much of it off his clothes as he could, resumed has fast walk up the road toward Glendale. As he approached the intersection with Pine Street, he saw a young couple that he knew coming toward him. There was no time to talk with them, but he couldn't ignore them either. The girl was the first to speak.

"Hello, Will," she said. "Where are you off to in such a rush?"

"Hello back, Francis," answered Will, a bit out of breath. "You too, Corbin," he added. Francis Sims was the daughter of one of Will's old baseball buddies, and Corbin Anderson was her boyfriend, someone Will did not know very well. "I'm off to catch the electric car in Glendale."

"Oh," exclaimed Francis, with a bewildered look.

"Missed the train in White Stone," explained Will, "and I got to get to Spartanburg. Sorry I can't talk with ya, Francis, but I can't waste no time." He waved good-bye and hurried on.

Reaching Glendale, Will scurried down the main street, looking for the streetcar stop. He knew it was in front of a grocery store and he was relieved to see two women standing near the stop.

"She ain't gone yet," Will surmised, and began to relax. He saw a Negro man working in the yard of a house next to the grocery, and he went over immediately to talk to him.

"Hello there friend," he began. "My name's Will Fair."

The yard worker was using some clippers to trim bushes that lined the sidewalk. He eyed Will with some circumspection before answering. He laid the clippers on top of the hedge. "Hello to you, too."

"I'm wantin' to catch the electric to Spartanburg. Has it come along yet?" asked Fair.

"It ain't come yet," replied the man. "Won't come for another ten to fifteen minutes, I reckon."

"That's good," said Will, breaking into a smile. " Afraid I'd missed it. Much obliged to you."

Will turned back and walked over to the grocery. Fruits and vegetables were stacked under the big window on which was displayed the name *Cathcart's Grocery*. Will selected a medium sized watermelon and lugged it inside to the counter where he paid the twenty-five-cent price. Back outside, he stopped by a low rock wall that extended just past the corner of the store. He smashed the watermelon, and breaking off a sizable piece, sat down to eat it. After a short conversation with a passer by, he broke off another piece of the melon and took it over toward the yard where the man was working.

"How about a piece of this here watermelon, friend? It tastes awful good, I'm thinkin'."

"Why thank you," said the man, extending his right hand. "That's mighty thoughtful. The name's Arthur Morse. I reckon Mrs. Cathcart won't mind me takin' off a minute or two."

"Surely not," agreed Will. "Glad to know ya, Arthur."

"What you doin' in Spartanburg?"

"Got to catch me the train to Wellford," explained Will. "Got a job out there."

"Wonder what that's all about," said Arthur, pointing down the street where a horseback rider was coming on fast.

"He's yellin' somethin'," said Will, who suddenly felt uneasy, "but I can't tell what it is."

———

When Abigail awakened, she had no idea of how much time had passed, nor could she really remember what had happened. She was lying on the floor of the coatroom, and the dog was licking her face. She saw blood on her leg where her skirt had pushed up, and she could see there was blood on her dress and on the floor. Her head was pounding, and it seemed like the pain was centered on her left temple. She pushed the dog away and tried to sit up.

She wondered what had happened, then remembered her fears from the previous night and the thoughts that the Negro man walking ahead of her had turned back and come into the house. That must be it, she thought, that man attacked me. She felt of her head. He must have hit her with something. She noticed a lath propped against the window frame that could easily have been the weapon. She struggled to her feet and made her way to the kitchen where she dropped into a chair.

"I've been raped," she screamed suddenly. "I need help."

She rushed through the house and out onto the front porch where she began to shout.

"Help! Help! I've been raped."

Her cry was heard by Ed Bolton, a White Stone farmer, who was returning from the store with a team and wagon. He pulled the team to a stop just past the walkway up to the porch where Abigail was continuing to scream. Jumping from the wagon seat, he ran quickly up the stone path. Bolton was a friend of Jacob Potter, and though he really did not know Abigail, he knew who she was.

"Mrs. Potter," he cried, stopping at the bottom step of the stairs that led onto the porch. "What has happened?" He wasn't sure whether he should go up and take her in his arms.

"Rape," screamed Abigail. "That black man raped me."

"Are you bad hurt," asked Bolton, still unsure of what he should do.

"Of course I'm hurt," she cried. "What do you think happens when a lady is attacked?"

"Where is the man who done it?" asked Bolton. "I don't see nobody."

"He's gone," answered Abigail, her screams now reduced to sobbing.

"We'd better call a doctor," said Bolton.

"And the police," added another voice, one belonging to Alan Wright who had arrived in a motorcar, coming from the other direction. "Is there a telephone in the house?"

"Yes," said Abigail, between sobs.

"You make the calls," suggested Ed, not too familiar with using a telephone. "I'll stay with her." Ed figured a man driving a car would know how to use these new-fangled inventions.

Wright mounted the steps and swerved around Abigail. Pushing through the door, he was pleased to see the phone in plain sight. He made the calls, deciding on the county police as the first call. Then he called Dr. W. B. Lancaster, whose office was not too far away.

In the meantime, Bolton helped Abigail to a sitting position on the top step as a small crowd began to gather on the lawn in front of the house. The word "rape" circulated among them. Mary Foster and her daughter Ruth had arrived after hearing Abigail's screams. Mary rushed up to Abigail, who was sitting next to Ed Bolton. He had finally put his arm around her shoulders.

"What is it, do you know?" she asked of Bolton.

"Says she was raped by a black man," replied Ed.

"My God, she was worryin' about that earlier. Let's get her inside and let her lie down."

They carried her into the parlor and let her stretch out on the couch. "Ruthie, get her a wet cloth for her forehead," directed Mary. "There should be water out in the back coatroom."

Vergie Moore and Annie Clowney were returning from the post office when they saw the people gathered on the Potter lawn. Curious, Vergie joined them, asking what was happening. The small crowd of white people turned to give the two black girls an angry stare.

"She's been raped by a black brute," barked the woman nearest to the girls. "You girls best get out of here right now."

Vergie was annoyed but knew the rules. A black person could not speak to a white person who had not addressed her first. She motioned to Annie, and they moved off down the street toward White Stone.

A man who had been standing at the edge of the crowd now walked away and mounted a gray mare he had left near Ed Bolton's rig. "I'm goin' to report this in Glendale," he shouted as he rode off toward the Glendale Road.

Andrew Beeson was feeling somewhat proud of himself as he rode into Glendale. He had information that he knew would be of interest. People on both sides of the street were watching intently.

"There's been a rape," he shouted but he did not slow down until he had nearly reached the bus stop. He reined in his horse and slid to the ground just at the corner of the grocery, tying the horse's reins to the hitching rail that extended down the alley to the side of the store. A crowd had gathered behind him, and he turned to face them.

"There's been a rape," Beeson said again. "A woman down at White Stone was raped by some big nigger." He shook his head as if to validate the importance and truthfulness of his news.

Will Fair could not hear all of what Beeson had said, but the words "rape" and "nigger" were clear. He felt a chill go up his spine, and he turned to Arthur Morse whose eyes betrayed his own fear.

21

"This ain't good Arthur," said Will. Both men were aware of the looks they were getting from the people standing between them and Beeson.

"That's for sure," answered Morse, who flashed a quizzical look in Will's direction. "Didn't you come from down that way?"

"I reckon I did," admitted Will. "But I don't know nothin' 'bout no rape."

Morse picked up his clippers. "'Fraid them white folks may be wonderin' about that," he remarked as he went back to his work.

Will found himself wishing there were some other black folks around as he watched two men make their way toward him from the other side of the street. They carefully avoided stepping on the rails of the streetcar track, thinking perhaps that the rails were electrified. A sound from down the track caused them to move more quickly, and Will Fair was much relieved to see the electric car approaching. The car screeched to a stop, its bell clanging, and sparks flying from the end of the pole on top of the car that connected with the high wire strung above the track.

Will waited patiently for the two white women to get on the car, before following himself. He felt conspicuous, and the apprehension showed on his face, as some in the crowd moved toward the car. He gave a weak smile to the conductor, handed him a dime, and moved to the back seat of the car. There were a half dozen people on board, including the two ladies who had just got on, and a county policeman. All watched as Fair made his way to the back. He sat down and stared at the floor, careful not to look at the policeman, thankful when the car jerked into motion. He could see one of the men on the sidewalk shaking his fist and shouting something. It was clear to Will that some of them were thinking that he might well be the rapist that Beeson had talked about. Even Arthur Morse seemed to have harbored such a thought. He wondered about the two women who had boarded with him.

There was nothing to do but wait through the ride to Union Station where he would be able to eventually board a regular train for Wellford. The time passed slowly for Will, who was becoming more agitated and distressed. It made him feel easier when the policeman got off at Pine

Street, apparently not paying any special attention to Fair. The man, whose name was John Williams, was known to Will. It was surprising, thought Will, that no words had passed between them.

When the journey finally ended, he waited as the others departed, noting the look from the two ladies who had boarded at Glendale. He was the last to get off the car, and he hurried into Union Station. He lingered near the door for a moment, watching the ladies who seemed to be walking with great determination down Magnolia Street.

Will went over to the ticket window.

"I need a ticket to Wellford," he said quietly to the agent, turning his head and surveying the room as he waited for a reply. The agent, who seemed annoyed at being bothered with such a request, did not answer, but opened a drawer and withdrew a ticket. He examined it carefully, then held it up and finally addressed the customer.

"The fare is fifty cents."

Will, who had expected the cost to be only twenty-five cents, fished in his pocket for a second quarter. He handed it to the clerk, who took it and pushed the ticket through the opening in the window. "You can wait over there," said the man, pointing to a bench on the far side of the room. "Boarding time is 30 minutes."

Shoving the ticket into his pocket, Will Fair walked slowly to the bench that he knew was reserved for black customers. He was feeling quite self-conscious, and he tried not to look at the three other people, all white, who were obviously waiting for the same train. He was the only person of his race in the room, and the awareness of his blackness enveloped and filled him with dread. He imagined the others were staring at him and accusing him.

"I wish I was on that train right now," Will muttered aloud but very quietly. "I wonder where them white ladies was goin'."

# FOUR

# Preparation

Jacob Potter had taken an early train from Hendersonville and arrived at the Spartanburg station shortly before ten o'clock. His father, Tom, was there to meet him, driving his recently purchased Model T Ford Touring Car. Tom was very proud of his new car and he stood back admiring it as his son came out of the station carrying a small bag.

"Hello, Jake," said his father happily. "Throw your bag in the back and hop in."

"Hi, Dad. Great of you to come pick me up." Jacob stopped to admire the car himself. "Course you'd do anything for a reason to drive this car," he added with a laugh. He was surprised then, when he saw the bits of dirt and straw on the back seat. He paused from dropping his bag in the back, and turned to his father with a quizzical look.

Tom picked up on the question before it was even asked. "Had to haul some hay out to the back pasture. This seemed like the easiest way."

"Haulin' hay in your brand new car? I don't believe it."

"That's what your Mom said," admitted Tom with a chuckle. "Don't worry, it'll clean up just fine."

Jacob dropped his bag into the back seat and the two men got into the car.

"I have to make a stop at Sims & Son and get some feed for your little sister's pig," explained Tom. "Then we'll get you home to that pretty wife of yours."

Jacob's little sister Sarah was only fifteen, and she was raising a pig to show at the county fair. He thought kindly of her, but was still annoyed at the delay in getting home. Abigail's behavior worried him at times, and he did not like to be away from her for any length of time. "Okay, dad," he said.

The feed store was close by on Church Street, not far from the square, and the stop took no more than 15 minutes, though it seemed longer to Jacob. His father found the turn down Pine Street and sped up as they moved toward the intersection with the Glendale-White Stone Road.

In a few minutes they had turned onto Union, the name given the street that fronted Jacob's home, passed the post office and approached the drive to Jacob's house. The view caused Jacob to become tense and stand up in the speeding car.

"What the hell," he exclaimed. "There's a crowd at the house."

"I see that," said Tom Potter. "Wonder what it is." He slowed and turned the car sharply into the drive, narrowly missing three men who were standing near the edge. Jacob vaulted over the low door before the vehicle had come to a stop and raced up the porch steps. Ed Bolton and Alan Wright were standing on either side of the front door, and Potter stopped between them, his face contorted in a look of bewilderment.

"What is going on? Why are you men here on my porch?"

"Well," began Wright, but Potter did not wait for the answer, pushing the door open and dashing inside. He stopped at the sight of his wife lying on the couch and Mary Foster kneeling next to her.

"What's happened, Mrs. Foster? What's happened to Abby?"

At the sound of her husband's voice, Abigail raised her head. "Oh, Jake, Jake," she moaned, before putting her head down again.

Mary Foster was not sure what she should say. "She'll be all right Mr. Potter, but she's had a bad time."

Jacob bent down to one knee and put is hand on Abigail's forehead. He looked in dismay at Mary before turning to his wife. "Honey, what is wrong, what happened?"

Abigail raised her head again. She began to cry, but managed to eke out the words, "I was raped."

Jacob put his arm under Abigail's shoulders and pulled her up into a tight hug. Her crying continued for a moment, before subsiding to a series of sobs. She had not intended to talk about the rape to him, but the words had just spilled out. Mary Foster withdrew and led her daughter Ruth into the next room.

Jacob continued to hold his wife, then gently placed her back on the couch so that she was sitting partially upright with a pillow behind her head.

"It's all right, Abby. It's all right. Just take your time and tell me about it."

Abigail said nothing for a brief time, but soon began to tell her story. She told him about the events of Sunday night as she remembered them, then explained about the rape. She ended with a detailed description of the black man and how he was dressed.

Tom Potter had come in to the room and heard the last part of Abigail's story.

"Let's take her over to my house, Jake, so Mom can take care of her."

Jacob thought this was a good idea, and he helped his wife to her feet. She was feeling stronger now that she had been able to confide in her husband. He lifted her into his arms and followed Tom Potter out the door and to the car.

"Lay her in the back," said Tom, shifting the luggage and wiping away the remnants of the straw from the seat.

"We're takin' you to Dad's place," explained Jacob as he laid Abigail down in the back seat of the Model T. "Wait a minute, Dad," he said, and walked quickly back toward the porch steps. He met Wright and Bolton who had followed down the stairs.

"Thank you for your help, men. And tell Mrs. Foster that I said to thank her as well."

"You're welcome," responded Alan Wright. "The police are on the way out here. We'll stay until they get here."

"Yes, that would be good," said Jacob. "And maybe you can keep them here, too," he added, indicating the crowd which continued to grow and fill the yard. He returned to the car, and waved at the people as they drove away.

Tom Potter's home was no more than a half mile away, and it wasn't long before they were moving up the driveway to a spot just short of the wide porch an the big farm house. A good portion of the crowd that was gathered at Jacob's house had followed along, some in cars, some on horseback, some in buggies, and others making their way on foot.

Tom and Jacob helped Abigail up the steps and into the house where Charlotte Potter met them.

"Here, Mother," said Tom, "help Abigail to lie down. She's had a bad time."

"Oh my," exclaimed Charlotte, looking quizzically at her husband and then her son. "What has happened? Do we need to call the doctor?"

"They've already called Dr. Lancaster," said Jacob, who had obtained that information from Alan Wright. "He should be here soon." Jacob could not bring himself to say more, incapable of saying the word "rape" to his mother.

"Just make her comfortable," advised Tom to his wife. "I'll explain it all to you later." With that, he and Jacob moved out to the porch to wait. It wasn't very long before they saw the two police cars coming up the lane.

———•———

Sheriff William James White was at his desk sipping coffee when the call came in. He had been late to arrive that morning even though his residence occupied the front part of the massive building that made up the jail. Everyone in Spartanburg was proud of the structure, built in 1895 at a cost of $40,000. Although he sometimes lamented the location of his home, White had to admit that it was spacious and attractive, facing Wofford Street and fronted by a nice lawn and a stone ledge that extended along the street. On the southwest corner of the residence, a hexagonal turret towered above the second floor. The cells were in the back part, occupying two floors, with a third floor that held a large hospital room and the scaffold for the execution of prisoners. The entire building was well ventilated, with steam heating, and electric lights throughout. A heavy, compact wall was attached to

27

the back of the residence on each side and surrounded the jail portion and its premises. Iron gates opened in the wall to a walkway leading to the Spartanburg County Courthouse. The sheriff's office was on the first floor of the courthouse.

Sheriff White's thoughts today, however, were centered on his wife, Viola, sequestered in the residence caring for two of his sons, who were suffering from typhoid fever. The older one, William, whom they called Junior, was feeling a bit better, or so he told his father, while the younger, Dean, remained quite ill. William suspected that Viola was sick herself, although she refused to admit it. The sheriff had been hoping that things stayed quiet so that he could return to the residence for lunch. His hopes sank when he was told about the rape out at White Stone.

His first call went to Moss Hayes, chief of the Spartanburg city police.

"Moss, we've got trouble out at White Stone. Some Negro has raped a white woman."

"The hell you say," exclaimed Hayes. "Anyone I know?'

"It's Tom Potter's daughter-in-law," answered Sheriff White. "I don't know the girl, but just about everybody knows Tom."

"You're right about that, and he'll raise holy hell I imagine." Hayes knew that Tom Potter was well liked and a fine man, but he could also be a pain in the neck for authorities he found wanting. "We'd better get somebody out there right away."

"I suggest we get a man or two each and go out there ourselves. We can each take a car."

The county police owned two Overland Touring Cars, as did the city. After hanging up the phone, Sheriff White strode out of the office, wondering who might be available to go with him. He strode across the yard between the courthouse and the jail, through the iron gate into the yard. Just as he entered the jailhouse, J. E. Vernon stepped out of the hallway that led to the second floor stairs.

"Ah, J. E., you need to come with me, we've got to go out to White Stone," exclaimed White. "Who else is around?"

"Well, E. L.'s upstairs," Vernon pointed out, "but nobody else is around. Williams is off somewhere." E. L. Wilson was the jailer.

28

"We can't take E. L., so I guess it will be just you and me," said the sheriff. "I reckon we'll be enough. You drive."

The county cars were parked in a small lot next to the courthouse, and the two men hurried out the door and angled across the lawn to where the cars were parked. Vernon was pleased that the sheriff wanted him to drive, for he considered himself to be the best at that job on the whole force.

"Hurry up," urged White. "The chief's on the way out there, too, and I want to be there before he is."

Vernon drove to the street and turned on the newly installed siren. He loved the sound and the feeling of power and importance it gave him. The sheriff was not so sure it was a good thing, but he was in a hurry and so he said nothing. It took less than twenty-five minutes for them to get to White Stone. A crowd continued to gather nearby and it included some angry looking men coming from the mills and farms. As he left the vehicle, Sheriff White noted that a variety of weapons were visible.

"By God, Sheriff," exclaimed Vernon. "Did you see that? One a them farmers has an old flintlock. What do you reckon he expects to do with that?"

"I guess they all think they're goin' to catch that guilty rapist. We may be in for some trouble here. Right now, though, we need to find out exactly what has happened."

As the sheriff pushed through the crowd and started up the walk to the porch of the house, a man who had been standing next to his automobile, hurried over and called out.

"Sheriff White, my name is Alan Wright and I'm the one who called you."

White looked the man up and down, as if that would determine the man's integrity. "Well, thank you for that. What can you tell me? Is the victim inside?"

"No," answered Wright quickly. "Her husband came home and took her over to his father's house."

"Did you talk to the woman? Do you know exactly what happened?"

"Not really," admitted Wright. "Ed Bolton there is the one who found her." He pointed to a man standing on the porch, behind the low rail that framed the porch floor on both sides of the steps.

"Did she tell you anything?"

"No, she just told Ed she had been raped by a black man."

A loud voice erupted from the crowd. "We better kill that nigger!"

"Got to catch him first," shouted another.

Ignoring the rising murmur around him, Sheriff White patted Wright on the shoulder. "Stay here. I may need to ask you some more questions."

Wright nodded. "Mrs. Foster and her daughter are inside. They talked with the woman and helped her. I told them they should wait for you, that you would want to talk to them."

"Thanks," said White and he ascended the porch steps with Vernon trailing behind. He stopped when he saw the city police car pull up near the walkway.

Chief Hayes jumped out of the car and waved at Sheriff White, who waited for Hayes to ascend the steps. Bud Bryson, a city policeman, emerged from the driver's side of the car and joined his boss.

"What've we got, Jim?" asked Hayes as he stepped up onto the porch. Although his first name was William, the sheriff's friends often called him Jim.

"The victim is not here," explained the sheriff, "but there's some women inside we need to question. Come in with me."

The two men went in together after asking their two deputies to stay on the porch. Mrs. Foster was sitting on the couch in the living room, and her daughter, Ruth, stood next to the door that led to the dining room.

"Are you Mrs. Foster?" asked Sheriff White, and when the woman nodded, he continued. "What can you tell us?"

"Not very much I'm afraid," answered Mrs. Foster.

"Can you tell us what happened?" Chief Hayes now entered the conversation.

"Mrs. Potter said she was raped by a Negro man. That's all I know."

"Did she describe the man?" wondered Sheriff White.

"I don't think so, least not to me." Mrs. Foster stopped for a moment, and closed her eyes, as if trying to visualize something. "Her husband came home then, and we left them alone. She might have told him something."

"Where did the attack happen, do you know that?" asked the sheriff.

"No," answered Foster emphatically. "Her husband did go through toward the back porch though. Then he came back and took Abigail over to his father's place."

Chief Hayes turned his attention to Ruth, who had remained silent.

"What about you, young lady? Can you tell us anything?"

Ruth looked at her mother and shuffled her feet before answering. She shook her head then said quietly, "She seemed awful scared."

"I'm sure she was," agreed the chief. "Anything more?"

Ruth shook her head and walked over to the couch.

"We need to talk to Mrs. Potter before we do anything else," said White.

"I agree," remarked Hayes. "There is a telephone out there and we should call in to tell our people where we are."

"You make the call," advised the sheriff. "I'm going to leave Vernon here to keep people off the scene and we'll take your man with us over to Tom Potter's."

———————

Sheriff White was the first of the new arrivals to make his way onto the porch.

"Hello, Sheriff," said Tom Potter. "Glad to see you." As he looked past to where Chief Hayes and Officer Bryson were coming, his eyes shifted further and his face wrinkled up a bit as he observed the number of others who had followed the police officers. "Looks like you brought a crowd along."

"Hello, Tom and you, too, Jacob." He turned to look out at the growing throng and shook his head. "Not much I can do, I guess, it is a free country."

"Maybe, but I ain't sure we need 'em all here just now," grumbled Tom.

"Here's the chief," noted White, as Chief Hayes came up the low stairs. Bryson did not follow, but turned to face the people who continued to gather in the yard. "They told us what happened, Jake, over at your house. How is your Mrs., is she okay now? We'll need to talk with her."

"She's restin' inside," answered Jake. "I really hate for you to disturb her. She told me everything that happened. That damned big black brute broke in and raped her, that's what happened."

"Yes, that's what we understood. Didn't see no signs of a break-in, but I left Deputy Vernon over there to check things out." Sheriff White grasped Jacob's right hand and squeezed it between his own hands. "I sure do feel for you, Jake, but we really need to talk to your wife."

"She gave me a description of the guy, isn't that all you need right now?"

"Well, it's a good start I guess, but we'll have to talk to her too."

"She said he was medium tall and stockily built," began Jacob in a voice loud enough to be heard by many out in the yard. "He had a black felt hat and a white shirt. His pants were dark and held up by suspenders."

"Anything else?" Chief Hayes wanted to know.

"She says she got up and looked out the window; she could see him headed up the road, like he was goin' to Glendale. She wanted to get my gun and shoot at him, but fainted instead."

"Is that how you found her?" asked Sheriff White.

"Well, no," said Jake. "She was in on the couch and bein' tended by Mrs. Foster. There was a bunch of people outside when I got there."

"If you don't mind my buttin' in, Jim," offered Hayes," I think we need to organize a search for this Nigra. We've got a good description of the bastard. You and me can question the lady later when things have calmed down a bit."

"Yes, I agree," said the sheriff. "We need to check in at our headquarters. Tom, do you have a telephone."

"I do," answered Tom quickly. "It's in the kitchen. Charlotte'll show you the way."

Hayes and Bryson walked over and stood next to their police car. "We'd better wait here until the sheriff comes out. He may have some new information."

"I reckon you're right chief," noted Bryson, looking out with some dismay at the gathering crowd. "I guess we'll have to start back at the scene of the crime, but what are we goin' to do about all these people around here?"

"We might be able to make use of some of them," said Chief Hayes, "but I suppose they could be a problem."

"Did you talk to the victim?" asked Bryson.

"No, her husband Jake said she wasn't up to it. We'll have to talk to her later, but we do have a description of the man, which is all we need right now. Here comes the Sheriff," noted Chief Hayes after a moment. "We'll get this search organized."

It was at this moment that a car rattled up the drive and pulled to a stop just short of where the two police officers were standing. The driver of the car was Alan Wright. He jumped down and walked quickly over to face Chief Hayes. Sheriff White was coming toward them with a look of surprise.

"We've got somebody for you," announced Wright, turning to point to where two men had emerged from the back seat holding a hefty, rumpled, and distressed looking black man between them. They pulled the man over to where Wright was standing.

"Here's your man, Chief," said one of the men, a wide and prideful grin lighting up his face. "We caught him just up the road from Jake Potter's place."

"They brought him in not long after you left," explained Wright. "Your deputy said to bring him here." These last words were directed at Sheriff White, who had come up next to the group.

"That's good, you did the right thing," said the sheriff. "What's your name, Boy," he asked, speaking now to the prisoner, who stood quietly with his head down.

"I ain't done nothin' wrong," muttered the man, not looking up. "I ain't done nothin'."

"That's not what I asked," said Sheriff White, speaking now a bit more gently. "What is your name?"

"Zeke Carter, that's my name."

Sheriff White turned to Chief Hayes. "What do you think, Chief? I reckon we'd best look into this right now."

"Yes," answered Hayes. "We'd better cuff him, though. Bryson, you got your cuffs?"

"I do, chief," responded Bryson, pulling the cuffs from his belt and moving quickly to where Carter was being held. "Put them hands behind you, Boy."

Tom and Jake Potter had both moved down so they could see and hear what was transpiring. Jake was eyeing Zeke Carter as if he was ready to tear him apart.

Seeing this, Sheriff White moved quickly up to the two men. "Jake, I'm afraid we are going to have to disturb your wife now. We have to see if she can identify this man as her attacker."

"I see that," agreed Jake. "But let me go and talk to her first before we make her face that brute." He stood for a moment staring at Carter.

"You do that, Jake," said White. "But we need to hurry. If he isn't the one, we've got to get moving on a search."

The crowd continued to grow, filling the yard around the house and pushing in close. Some were beginning to cry out against Carter, whom they quickly assumed was the rapist.

"String him up," was the cry. "Let's lynch that nigger right here," yelled one man. "Skin him alive," shouted another.

"This isn't good, Chief," remarked the sheriff, watching as Bryson began pulling Carter toward the stairs to the porch.

"I agree," said Hayes. "This crowd ain't far from bein' unruly and mighty ugly. We need to get this man inside right away."

Sheriff White turned to the crowd and help up his hand. "We want you folks to remain calm, now," he began. "We have a suspect, but we have to question him, and see if Mrs. Potter will identify him. We may need you later to help in our search if it turns out he ain't the man."

Turning away now, the sheriff addressed himself to Wright and the other two men. "Thank you, men, for bringing this man in to us. I hope this is the end of it, but it may not be. If you don't mind, I'd like you to stay here until we know something more."

"Glad we could help, Sheriff," said Wright and the other two nodded their agreement, hoping, of course, that they had the right man and looking forward to the acclaim they reckoned they deserved.

———————

After getting off the streetcar at Pine Street, County Police Officer John Williams had made his way over to his mother's house, which was only a short distance from the Pine Street stop. Since he was expected at the jail, he thought it wise to call in to let them know where he was. Fortunately, his mother had a telephone. When he reached Wilson at the jail, he was surprised to hear about the rape out at White Stone.

"God," he shouted at Wilson, "I ain't too far from White Stone. I ought to get over there."

"That'd probably be good," said Wilson. "Vernon's out at the Potter house right now."

'Mom's neighbor's got a car," remembered Williams. "I bet he'd let me borrow it for police business. Talk to you later."

Slamming down the phone, Williams hollered at his mother. "Mom, do you reckon old man Waters is home? I need to borrow his automobile."

"What, John? What are you saying? I'm fixin' you some lunch."

"Got no time for lunch, Ma. I've got important police business. Do you think Mr. Waters is at home?"

Mrs. Williams appeared in the dining room where the phone was located. "He's always home. I've already fixed you a ham sandwich, honey. It's on fresh white bread. Surely you've got time to eat that."

The thought of a piece of thick ham on his mother's fresh bread brought John up short. "I'll take a sandwich with me, Ma, but I've gotta run."

Darting into the kitchen, Williams grabbed a sandwich and kissed his mother on the forehead. "Thanks, Ma, I love you." With that he was gone.

Mr. Waters was glad to loan his car and, in a few minutes, John Williams was driving up to Jake Potter's house. There were still a number of bystanders in the yard and Officer Vernon was on the porch.

"The Sheriff's over at Tom Potter's house," said Vernon as Williams parked nearby and shut off the engine.

"What do you know, J.E.?" asked Williams, remaining behind the steering wheel.

"Not much, but we do have a description of the man. I talked to the sheriff on the phone."

"So what did he look like?" John Williams could not help thinking about Will Fair, who he had seen on the electric car.

When Vernon finished with the description as he understood it, Williams immediately started the engine. "I know who that is and I know where he is," he shouted loudly over the engine noise. "Tell the sheriff I'm goin' to Union Station to arrest Will Fair."

Vernon shook his head as he watched Williams drive off. "I hope he knows what he's doin'."

As he waited at the train depot, Will Fair thought about his day. A lot had gone wrong, although he still had a chance to get to the job waiting for him in Wellford. He was filled with dread. The announcement in Glendale about the rape had unnerved him, and he knew that some people there suspected him of being the rapist. His own demeanor had contributed to that he knew, and he was especially worried that the two ladies on the electric car might take some action against him. Then his worst fears were realized. The county police officer, John Williams, had entered the waiting room. He looked around, then headed straight over to where Will was seated.

"Hey, Boy," shouted the officer. "Stand up and keep your hands up where I can see 'em."

Will stood and raised his hands up and out to the side. "Are you speakin' to me, sir?" he managed to stammer

"You're damned right I am," said the policeman. "You're under arrest for rapin' a white woman down at White Stone."

"I ain't the man, sir," Will replied. "I ain't the man."

"Tell that to the judge," shouted Williams. "I'm takin' you to the jail."

At Tom Potter's house, there was considerable excitement. The crowd, which continued to grow, was buzzing with the news that the rapist had already been captured. The people watched while the three police officers led the suspect up onto the porch. The officers were met by Jake Potter, who had just come out from talking with Abigail. His father stepped aside.

"She'll talk to you, but you need to treat her gently," cautioned Jake. "She's still mighty upset."

As Sheriff White reached for the door handle, Jake grabbed his arm. "I'm goin' to be there too, Sheriff, and if she starts cryin', the interview is over."

The sheriff suppressed a retort, nodded his head and opened the door. Jake followed him in, then Chief Hayes. The trembling suspect was pushed in by Officer Bryson. Once inside, the sheriff stopped them in the outer hall.

"Chief, I think we should take off the cuffs now. It wouldn't really be fair to have him cuffed when we're showing him to the victim. She needs to see him in a more natural state."

"You're right, I guess," agreed the chief. He nodded at Bryson, who removed the cuffs.

Jacob Potter led them to a bedroom at the back of the house. His mother Charlotte stood next to the bed, holding a wet rag against Abigail's forehead.

"Darling," said Jacob softly. "They've brought in the man I told you about. They want you to tell them if he is the one."

"Okay," murmured Abigail. She scooted up in the bed and leaned back against the pillow. She pulled the covers up high around her shoulders.

"We're sorry to bother you like this, Mrs. Potter," said Sheriff White in an apologetic tone. "We need you to tell us if this is the man that assaulted you."

Charlotte Potter had removed the cloth and stepped out of the way. Chief Hayes took hold of the suspect's left arm and pulled him toward the bedside. The man tried to look away, not wanting to look at Abigail or have her look at him.

"Stand straight, man," said the chief. "Let her get a look at you."

Abigail stared at him for a moment, before nodding slightly. She raised her hand and motioned that she wanted him to turn around.

"Turn around, Boy," barked Officer Bryson. When the man was slow to respond, Bryson grabbed him and turned him roughly. The officers all looked expectantly at Abigail.

"That's him," she said softly, then louder. "That's him."

Sheriff White and Chief Hayes shared knowing and satisfied glances.

Upon hearing her words, the black suspect suddenly straightened and turned back to face her. "No, no," he shouted, "it ain't me, it ain't me." With these words he began ripping at the buttons on his shirt and before anyone could say anything he had torn the shirt off and threw it on the floor. The bystanders were surprised to see that he still had on a shirt that was identical to the one he had removed. Just as quickly, he began unbuckling his belt and the top button of his pants.

"Wait a minute," cried Bryson, but before he could say or do anything more, the pants of the accused man were pushed down, revealing that he had on a second pair of pants. Stepping out of the first pair, the man turned a complete circle, then looked at Chief Hayes, his eyes wide and pleading for understanding.

Abigail could not muffle a shouted "Oh!"

"Are you sure he's the one, Mrs. Potter?" asked Sheriff White.

A look of amazement had taken over Abigail's face. She bowed her head and began to sob. "He's not the one," she managed to say between sobs. "It's not him."

"Are you sure honey?" asked Jacob, stepping in and taking his wife's hand. "Are you sure."

"I'm sure," she said, bursting into tears.

"What do you think, Jacob?" inquired White. "Do we have the wrong man?"

"I'm afraid so, Sheriff. She seems pretty sure now. I think it would be good if you all left us alone now."

"All right, we'll go. We may have to talk to her again, Jacob."

"I know, Sheriff. But no more today, please."

Sheriff White nodded in agreement and spoke to Chief Hayes.

"Well, Chief. I didn't think it could be that easy anyway. We'd better explain things to that crowd out there, or they'll tear this poor fellow apart."

The three officers led Zeke Carter out onto the porch. Immediately a cry came from out of the crowd. "Hang him. String him up!"

Others began to take up this cry, but Sheriff White stepped forward and held up his hand.

"No," he shouted. "This man is innocent. The victim is sure this is not the one who assaulted her."

"String him up anyway," came a cry from someone. "He's prob'ly guilty of somethin'." This remark was followed by a large guffaw, and a sprinkling of laughter from the rest of the throng.

Charlotte Potter came to the door. "Sheriff, there's a phone call for you. It's your deputy down at the jail."

"Now what?" exclaimed White.

As the sheriff went back in to take the call, Chief Hayes turned to Officer Bryson. "We need to take this man to his home and away from this mob."

"Right, Chief."

"Wait," called Sheriff White, rushing out onto the porch. "We've got another suspect. John Williams arrested a man down at Union Station and put him in the jail."

"Well, I'll be damned," exclaimed the chief.

# FIVE

# The Mob

When Andrew Beeson returned from Glendale, he was happy to see that a crowd continued to gather in the yard in front of the Potter house. The closer he came to the scene of the crime, the greater grew his wrath against the unknown black beast who had carried out such a horrid act. It was an affront to all of white civilization, he thought, and it demanded a violent response.

Beeson surveyed the crowd, looking for someone he knew. A number of the faces were familiar, but he was searching for one of his friends who he knew would share the outrage that was driving him now. When his eyes fell on Jacob Turbett, he smiled, tied his horse to the porch rail and pushed through the knot of people milling around in front of him.

"Hey, Jacob," he shouted. "Jacob Turbett. It's good to see you."

Turbett looked up to see who was calling out to him. Delighted to see his old friend Beeson, he moved to meet him. Turbett was tall and slim, and he walked with a limp, which had continued after he cut off his big toe with a spade two years earlier.

"Hey, Andy," he called, "where've you been? Do you know about what's happened here?"

"Yep, I know. Just got back from spreadin' the word up at Glendale."

"This is bad stuff, Andy," said Turbett. "We can't have them blacks treatin' our women like this."

"You're right about that Jacob," returned Beeson, glad to find that his friend already shared the feelings that had welled up in him as he rode back from Glendale. "We need to do somethin' about it and real soon."

Turbett turned and pointed at the others concentrated in front of the porch. "We ain't alone with such thoughts."

"Do they know who done it yet?" asked Beeson.

"The sheriff was here and picked up his deputy. They locked up the house and told us to go home."

Just then a car drove up and Dillon Foxx jumped out.

"We've just been to Tom Potter's house," he announced. "They arrested a guy, but let him go."

"What?" came the cry from the crowd, almost as if it was one man, the people gathering close around Foxx.

"She said he wasn't the one," explained Foxx.

"Who said that?" demanded Andrew Beeson, who had pushed his way to the front.

"Why the victim, Mrs. Potter," answered Foxx. "She said it was him first, then changed her mind."

"Don't sound right to me," shouted Beeson, turning to face the throng, which was growing as more people returned from the other Potter farm.

Seeing that he was losing the crowd's interest, Foxx offered up another piece of information. "Somebody said he thought the sheriff got a call—maybe they arrested some guy downtown in Spartanburg."

"That sounds better," said Beeson. "Come on folks, we need to go up to the jailhouse and see what's goin' on."

"He's right," came a call from the crowd.

"Bring your weapons," shouted another.

---

Sheriff White sat at the little desk in a small room off the main corridor of the jailhouse ground floor. Although it wasn't his main office, he liked to use it when in the jail. He had entered the name of Will Fair in the logbook he kept there, noting that the man was suspected of rape. Although the official record of arrests was kept at the main desk, he liked to keep his own version. Officer Williams had filled in the official entry, and Sheriff White had just returned from a short visit to the cell where Fair was being held. It was on the second floor at the suggestion of jailer E. L. Wilson. White knew what was on Wilson's mind, for it was on his as well. He and Chief Hayes had agreed that it would be best to keep a lid on what was happening for as long as possible.

Fair had insisted that he was innocent, a common argument and readily ignored by the sheriff. White did notice that there was nothing suspicious about the clothes worn by Fair, they were neither bloody nor torn. He made a mental note to talk with Officer Williams about that. His thoughts kept returning to his wife and children, and he decided that this might be a good time to check on them. His plan was disrupted when J. E. Vernon rapped on the door and stepped in.

"Hey, Boss. Captain Hall is here to see you."

R. C. Hall was a captain of the Spartanburg city police. He followed Vernon into the room and did not wait to be greeted by Sheriff White.

"Hello, Sheriff," he said, smiling broadly. "The chief thought I should come and talk to your prisoner."

"You're welcome to it," replied White. "Do me a favor, though, will you? Check him out real good, check his clothes and body for any kind of sign he was in some struggle."

"You sure he didn't change his clothes somehow?" wondered Hall.

"I think he's just the way he was when John Williams brought him in, but I'll check with John again." Hall nodded his assent and White addressed Vernon.

"Show him the way, J. E."

Sheriff White made his way to the main desk where he encountered the jailer, E. L. Wilson.

"Hey, E. L. Did you put the prisoner in his cell or did John do it?"

"We both took him up, Sheriff."

"Did you see any blood on him? Any tear in his clothes?"

"None that I could see."

"Could he have washed or gotten rid of anything?"

"Not since I seen him and John would've never let him do anything like that either." Wilson eyed the sheriff for a moment, before offering another thought. "I suppose he could have done somethin' ahead of when John caught up with him."

White did not know enough about Fair's movements to know what could be said about that. He really hadn't come to any conclusions about the guilt or innocence of Will Fair. There was a worry nagging at the back of his consciousness, but he tried to block that out. He decided to make a quick visit to his office at the courthouse, then go to his residence.

Audrey Brown, his receptionist, was ready with a message when White appeared at his office.

"Hello, Sheriff," she said, greeting him brightly. "Solicitor Hill called and wants to see you. He'll be over soon. Oh, and Mr. Gantt wants to talk to you, too." Robert Gantt was the county magistrate.

"Thank you, Audrey," replied the sheriff, slumping into his chair with a sigh. Solicitor A. E. Hill was the city and county attorney and the Solicitor for the 7th Circuit. White wondered how Hill had learned about the arrest, for the sheriff's office hadn't yet notified him. Perhaps Chief Hayes had called.

"This ain't good," thought White. "Won't be long 'til the whole town knows."

---

It was nearly suppertime before Sheriff White made it to the family residence. He came all the way around to the front entrance, not his usual practice, but something he felt compelled to do.

His chat with Solicitor Hill had not lasted long. White informed Hill that a Will Fair was in custody, but not much was really known yet about his movements.

"John Williams is pretty sure he's our guy," explained the sheriff. "He saw him on the car in from Glendale."

"I expect you've got the damned rapist all right," agreed Hill. "Should be an easy case to prosecute."

The two men talked for a while longer, exchanging what information each possessed.

"Who knows that we've got this man in the jail?" asked White as their conversation drew to a close.

"Chief Hayes called me," replied Hill. "Said you had asked him to do that. I don't know who else heard this, but I expect the news is out and will be all over town before long."

"That's what I was afraid of," said White. "The chief and I wanted it kept quiet for as long as we could."

"I know what you're thinking," said Hill. "There was a lynching last week down in Laurens County."

Laurens County was the neighbor county to the south and Sheriff White was well aware of what had happened there. He had talked with the county officers, who had explained there was nothing they could do to stop the huge mob from dragging the prisoner out of the jail. White had been sympathetic, although he had his own doubts about how dedicated the officers had been toward protecting what they figured was a guilty Negro man.

Robert Gantt had supplied the warrant for Will Fair's arrest. He informed White that he would like to take the prisoner out to begin an investigation, but had decided against it.

"Maybe it's best we not remove him from the protection of the jail just now," Gantt had remarked.

"I agree with that, Robert," said the sheriff. "You can take Officer Williams with you tomorrow."

"Good. We need to check on all his movements," replied Gantt, who returned to his office.

There was no one on the ground floor when White entered the residence, so he climbed the stairs, expecting to find his wife in the boys' room. She was there, bent over the bed where young Dean was lying, applying a wet cloth to the boy's forehead. The sheriff nodded at his son, William, Jr., who was propped up on his own bed and reading a book.

"How is he, Mama?" asked White, who leaned over and kissed his wife on the back of the neck.

"Not good," replied Viola, not responding to her husband's attempt at affection. "His fever's pretty high," she added, straightening up and turning to face William.

"I'm sorry, Vi, wish I could do something to help."

"Dr. Blake was here earlier. He didn't help much either." Viola was not well herself, and she wasn't feeling kindly toward anybody.

Junior put down his book, and hoping for support from his father, appealed to his mother. "Mama, can I get up now?"

Viola sighed and walked over to where her other son was lying. She put her hand on his forehead. "No," she said, shaking her head. "You've still got some fever. You stay in the bed. I'll bring you some soup."

Although tempted to interfere, the sheriff thought better of it. "You listen to your mother now, Junior, and stay quiet. I'll come and see you later tonight."

White followed his wife down the stairs and into the kitchen.

"I haven't had time to fix you any supper, James," declared Viola, who usually referred to her husband by his middle name. "You'll have to wait."

"That's fine, honey," replied White. "I want to talk to you anyway. Just do what you need to."

"Well I've got some chicken soup I want to give to Dean, then I'll fix something for you."

"The soup will be fine for me too if you've got enough. You got any bread?

"There's some left from the loaf I baked yesterday."

"Where are John Earl and the baby?" Sheriff White had just realized there was no one else around. Nine year-old John Earl was the oldest of the White children, and the baby was one year-old Mary Eloise.

"I sent 'em over to your brother's house. I'm hopin' they don't catch what the boys have got."

William watched as his wife went about her work. He realized what a gem she was and he just liked looking at her.

"What did you want to talk about," she asked after a while.

"Did you know we've just put a Negro in jail who is charged with raping a white woman?"

45

"God, no! Who was the woman?"

"Well, you know we don't say that in public, but I guess I can tell you. It was Abigail Potter, Jake Potter's wife."

Viola shook her head and looked at her husband with a look of disbelief. "Do you have the right man?"

"Probably, but we're still studyin' it."

"James, I'm scared," exclaimed Viola, expressing aloud the same worry that had been bothering White all afternoon. "There was a lynching just last week down in Laurens County."

"I know, dear, and I'm afraid the word is out. There was already a crowd out at the Potter house."

"What will you do if they come?" asked Viola, already afraid she knew the answer.

"You know what my duty is, Vi. I have to protect the prisoner."

"Even if he's a Negro and he is guilty?"

"Even then, dear. We don't know yet if he's guilty, but it really doesn't matter."

"Nobody would blame you if it happens, James. What about us in here? Would we be in danger if a mob storms the jail?" Viola admired her husband's principles, but there was such a thing as discretion and wisdom. "I read about a case in Texas where the mob burned down the whole jail and courthouse tryin' to lynch an inmate."

"That wouldn't happen here in South Carolina," said White. "I need your support, Vi, for whatever I do." The sheriff went to his wife and pulled her into an embrace. "You and the boys will be safe here."

Viola couldn't hold back the tears, but she managed to get in the last words. "I love you, James. But I'm still scared."

---

Solicitor Hill was right--the word was out. One of the city policemen, Claude Bobo, had stopped in at his favorite barbershop, Phillips and Harper on east Main, and confided in his friend, Arthur Phillips.

"We may have trouble brewing, Arthur."

"What are you talking about?" asked Phillips.

"They've got a black man down at the jail and they say he raped a white woman."

"So, what? Are you worried about a mob?"

A customer on the way out stopped long enough to hear what Officer Bobo had said. After that, the word spread quickly.

Andrew Beeson and his friend, Jake Turbett, had returned to Glendale and waited outside the gate at the Glendale Mill. Beeson had worked there for a while before getting crosswise with a foreman. His firing had left him furious, and then depressed. For a while he had considered violent revenge, but his wife had talked him out of it. He had weathered the period of depression, then found work as a farm laborer. When that job had been lost to the hiring of a Negro at a lower wage, Andrew had sought out a friend that he knew was in the Klan. It was this friend that Andrew and Jake were awaiting at the Mill.

The man's name was Jordan Goode, and he came through the mill gate along with a crowd of workers at the 6 o'clock whistle. Immediately, he caught sight of Andrew Beeson, and his first thought was to scoot away through the stream of men to the other side where Beeson couldn't see him. The man had become a bit of an annoyance for Goode, bombarding him with complaints about the blacks and pushing for action from the Klan. It was too late, however, for Beeson had seen him and was waving vigorously.

Beeson and Goode had become acquainted when they were teammates on the mill baseball team. The firing had been a blow to Beeson and Goode well understood his friend's anger and frustration. Even so, he thought, it was time for Beeson to give it a rest. Instead, he had become worse.

"Jordan, Jordan," cried Beeson as Goode came near. "Have you heard what happened?"

"I think I'm about to," replied Jordan, eyeing Turbett, who had crowded up close to where the other two were standing. "What is the news, Andrew?"

Noting the look on Goode's face, Beeson pointed at Jake and said, "This is my good friend Jake Turbett. We're here because a big nigger raped a white woman down at White Stone. Did you hear about it?"

Jordan nodded at Jake, then turned to Beeson. "There was some talk over on the line across from us, but we never heard any details."

"Well, we hear they got a man in the jail up at Spartanburg," explained Andrew, "and we figure that damned brute deserves to be lynched. It's a job for the Klan, and we figured you was the guy to get things goin'."

"Andrew, I've been tryin' to tell you, the Klan is layin' low right now, and won't be officially involved in any hangings."

"They was involved down at Laurens so I heard tell, wasn't they, Jake?"

"It's what I heard," agreed Turbett.

"There was Klansmen in the mob, no doubt," admitted Goode, "but I'm tellin' you, it weren't no official Klan job."

"I guess it don't matter none," proclaimed Beeson. "The brute needs to be strung up, and I figured you'd want in on it."

As he thought about it, Goode had to agree. The rape of a white woman by a Negro man was just about the worst crime any good white man could imagine, and Goode had no inclinations to grant such a person any shadow of doubt about his guilt. Still, he had to ask the question. "Do they have the right man?"

"There's no doubt, far as I know," said Beeson with confidence. "They said the woman described him perfectly. He was down at the train station, tryin' to git outta town." He supposed he might be stretching things a bit, but this was not the time to worry about that. "There's a crowd gatherin' at the jail right now, and we need to be there."

Jake Turbett figured Beeson was saying a lot more than either of them knew, but he remained silent.

"Well, my car is over here," said Goode, who realized he wouldn't want to miss out on what might be happening in the town. "We need to stop by my house and get my gun, and so I can tell the old lady where I'm goin'."

As darkness fell, a mass of men was gathering in Morgan Square in downtown Spartanburg. More were arriving every minute. Some came by street car, some arrived by auto, others came by horse and buggy. Many just seemed to appear out of nowhere. There were young men not much more than boys, and a good number of mill workers just off their shifts. All kinds of weapons were in evidence, including clubs, pitchforks, axes, and a variety of firearms. A long line was moving down Magnolia Street and gathering on the courthouse grounds.

Officer Vernon had come out of the jailhouse and was standing along Wofford Street where he could see the growing crowd on the courthouse lawn. To his right he could see men coming up Choice Street which bordered the jail and the sheriff's residence on the west side.

"This ain't good," he muttered as he turned and headed back to the big iron gate in the high wall that surrounded the jail. He found the sheriff in his little jailhouse office.

"Things are not lookin' so good, Sheriff," reported Vernon. "There's men comin' in from all directions."

"Well, it's what we expected," answered White. "We need some help. I'm gonna call Chief Hayes."

E. L. Wilson looked up as the sheriff walked in, noting the worried countenance.

"We've got trouble comin', E.L."

"Not surprisin'," replied the jailer. "What do you want me to do?"

"Just hang tight for the moment," directed the sheriff. "I'm goin' to call the chief and see if he'll send some help."

White went to the phone that hung on the wall at the end of the counter, removing the receiver and speaking to the operator. In a moment the voice of Chief Hayes could be heard.

"Chief," began White, "we need some help down here at the jail. There's a mob forming outside."

"I know that, Sheriff," answered Chief Hayes. "But the mayor has told me he wants us to keep out of it."

"Damn," cried White, allowing himself this bit of profanity. "What is he thinking?"

"Don't know, Jim. Coverin' his ass, I guess. He did shut down liquor sales in the city. Maybe I can send you a couple of guys anyway."

"Whatever you can do, I'll greatly appreciate it, Chief."

After ending his conversation with Hayes, Sheriff White asked the operator to connect him with one of his close friends and baseball buddies, John Story.

"John, this is Jim White."

"Yes, Jim," replied Story. "You don't sound good. What's up?"

"I may need your help, John. Have you heard what's goin' on here at the jail?"

"I heard there'd been a rape and there'd been an arrest."

"Well, we've jailed a suspect, but I'm afraid we may not have him much longer. A mob is here now and I know what they're goin' to demand."

"Oh, God, Jim. What are you gonna do?"

"I'm going to do my duty, John. I can't let them take my prisoner and lynch him. This ain't Laurens County."

"I know you, Jim and I'm not surprised at your take on this. But nobody would hold you responsible if you can't stop the crowd. What about Vi and your kids? Where are they?"

"Vi and two of the boys are at the residence. The boys have the fever."

"Your first duty is to them and yourself, Jim. You can't risk any lives to save a criminal."

Sheriff White was quiet for a moment. His friend was probably right. At least he should get his family out of danger. "What can I do, John?" he finally asked.

"Let me come and get your family out at least, Jim," pleaded Story. "I've got a car."

"Good," said White. "And see if Miller can come with you." The sheriff was speaking of R. E. Miller, a neighbor of Story and another good friend.

In the end, Chief Hayes sent four of his officers to the jail, Claude Bobo, Bud Bryson, W. W. Littlejohn, and B.J. Alverson.

Rosa Fair had been thinking about Will when the knock came at the door. She wasn't expecting Will to be back, for his job at Wellford would keep him there for the entire week. She hoped he had made it there in time, for she was well aware that he could have missed his train. Their son, Tom, had returned from his day's work at Thompson's clutching the promised dollar. He had given it up reluctantly to his mother when she demanded it. It was really his, he thought, but he also knew how much the family needed whatever money came their way. He was surprised when his mother gave him back two shiny dimes.

"Who could be knockin' at this hour," wondered Rosa, speaking out loud as she often did. "Come on in," she hollered.

She was surprised to see Nathan Black and Isaiah Clowney stepping through the door, hats in hand. She nodded at Clowney and spoke to Black.

"Nathan, what you doin' here?"

"We've got some bad news, Rosa. It's about Will."

Rosa's face broke into a slight smile in spite of Black's words.

"What's that big fool done now, Nathan?"

"It ain't nothin' funny, Rosa," said Nathan, noting her smile. "We hear he's been put in the county jail up in Spartanburg."

"Jail? What for?" Rosa's pleasant look was gone.

"They say he raped a white gal," answered Nathan.

"We don't believe it, Mrs. Fair," interjected Clowney, acting in his role as a preacher. "We know he's a good man."

Although Rosa often accused Will of infidelity, she didn't really think he would be guilty of rape. "He went on the train to Wellford," she remembered. "How could he have been arrested?"

"He missed that train, Rosa," explained Black. "I saw him right after and he went on to Glendale to catch the electric."

"My daughter, Annie, saw him walkin' along Union near the house where the white woman lived," added Clowney. "At least Vergie Moore thought it might have been Will."

"Vergie?" cried Rosa. "That silly girl don't know nothin'."

"Well, they saw a big crowd of white people gathered by that house later, so they knew there was big trouble." Clowney realized he wasn't helping matters. "But they were sure Will never went in that house."

"What should I do?" Rosa pleaded. "What should I do?"

Clowney took hold of Rosa's hand and patted her on the shoulder, but words failed him as she began to sob. After a moment she turned to Black.

"Should I try to go and visit him, Nathan?"

"No, no, Rosa, it wouldn't be safe. No tellin' what them crowds might do if they saw you goin' into that jailhouse."

"You need to just stay here, Mrs. Fair." Preacher Clowney had finally found his voice again . "Mrs. Clowney will come up and stay with you."

Rosa slumped into a kitchen chair and laid her head on the table. "My poor Will," she mumbled, amidst the tears. She raised her head up suddenly as another thought came to her. "My God, will they lynch him?"

Both men knew that she was thinking about what had happened in Laurens County. They held the same fear, but they couldn't affirm that just now.

"They can't get in there, that jail has a big wall." Nathan Black knew the jail quite well, having spent a night or two in there himself.

"God will protect him," said Clowney, feeling that was a necessary answer, although he was hoping the sheriff would be up to the task as well.

"Will you pray for me, Reverend?" asked Rosa.

Although he didn't really feel he was an authentic "reverend", Clowney knew such an admission would be of no help to Mrs. Fair. "I sure will."

The prayer was long and followed by Black's hearty "Amen." The two men left and Rosa called her four children together. "Your Pa won't be home for a while," she said, with no further explanation.

# SIX

# The Attack

The mood of the mob was growing ugly. Shouts and epithets were hurled at the jail as the men pushed together at the gate to the jail yard.

"Send that damned nigger out here! We'll take care of him."

"We demand justice for our white women. Come on, Sheriff. Give him up."

"That damned rapist deserves to die. You know we'll get him in the end."

County policeman J. E. Vernon stood close to the gate but out of sight of the gathering crowd. Sheriff White stood on the other side. "It's gittin' pretty rough out there, Sheriff. What are we going to do?"

"I don't rightly know, J. E., but we can't just give in to them. My duty is to protect everybody, and that includes my prisoners. Surely they'll quiet down and go home when it is clear we ain't going to send the prisoner out." Although he had almost said "the nigger", Sheriff White realized he had to be more careful how he referred to Will Fair. He needed his deputies to regard Fair as someone who needed protection. Although he had great confidence about where his jailer, Wilson, stood, he was not so sure about Vernon. The deputy had been known to be pretty rough on blacks he had arrested in the past. His own thoughts on the matter weren't as clear as he made them seem, White realized. He had to consider the safety of the other prisoners, not to mention his own family. His friend, John Story was probably right. No one would blame him too much if he gave in to the mob.

"Keep a close watch on things, J. E. I'm goin' to check on my family. I'll be back shortly." White turned and went back toward the side of the jail next to his residence. He noted the city policemen had taken places that he had suggested. One, along with Vernon, remained near the gate, one was just inside the building door, and another had gone upstairs to join the jailer, Wilson. The last one, Officer Bobo, was stationed near the heavy door that went into the sheriff's living quarters.

"I appreciate your being here, Officer," said White as he opened the door. "Be right back."

Passing through the kitchen and dining room, James went through the parlor to the front door. He was hoping to see John Story driving up, but met with disappointment. On the second floor he found his wife sitting between the boys' beds, reading. The two patients were asleep.

"Hey, Vi. How are things?"

"At least they got to sleep," answered Viola, nodding at the children. "What's goin' on out there? I can hear some shouting."

"A mob has formed, I'm afraid," said James. "They're gittin' restless. I've called John Story and I hope he can get you and the boys out of here before anything happens."

"That won't work, James. The boys can't be safely moved just now. Do you think we are in danger?"

"Not really, dear, but I'd like to be safe about it."

"How can you stop them? Do you have any help?"

"We've got J. E. and E. L., and four city policemen. Plus that's a damned big wall. It won't be easy for them to get in."

"But they'll get in if they want to bad enough." Tears came to her eyes as she spoke. "It ain't worth your life, Jim, please remember that."

"Honey, I promise I won't do anything foolish, but I've got to do my job. You stay up here unless John comes to get you out. I think he may have just drove up, so I've got to go. I'll post a man at both doors to the residence."

"Go then, James, but be careful."

The sheriff started to go, then went to his wife, taking her hands and pulling her upright. He squeezed her tight against him and kissed her deeply.

"I love you Vi," he said quietly, "and I promise to be careful."

Hurrying down the stairs, White rushed to the front door and stepped onto the porch. John Story and Ron Miller were coming up the steps from the street through the short stone ledge and onto the walk in the front yard. Story's car was parked along the street just below. White waited for them, noting that there was a crowd of men along Choice Street.

Story was the first to speak. "Jim, we had a hell of a time getting here. You can see there's a crowd back here, too. I'm not sure it is safe to try to get your family out this way."

"No, John, I think you're right," agreed the sheriff, nodding to Miller. "Hello Ron. Vi doesn't want to move the boys anyway. Come on in."

Once inside, Sheriff White had a request to make of his two friends. "I'm needing some help, men. I'd like to deputize you both. Are you willing?"

"You know we are, Jim," replied Story with Miller nodding his agreement.

"All right. Come on back, and I'll swear you in."

———•———

The mob had no leadership, but that was about to change. Andrew Beeson, Jordan Goode, and Jake Turbett had arrived at the courthouse and pushed their way through the crowd until they were near the big iron gate that opened into the jail yard. Along the way, Goode recognized one of the Klan leaders, Howard Walters, a 50-year old undertaker who owned Walters Funeral Home. The two men acknowledged each other and Goode led his friends over to where Walters stood a few feet from the gate.

"Hello, Howard," said Jordan, holding out his right hand which Walters quickly grasped. "You thinkin' what I'm thinkin'?" continued Goode.

Walters nodded, but was slow to speak. His hatred of the Negro race had found its expression in his activity in the Ku Klux Klan. His father had fought with a South Carolina regiment in the civil war, and although not a slave owner himself, he blamed the Negroes for the terrible conflict and the hardships it brought. His attitudes had passed to his son as had his business.

The current circumstances provided a perfect opportunity for Howard. His time in the Klan had led to leadership chances and he had made the best of them. He felt quite confident in his abilities, and he could see how they could be put to work now to achieve the desired action against this black prisoner. There was no question that the man was guilty, and in Howard's view that really didn't matter much. The crime of rape by a black man against a white woman required immediate and severe response. A Negro needed to die as a clear warning to the others, for they must be kept in place.

"The man must be lynched," Walters said finally in answer to Goode's remark. "Help me get this crowd organized." He moved quickly toward the gate, with Goode, Beeson, and Turbett trailing behind.

Some of the people seemed to recognize Walters and they moved aside, as if expecting him to take charge. A burly man was standing just to the right side of the gate, yelling at the sheriff to bring the prisoner out.

"Any answer from inside?" Walters asked of the man, whose name was Jason Calo.

"Not a damned word," answered Calo.

"Not surprising. White would think he has to protect the brute." Walters had no reason to dislike the sheriff, but he had always sensed a difference of opinion with him on the Negro question.

"Yeah, he's a damned fool," said Calo. "I've played ball against him, and I don't like him much."

"We need something to batter down that gate," said Walters.

"I know where we can get a railroad tie," answered Calo, who had only recently been working near the rail station.

"Take some men and get it," advised Walters. "And be quick about it."

Calo turned immediately and angled across the yard toward Magnolia Street. The railroad was only a couple of blocks down that street. Four men ran with him. Walters began shouting at the people standing near, urging them to increase the yelling at the jail, telling them they needed to be ready to charge through when the gate was knocked down.

"This is gonna be great," said Beeson excitedly to Goode. "We'll have him out here in no time."

"We'll see," cautioned Goode. "We ain't close to bein' in there yet."

It wasn't long until the men returned carrying a big eight-foot railroad tie. The people crowded in around them as they began battering away at the gate. The noise increased, and the gate rattled as the heavy beam banged against it. Inside the yard, the sheriff and his deputies took notice. Sheriff White, who was standing back near the door into the jailhouse, started toward the gate, when his friend, John Story, grasped his elbow and pulled him back.

"Don't go up there, Jim," pleaded Story. "They've got weapons out there and some fool might take a shot at you."

"I must do something, John, before they knock that gate down." White pulled away and with steely determination, marched toward the gate, fully visible to the crowd outside. As the people recognized him, a volley of shouts greeted him.

"Give him up, Sheriff. We're goin' to git him anyway."

"Send that damned brute out to us—he ain't worth your time."

"Men, Men," pleaded White. "Think about what you're doing here. Let the law take its course, justice will be done."

"Justice will be done when that nigger's hangin' from a tree," came the reply.

The men had dropped the railroad tie as the sheriff had begun to speak. White recognized some of the people, especially Howard Walters, whom he knew quite well. He directed his comments to Howard, although he did not single him out by name.

"You're fixin' to damage that gate, and the taxpayers will have to pay for that. We don't want anyone to be hurt, but all this shouting and banging is going to lead to that if you don't stop. My family is upstairs in the residence and you're scaring them to death. My two boys are in bed sick with the typhoid."

"We ain't after your boys, sheriff," shouted Beeson. "Just send out that black son-of-a-bitch and all will be quiet."

"You know I can't do that," answered White. "I'm duty bound, fellows. You're my friends, but I can't let you in."

"Then you go to hell, cause we're comin' in," cried Calo, who signaled for the battering ram to be picked up again. "We're comin' in."

With that, the big beam was rammed against the gate with great force, although the gate held up without weakening.

"Get something stronger," came the cry from the crowd. Walters nodded his head, and the men holding the tie dropped it, waiting for more instruction.

"There's some loose rails down by the track," pointed out one of the construction workers.

"Get one," said Howard. "That might do it. That gate has to come down."

The shouting continued, becoming more ugly and profane, but the mob had retreated a bit, waiting for the men to return with the rail. Sheriff White huddled with his deputies in the jail yard, and they moved closer to the gate, allowing the men outside the gate to see them loading their weapons. Not really aware of what the crowd was waiting for, the sheriff began to hope the worst was over.

His hopes were soon dashed as the iron rail was brought up and thrust against the gate. The sound of iron against iron rang out above the noise from the throng, but the gate continued to hold.

Back on the edge of the crowd, Ralph Carson came out from his law office on Magnolia Street and stood next to Sam Nicholls, whose own office was just down the street from that of Carson.

"Doesn't look good, Sam," observed Carson. "I think Sheriff White will try to hold on, but expect the mob to win in the end."

"I think they've got the right man in jail," observed Nicholls. "I was out at Glendale earlier today and we talked to this Negro man who had seen Will Fair."

"Fair is the prisoner's name?" Carson had not really heard much about what had transpired. "What did the man tell you?"

"He claimed he had seen Fair within 200 yards of the crime scene and that he had gone up to Glendale. The thing was, he gave a description of the man that was exactly like that given by Mrs. Potter."

"How do you know that, Sam?"

"Bob Kassen was riding with me and he was at old man Potter's place where he heard Jake Potter tell what his wife had told him."

Carson thought about that for a moment. "Wouldn't hold up too well in court, probably," he concluded with a chuckle. "But then again, maybe so when you consider it's a black man who's raped a white woman."

"I wouldn't want to be his defense lawyer," noted Nicholls. "Somebody will be assigned I suppose. Could be you, Ralph."

"Not a plum assignment for sure," agreed Carson. "Right now I'm more worried that some of our good citizens may get hurt before this is over."

———————

There were 34 prisoners in the jail, four of whom were women. The shouts from the outside were loud enough to be heard by the inmates, and they began to get nervous. On the second floor and across the hall from the cell that held Will Fair, a man called Jock directed his remarks at the alleged rapist.

"Why don't you give yourself up, you nigger bastard? You'll get us all killed."

"That's right," cried another. "You know they're goin' to git in here anyway."

Will Fair wanted to shout back at them, but he knew that would just lead to more of the same. He couldn't completely stop himself, however, and he finally answered quietly. "I ain't guilty."

"Yeah, we know. Ain't none of us in here's guilty, right. But they know you're guilty, and that's all that matters," said Jock, who then hollered at Officer Wilson at the end of the hall. "Come and get him, Officer. He wants to give himself up."

"Shut your mouth," cried a black inmate in the cell next to Fair.

Will Fair sank back on his cot and listened as the prisoners began screaming at each other. "I'm a dead man," he thought, "and Rosa won't even know what has happened to me."

A loud roar came from the crowd outside and then shots rang out. The men holding the rail at the gate, backed up and dropped the rail as the rest of the crowd sank back. Many began to run away.

"Blanks," yelled Jordan Goode. "They're shootin' blanks, men. Come on back."

It was true, Sheriff White had ordered his men to load their weapons with blank cartridges, and he watched as the crowd moved back.

"They're backin' away," said Officer Alverson, one of the city policemen.

"Not for long, I'm afraid," answered White. "Once the crowd figures we're shooting blanks, they'll be back."

Word had quickly spread among the rioters, and some began drifting back. Goode and Walters were urging another attack as Calo and others picked up the rail once more. Some half-hearted attempts were again made at bashing down the gate, but there was no success. Walters huddled with Goode, Beeson, and Calo. When they broke the huddle, Calo motioned to one of his fellow construction workers and the two men ran off toward the rail station.

Sheriff White passed the word to his deputies that they should now load their weapons with regular ammunition. Ron Miller, who had agreed to stay in the residence and keep his eye on the front door facing Wofford Street, suddenly appeared in the yard where he found the sheriff.

"Ron, what are you doing out here," White demanded to know. "I need you in the residence."

"Vi wanted me to find you and tell you they're all right, but really scared."

White resisted the urge to utter some angry words at Miller for deserting his post. "What did she say about the boys? I hope she doesn't need the doctor."

"She says they're no worse, but the shooting and yelling has them mighty upset. She's worried about you, Jim."

"Get back and assure her that I'm fine. There may be a lot of noise, but I don't think anybody will bother the residence. But tell her we can't get anybody in or out right now."

"She knows that, Jim but she keeps sayin' she thinks you might do something stupid and get yourself hurt or killed." Miller didn't add that he was thinking that himself.

"Tell her I'll be careful." White grabbed Miller by the right elbow. "Ron, I'm countin' on you to protect my family. Get a gun from Wilson and get back to the house. If any fool tries comin' in that front door, I want you to shoot. Do you understand."

"I've got you, Jim. Nobody's comin' through there." Miller turned and went back inside the jail.

Another cheer came up outside the walls, a reaction to the return of Calo and his companion. They were carrying something and the men nearest the gate soon figured out that Calo had a pack that contained explosives.

"Dynamite!" The word ripped through the crowd like a flash of lightning. People began coming back toward the gate, eager to see what might happen after the application of dynamite. Calo placed some of the explosive along the base of the wall and they tied a fuse of some length to it. "Light it," came the cry from the crowd. It went off but it was disappointing, for it opened only a small hole in the wall.

Aware of what was going on, Sheriff White, along with Officers Vernon and Alverson moved toward the gate, and when the charge went off, they began firing their weapons. They deliberately fired high enough to avoid hitting any of the mob, but some bark flew off of one of the small trees growing in the yard. It quickly registered with the crowd that the officers were now firing real bullets. This interrupted the surge of the men somewhat, and Howard Walters began again to urge them forward. He sought out Calo and offered some advice.

"You've got to set a heavier charge, man. Put it at the gate and see if you can blow it off its hinges."

Calo conferred with some of the railroad workers, knowing they had some experience with explosives. A new and stronger charge was placed under the gate at the hinged end. The crowd moved back. When the fuse was lit, the resulting blast was enormous, and the gate went down.

"It's down," was the cry and when the dust had cleared, a gang led by Calo and Goode began to run toward the opening. They were brought up short by the appearance of Sheriff White, who was pointing his revolver directly at the center of the chasm left by the fallen gate.

"Friends, and you are my friends," shouted the sheriff. "I don't want to do it, but I'll kill any man who comes through that open gate." Officers Alverson and Vernon had taken up positions at each edge of the opening, also pointing their weapons.

"The hell you will," replied Calo. "You wouldn't dare shoot one of us. The rest would tear you apart."

"Maybe so, Jason," said the sheriff, who knew Calo by name. "But which of you is going to put me to the test? Will it be you?"

The line of men approaching the gate had stopped. "Rush him," someone shouted from the back, and a shot was fired from somewhere in the rear. Suddenly there was a scuffle from off to the side as Captain Hall and Frank Johnson of the city police, both dressed in civilian clothes, pushed in among the men clustered near the gate. Johnson attempted to grab a revolver in the hand of one of the mob, when another man hit him in the head with a stick. Hall tried to arrest him, but the man escaped back into the crowd. As Hall started after the attacker of Johnson, he was grabbed from behind by a young man who was trying to get Hall's pistol. Turning quickly, Hall slammed the man against the wall, injuring the arms of both men, then pulled away and tried to resume his chase of the first man. It was too late for that, and Hall came back, helping Johnson to his feet.

Officer Alverson had seen these altercations, and when he stepped out into the edge of the crowd, he saw a group of rioters pulling at the fallen gate, trying to get it out of the way so as to widen the opening. He went among them, and pushed one of the men down. As he did this, he was attacked from behind, the assailant pulling him back and down.

"Take him down," called out a bystander, and a cheer arose from those watching. "Get that stupid cop," yelled another. "Take him out!"

Alverson had drawn his revolver, and as he was being pulled backward, he whirled and fired his gun, the shots going backward and downward. One of the bullets passed through the trousers of Will Turner, who was standing near, and slammed into the leg of Frank Eppley. A second bullet found its way into the hip of J.C. Owensby. Both Eppley and Owensby let out a howl, and dropped to the ground. This had a chilling effect on the rest of the mob, which once again retreated from near the jail yard wall. Answering shots came from back in the crowd. Then all was quiet.

Eppley and Owensby had been standing at the edge of the crowd and near Wofford Street. Unfortunately for them, there had been no one between them and Officer Alverson. Captain Hall saw them go down and went to their aid. He drafted some men nearby to help

"I don't think their wounds are too serious," Hall explained to the men, "but they need treatment. Do any of you have a car nearby?"

When he was assured that there was no automobile available, Hall asked Johnson to stay with them while he went to arrange for transformation. "We'll have them taken over to the K. W. N. Pharmacy." He hurried away to find a telephone.

The quiet remained for a few minutes, but then a stick of dynamite sailed over the wall and exploded in an open grassy area. "Damn!" shouted Sheriff White. "We need some help."

He ran to the door and instructed Officer Bryson to call the mayor. "Tell him we need more police, or better yet, have him send the firemen who can put a hose on this howling mob. Tell him we have some injuries and we've got to get this thing stopped before somebody gets killed."

Bryson ran inside, wondering whether he should call Chief Hayes first. He found the phone and talked to the operator. "Get me Mayor Johnson—it's an emergency."

The mayor, who was aware of what was going on, was in his office and he answered the phone quickly.

"This is Mayor Johnson. Who is this?"

"It is Bud Bryson, Mr. Mayor. I'm down at the jail and the sheriff asked me to call. We've got big trouble and he wants you to send help."

The mayor had been talking with some of his advisors for much of the evening, and he was prepared to react to this call. However, he decided to stall a bit first.

"What kind of help does he want?"

"There's a lynch mob here, sir, and there aren't enough of us to keep 'em out. We need you to send the firemen here with their hoses. The sheriff thinks they could get the mob to disperse."

"I can't do that, Officer," said the mayor. He and his advisors were well aware of the upcoming election. "It's not advisable for me to intervene to save a guilty Negro."

"It ain't the Negro you'd be helpin', Mayor. It would be helpin' the sheriff and the rest of us who are here trying to stop this mob."

"The best thing is to let them have their way," replied Mayor Johnson. He wasn't feeling too proud of himself, but he was sticking to what had been decided. "Tell Sheriff White I'm sorry, but he needs to protect himself and you deputies, not the Negro." With that, the mayor hung up.

"What the hell?" exclaimed White when Bryson told him what the mayor had said. "Did he really say that?"

"Who said what?" The sheriff was startled by this interruption, but happy to see the speaker, Robert Gantt. He might have need of the county magistrate before the night was over.

"Hello Robert," remarked White. "I'm really glad to see you. Officer Bryson was telling me about his talk with Mayor Johnson."

"And what did our good mayor have to say?" Gantt was not a big supporter of the mayor.

"Said he couldn't help us," replied the sheriff. "How did you get in here, Robert."

"Sounds like our mayor all right. I came in through the residence, but it wasn't easy getting past your man Miller. He wasn't going to open the door until he was convinced who I was."

"He's protecting my family, Robert." White was comforted at this report on Miller's protective behavior.

"You've attracted quite a mob, James," observed Gantt. "There must be over 500 men out there, that's why I came around to the side."

White was moving back toward the fallen gate and Gantt went with him. Officer Vernon stood near the wall, pointing his shotgun at the opening. "How have you managed to keep them out?" Gantt wondered.

"I promised to shoot the first man who tried to come through," said White.

"I think we need more help," advised Gantt. "Let me wire the governor and ask for some troops."

"Do that Robert, and do it quick." White was doubtful that troops would arrive in time, but maybe he could use them as a threat.

"I'm on my way!"

The shooting and the unyielding promise from the sheriff that prompted shouts of "he means what he says" had cooled the ardor of the mob somewhat. There had been a cautious movement away from the wall, and some of the men had begun to leave the scene. Realizing that the moment of success was receding, Howard Walters convened a meeting of several of the most determined lynchers, including Calo, Goode, Beeson, and Turbett.

"You men go out among the crowd and get them back into the mood of storming that wall. The sheriff and his men can't stop us if we make a bull rush at that opening."

"Trouble is, Walter, he can stop one of us," Goode pointed out. "Who will it be?"

"That ain't the right attitude, Jordan," said Beeson.

"Then you go first, Andrew," urged Goode. "We'll be right behind you."

"Stop it men. Stop that talk," demanded Walters. "That gets us nowhere. There's still a pile of men around here, we just need to get them behind us again. Now get at it."

Walters waved them off and began shouting as loud as he could. "We want that nigger. We mean to have him, so send him out."

Others took up the cry and it seemed for a while that the mob would make another determined effort to force its way into the jail.

In the jail office, Robert Gantt contacted the Western Union operator and gave the following message:

*Governor Cole L. Blease, Columbia, S.C.*
*Peace officers and mob in battle at the jail. Mob using*
*dynamite. Sheriff's wife and two children within*
*walls. Wire authority to call out militia.*
*Spartanburg County Magistrate, Robert Gantt*

It wasn't long until Gantt received the governor's reply. It ignored the request for militia, but promised that he would order a special term of court for the first week of September. Disappointed, Gantt now got on the phone to Solicitor Hill at his home.

"A.E., this is Bob Gantt. Sorry to bother you so late."

"It is late, but I've been told there is trouble down at the jail." Hill lived too far away to have easily heard the shooting, although he did think he had heard an explosion.

"You're right about that. We need your help." Gantt went on to explain what had been happening and that the mayor refused to help, as had the governor.

"You know Governor Blease, don't you A.E.? Can you call him and see if you can get him to authorize calling out the militia."

"I know him Robert, but I doubt he'll do that. He's not going to sympathize with saving a Negro."

"It's not the Negro we're worried about, it's the sheriff and his deputies. Not to mention people in that mob that could get hurt too. They're using dynamite."

"I'll call him, Robert, but don't expect too much. Is he at his home?"

"I don't know, A.E. He did answer my wire pretty fast, so I don't think he is sleeping."

Hill managed to reach the governor without much trouble, and spent some time trying to explain to him exactly what was going on at the Spartanburg jail. The governor promised an answer by wire. It followed in only a few minutes.

*Columbia, S.C., Aug 19, 1913*
*Solicitor Hill, Spartanburg, S.C.*
*Your request for special term of court to be held*
*first week in September at Spartanburg*
*has been granted and order issued.*
*COLE L. BLEASE, Governor*

Outside the walls, the efforts to restart the assault on the jail had fizzled. The sight of Sheriff White and his deputies standing in front of the gate opening with their weapons drawn was enough to discourage the attackers. Jason Calo pointed out that there were plenty of weapons available, and enough firepower to eliminate the defense. Somehow the idea of bashing down a wall was more acceptable than shooting peace officers, and in the end, the crowd simply drifted away. Although a few clusters of men continued to hang around, the danger to the jail and its inhabitants was over, at least for the night.

It was more than an hour past midnight when Spartanburg Police Chief Moss Hayes had made his way into the jail yard. A watch had been placed at the opening, and the other defenders had gone inside the jail. After a quick visit to his wife and children, Sheriff White had returned to the main jail office where Chief Hayes found him.

"You've had a rough time here, Jim," noted Hayes. "But you held out. Congratulations."

"Thanks for your help, Moss. Your men were a Godsend."

"Sorry the mayor didn't let us do more. I think we need to move the prisoner out of town, Jim. That crowd may well come back with more men and more determination.

"I agree completely, Moss. I don't want another night like this one. How do we do it?"

"I think there's a train out to Charlotte at 3:00 or 4:00 this morning. Once there, we can get him to Columbia."

"Can you make it happen, Moss?"

"Don't see no reason we can't. I'll take him there myself."

# SEVEN

# The Better Part of Valor

Jason Calo was quite unhappy that the opportunity to get Will Fair out of the jail had passed them by, at least for the immediate future. He continued to badger Howard Walters to try to renew the effort. Beeson had joined him but Walters was ready to give it up.

"We've lost the crowd, Mr. Calo," was his answer.

"It will come back," snapped Calo. "We can get more men to come in from out in the county. I bet we can get help from Laurens County too."

"That might be so if he's still here by the time we get those people here."

"What are you talkin' about, Howard. Why wouldn't he be here?"

"Because I'm guessing they will try to move him out of Spartanburg County." Actually, this thought had only come to Walters in the last few minutes.

Brought up short by this new idea, Calo chastised himself silently for not having thought of it himself. Andrew Beeson, who had not been listening at first, now spoke up.

"My god, we can't let that happen!"

"Hell no, we can't," agreed Calo. "We need to get the word out about this."

Howard Walters was now back in the game. Organization was needed and all thoughts of going home were gone. "There's still enough men around here to prevent them moving him. Get some of them over here and let me talk to them."

"Where's Goode?" asked Calo.

"He went home," said Beeson. "Said he had to get some sleep because he had to be at work extra early tomorrow."

"Damn!" shouted Calo. "This ain't no time to be goin' home. We need every man we can find."

"How will they do it, do you think?" asked Beeson, speaking to Walters.

Walters did not answer immediately, but stood looking at the jail for a time. Finally, he offered a thought. "If I were doing it, I believe I would try to get him to Columbia."

"By car?" wondered Calo.

"No, I think by train," replied Walters. "In fact, I'm sure of it. They can sneak him out the back and down Choice Street."

"We'd better get some people down there right now, then," said Calo.

"Does anybody know the train schedules" asked Walters.

"I think there's one real early, like three or four o'clock," announced Jake Turbett. "I put my mother-in-law on there one time," he added, responding to the surprised looks from the others.

"What time is it now," asked Beeson.

Walters drew a watch from its pocket in his pants, but it was too dark to see it properly. They moved back to a porch on the backside of the courthouse, dimly lit by a single bulb. "It's about one-thirty," Howard concluded. He pointed at Turbett. "You go down and keep watch on Choice Street. We need to know if they come out and head over to the train station. I'll send somebody else down to help you, but right now we need to gather some more men to join us. Calo, you and Beeson go over to Morgan Square and round up some guys. I'll see who is up here at the courthouse."

69

In the jailhouse, the inmates, who had been worried for their own lives, had begun to calm down.

"You should have seen them, Sheriff," remarked the jailer when Sheriff White came back into the jail. "The inmates, I mean. They were crying and begging us to protect them from that mob. I felt pretty sorry for the gals."

Four of the inmates were white women, and it was they of whom Wilson was speaking. "Those damned fools wouldn't have even worried about harming those women, I suppose," continued Wilson, who was quite worked up himself.

"It's all right, E. L.," said White. "The big danger is past now, I think. You can tell them that they're quite safe. Do we still have someone on the second floor?"

"Officer Littlejohn is up there," answered Wilson.

"We're going to get Will Fair out of here, E. L. That crowd could come back tomorrow, and I don't want a repeat of what's just happened. Go up and explain that to Officer Littlejohn and to Fair as well."

Will Fair was pacing in his cell, knowing that the jail was under attack but unaware of the actual situation outside. He saw the jailer in the hall motioning for Officer Littlejohn to meet him outside Fair's cell. A stab of fear penetrated his thought. "What 's this about?" he wondered.

The two officers met outside the cell as the prisoner watched, unable to hear what they were saying to each other. Someone from across the hall shouted an obscenity, calling for Fair to be given up.

"Shut up," cried Wilson. "You're all safe right now." He turned to address Fair. "Get yourself ready, we're gonna get you out of here."

"What do you mean?" answered Will, thinking maybe the sheriff had decided to give him up. "You can't let them have me."

"We'll get you out of Spartanburg," said Wilson. "You'll just have to wait until we're ready."

"I know there's a big mob out there," protested Fair. "I don't want to go out there."

"The mob's mostly gone. We'll get you out." Wilson was becoming disgusted with the Negro's attitude. He turned and went back to the stairway, nodding to Littlejohn as he went. "Stay here and keep him quiet. I'll let you know when it's time."

"What about my wife?" hollered Will to the departing jailer. "Does she know what's happened to me?"

Wilson stopped and turned back. "I have no idea," he barked. "We've got enough to worry about with you." With that he left.

---

Spartanburg police chief Moss Hayes was huddled with Sheriff White in the little room off the main hall. They had learned that a train would leave for Charlotte at 3:45, which was just a bit more than an hour away. The problem they were discussing had to do with getting Fair to the train station without being seen.

"There's still some men around the courthouse, and probably some watching on Choice Street," remarked the sheriff. "If we get him out in the open, we might not be able to keep those idiots from taking him."

"We need some way to throw them off," said Hayes.

Ron Miller appeared at the door. "There's a man at the residence, Jim," announced Miller. "Says his name is Frank Metcalf."

"Somebody you know?" asked Chief Hayes.

"Yeah, I know him," answered the sheriff. "He was a constable over in Wellford a while back. I worked with him a bit."

"Should I let him in?" Miller wanted to know. "He says he wants to help."

"Bring him back here, Ron," said Jim White. "We'll see what he's got to say. Then you need to get back to the residence."

It wasn't long until Miller appeared again with Metcalf just behind him.

"Hello, Frank," was the greeting from White, who stood and extended his hand to Metcalf. "What's on your mind?"

Metcalf shook the sheriff's hand and nodded at Hayes. "I had a call from Joel Gentz who told me what was going on here. Woke me from a sound sleep. Anyway, I thought I might be of some use to you. So might Joel—he's a good friend and an officer with the Guards."

71

Metcalf was speaking of the Hampton Guards, Spartanburg's own National Guard organization. The name struck Sheriff White with immediate regret. "By God," he exclaimed. "I should have thought of them."

Chief Hayes was on his feet now. "I know how we can use the Guards."

"What are you thinking, Chief?" asked White.

"We need a diversion," replied Hayes with excitement. "There's weapons and ammunition at the Armory, and the Guards can get in there."

"Can your friend get some of the Guards out real soon, Frank?" asked White.

"Sure, I think he's already calling some of them."

"So how do we use them?" This question was directed to Chief Hayes.

"Have the Guards load their rifles with blanks and start shooting. That ought to get everybody's attention." Chief Hayes was feeling quite proud of himself.

Sheriff White was not quite so sure that the ruse would work. "But what if they leave a bunch of people here to watch the jail?"

"My guess is that they'll think we are trying to move the prisoner out of town by car."

"Well, I hope you're right, Chief, but I guess it's worth a try." White turned to Metcalf and directed him to contact his friend. "Tell him we need as many men as he can get out to the Armory, but it must be quick."

Metcalf went immediately to the phone and called Joel Gentz. As soon as he had completed the call, he reported the result to White. "He thinks he can get 8 to 10 Guards out there in less than twenty minutes. He's already called several of them. I'll go down there right now, I've got a key."

Metcalf started to go back toward the residence when the sheriff stopped him. "Go out the jail yard gate," he advised. "There's probably somebody watching to see if we send anyone out toward Choice Street. I'd rather they think you're still in here."

After following a circuitous route and slipping by several clusters of men, Metcalf arrived at the Armory and let himself in. He located some stores of ammunition and was gratified to find several boxes of blank cartridges. It wasn't long until Joel Gentz joined him.

"Hello, Frank," said Gentz. "Some of the Guards said they didn't want to help no Negro rapist, but I've got about ten men coming. They should be here in just a few minutes. What do you want us to do?"

"Thanks for your help, Joel. The sheriff wants us to create a ruckus so they can get everyone away from the jail. They want to get the prisoner on the train and out of town."

"I reckon that is important to do. How did they manage to fight off that mob anyhow? I heard there was a thousand people stormin' that jail."

"Don't know any more than you do," answered Metcalf. "We didn't have time to discuss what happened, but they're mighty anxious to get that Negro out of town, that's for sure."

"So what do we do here?"

Metcalf held up one of the boxes of blanks. "We'll use these. Chief Hayes thinks that if we start a bunch of shooting, the mob'll think they're tryin' to get the man out of town by car, and they'll come down here and try to stop them."

Gentz nodded in agreement and went to open the door for the Guards who had begun to arrive. Eleven men showed up and it wasn't long until each had obtained a rifle and loaded it with blanks.

"All right, men," shouted Gentz. "Let's go out and make some noise."

———————

Andrew Beeson was glad to see that there was still a sizable crowd gathered in Morgan Square. The men were milling around, exchanging stories about what had happened around the courthouse. Andrew and Jason Calo moved among them, informing them of the opportunity that still existed in grabbing the prisoner as the sheriff tried to move him out of town. They did not fail to notice, however, the presence of a number of city policemen on the street.

"What are all these cops doin' here?" Calo asked one of the men near him.

"There was a bunch tried to break into a hardware store," the man explained.

"Hell, how stupid is that? What hardware?"

"The one over there," said the informer, pointing across to the other side of the square. "Montgomery and Crawford's I think."

"They arrested somebody," chimed in another man.

"Well, we gotta get some men over to the jail and right soon," said Calo. "We're pretty sure they'll try to get that nigger brute onto a train. We can grab him real easy."

"That's right," shouted Beeson. "Come on, you men. Come with us right now."

A few more minutes of pleading resulted in a gang of twenty men following after Calo and Beeson. Each man was armed with a weapon of some kind, mostly rifles and pistols. As they moved down Magnolia Street, their march was interrupted by the eruption of several gunshots coming off to their left

"Somebody's shootin'," cried Beeson.

"Where's it comin' from?"

"I think it must be from the Armory." A new voice had entered the discussion. It belonged to Henry Fernandes, the manager of the Goodlett Gun store and a good friend of Howard Walters. He was feeling unhappy with himself for not being a larger part of the action at the jail. "Maybe they've taken that scoundrel down there, tryin' to get him out of town."

" Could be," agreed Calo. "We might be wrong about the train."

"Let's get down there," shouted Beeson. "Come on men, to the Armory. Let's get that bastard."

The group of twenty had become thirty, and it turned toward the Armory.

Jake Turbett was not sure what he should do. He had stationed himself down near the intersection of Wofford and Choice Streets where he could see the entrance to the sheriff's residence and also have a view down Choice Street toward the rail station. Howard Walters had promised to send someone down to help him keep watch, but so far no one had appeared. There were a few people stirring around on the courthouse lawn, but they were paying no attention to anything in his area.

Now he had heard the shooting coming from behind his position and it left him with a dilemma. He had seen someone go into the residence, but nobody had come out, as least as far as he knew. So what could the shooting be about and how should he react? His first thought was that somehow the prisoner had been brought out and had been discovered trying to get out of town. It didn't seem possible, but maybe they had taken him out of the jail before he had taken up his position. He supposed he should stay where he was, but the desire to find out what was going on with the shooting was hard to resist. More shots rang out, and it made the decision for him. Jake thought he could go a ways down Choice to the southeast to see if he could see what was happening, then return to his post before anyone knew. He acted on that thought.

Ron Miller was aware that a man was watching the house from across the street, and he saw Turbett move off toward the sound of the shooting. John Story had joined him at the residence, and Miller informed Story immediately when Turbett left his spot.

"John, the man watching us has run off to see what the shooting is about. This is the chance Jim White has been waiting for."

"Are you sure he hasn't been replaced, or there is another spy posted out there somewhere?" Story had been sent to Miller by the sheriff for this very purpose. He was in plain clothes and would not be recognized as being with the police. "Let me go out and take a look around."

"That's good," replied Miller. "I'll go and tell Jim that we might have a window right now."

As Story went out the door, Miller hurried back through the residence and went straight to the office where White and Hayes were waiting. He was surprised to see Will Fair standing in the hallway, flanked by the jailer, Wilson, and Officer Littlejohn.

"Jim, we think there is no one watching on Choice Street just now. John is out checking, but the man who was there has gone off toward the Armory."

"Thanks, Ron," shouted White excitedly, jumping to his feet. "Let's go right now."

"Come on," grunted Wilson, grabbing Will Fair by the arm. "We're takin' you to the train."

Fair was not happy, thinking he was safer in the jail than out on the street. Sheriff White had explained carefully to him what they intended to do, but he couldn't shake the idea that maybe this was just a plan to get rid of him and let the lynch mob have him. He didn't resist however and was greatly relieved when the little party made it out and onto Choice Street that remained completely deserted. They hurried down to the train station where the stationmaster, John Chapman, met them as they neared the platform and hustled them to the western end of the building, avoiding the waiting room. Sheriff White, who had explained the situation to Chapman by phone, now huddled with him in order to map out their procedures while waiting for the arrival of the train. Hayes and Wilson took Fair around the other side, out of sight of the two customers in the waiting room, and anyone watching from the town side. The three of them went through a door that led into a small baggage storage room. Officer Littlejohn kept watch out front.

"The train will be here in about 10 minutes," advised Chapman. The stationmaster was uneasy about what might happen if there was trouble getting the Negro on the train without being seen.

"How long will the train be in the station?" White asked.

"No more than 15 minutes," was the answer by Chapman, who quickly answered, "I hope."

There was nothing to do now but wait. The two men waiting for the train talked quietly to each other, wondering about the presence of the policeman they had seen outside.

The shooting had stopped at the Armory, and a growing crowd of men had it surrounded. Jason Calo was among the first to arrive and when he could see nothing unusual, he turned back to meet Howard Walters, who was close behind.

"What's going on here, Calo?" asked Walters. "Who was shooting, can you tell?"

"There's nobody out here but us, Howard. Maybe they've got the nigger inside."

"They're inside," someone yelled near the back of the mob.

They were inside. The Guards had moved inside quickly once they saw the men coming in from the area of Morgan's square. Gentz advised them to replace the blanks with live ammunition, although he certainly hoped it would never be used.

"They got him inside," was the cry that arose again from the back of the crowd.

"Let's go in," shouted another. "There's a stash of rifles in there." There was a rush now toward the door, but it was locked and there was a momentary lull.

Inside the Armory, Joel Gentz and Frank Metcalf were huddled, trying to decide how to proceed. "They think we have the prisoner in here with us," noted Gentz.

"Yes, and that's good. The sheriff needs us to keep the mob here so they can get the man on the train without being seen." Metcalf was feeling good about his part in this charade. "I don't see how they can break in here, do you?"

"It wouldn't be easy," agreed Gentz. "Still, it might be good to talk to them and make them think we do have the guy with us."

"How do we do that without opening that door and givin' them a chance to get in here?"

Gentz motioned for three of his fellow Guards to follow him to the door. He placed them behind him with guns at the ready, then pushed open the door and stepped into the opening. He pointed his rifle at Jason Calo, who was closest to the door, and addressed the crowd.

"I know you think you want to get in here, but I'm tellin' you that ain't gonna happen. I'll shoot the first man who moves toward this door and I'll shoot to kill."

Calo stepped back and Howard Walters stood his ground but spoke up. "All we want is that damned rapist. Put him out and we'll go away."

"As I said before, that ain't goin' to happen." With that, Gentz stepped back and slammed the door shut again.

"We missed our chance," muttered Calo. "The damned door is shut again."

"Didn't see you movin' forward too fast," said Henry Fernandes. Nobody else said anything for a moment. Then more shouting came from the gathered men, demanding action. Jake Turbett had arrived at the rear of the crowd, just in time to see Joel Gentz aiming his rifle at Calo. He realized that the men thought Will Fair was inside the building, but Jake couldn't see how that could be true. There was no fighting now, and Turbett realized that he should be back at his original post. He knew he'd better get there before the others discovered he had left it, and he turned and began running back, hobbled by his limp, but in a hurry.

It was now that Andrew Beeson appeared near the door with another man just behind him. "Howard, I think you need to talk to this man," he said to Walters. "His name is James Harrison, and he has a strange tale to tell."

It was quite dark, but Walters could see that Harrison was not living on the high side of life. His overalls were ragged and dirty, and he wore no shirt. Someone produced a lantern, and in the dim light, Howard could see that Harrison's face was wrinkled and unshaven, and it was obvious that Harrison was far from sober.

"I don't wonder," remarked Walters. "So what is it man?"

Harrison looked at Beeson who nodded, then began to speak in a voice that was quivering and slightly slurred. "There ain't no nigger in there," he managed to say.

"What?" exclaimed Walters. "How do you know that?"

"I was over there," answered Harrison, pointing to some bushes at the edge of the lawn in front of the building

"So what did you see, Jim?" demanded Walters, who took the lantern and held it up close to Harrison's face.

Tilting his head slightly and looking down, Harrison spoke quietly but with increasing clarity. "A man came and opened the door, then others came and went inside. They was all white men."

"How could you see that, you old fool? It's all dark." Howard did not want to believe the man, but he was afraid that he was telling the truth.

"The door was open and they turned the lights on. I could see 'em just fine." Harrison, in spite of his condition, was feeling important and quite sure of himself.

"Well, go on then. What else did you see?" Calo had joined in the questioning.

"A bunch of 'em came out and started shootin'."

"What were they shooting at?" asked Walters.

Harrison shook his head. "Don't know, mostly seemed to be just shootin' at the sky."

"I'm thinkin' we've been had, men," said Walters, looking off toward the railroad station.

"What do you mean?" asked Henry Fernandes.

"They're gonna' put him on a train," responded Walters. "This stuff here was to get us lookin' in the wrong place."

"Well, Jake woulda seen 'em," put in Beeson.

It was then that the shrill whistle wailed at them from somewhere just short of the railroad station. "They're going to put him on that train," shouted Walters. "We'd better get over there right now!"

———•———

Sheriff White had soon realized that the presence of him and the other officers would be a giveaway if part of the lynch mob showed up at the station. He spoke to the station manager, a man he trusted to do the right thing, informing him of his decision. Next, he notified Chief Hayes that he would be left alone to take care of Will Fair, and gathering the others at the back of the building, he led them out of sight on a round about return to the jail.

The train whistle was a welcome sound to Hayes, huddled with Fair in the baggage room. The two of them did not speak, although Will was now satisfied that the sheriff and the chief were acting in his behalf. John Chapman poked his head in and spoke quietly to Hayes.

"The train is almost here. There's a Pullman car near the back, and we'll put you on there in a closet until the train gets well out of town."

"Thank you, John," exclaimed Hayes. "Is there any sign that anyone knows we're here?"

"Not as far as I know, Chief. There's a pair of guys in the waiting room, but they never saw you, I'm pretty sure. Sheriff White and the others have all left." Chapman closed the door and moved out on the north platform as he watched the big engine come into sight and began to slow to a stop.

The officers had all agreed that Chief Hayes was the right person to take Fair to Columbia, and Hayes was quick to agree. He couldn't completely suppress his fear, however, for he knew that if the mob reappeared and believed that Fair was on the train, his own life would be in danger. He could hear that the train had arrived, but he resisted the urge to open the door. He would wait for Chapman to give the okay. The familiar sounds of the steam engine coming to a halt and the other noises associated with the arrival of a passenger train were pleasant to the chief's ears. He loved everything about the railroad, never completely forgetting his boyhood desire to be a locomotive engineer.

A few short minutes passed as Hayes and Fair waited anxiously for some signal to board the train. The door opened and the stationmaster stood there with the train's conductor.

Chapman nodded at his companion. "This is Bernard," he said to Chief Hayes. "He'll put you on the train."

The conductor, Bernard, was a short, portly man with a serious manner. He said nothing at first, but motioned for Hayes and his prisoner to follow him. As they stepped out, the smell of thick coal smoke hit them before a quick breeze took it away. Down the track to their right the men could see sparks in the smoke coming from the engine's smokestack. There were six cars behind the locomotive and its tender. The conductor led them to the last car, a Pullman sleeper.

Bernard went all the way to the back and stepped up on the short stairway to the platform at the end of the car. He motioned for Hayes and Fair to join him as he pushed open the door.

"Hurry up and be quiet about it," he whispered. "Mr. Chapman says we need to get you on here real quick and make sure nobody sees us." The conductor was not at all happy about what he was being asked to do, but he wanted no trouble with the stationmaster nor with the county police. Besides, he considered himself a clever man, and he was glad to have an opportunity to show that.

It was very dark in spite of the two small lights on the top corners of the car, and Chief Hayes was thankful for that. As he ducked into the door just behind Will Fair, he could see no sign that they had been seen by anyone back toward the jail. Bernard ushered them into a small closet on the right side of the car just inside the door. The two men could see that there were others in the car. Sleeping berths had been pulled down on the left side, and two nuns were seated facing each other, halfway up the right side. In the dim light generated by the car's interior lighting, Hayes thought that the passengers appeared to be asleep.

"You're in here until we are well out of town," cautioned Bernard, who reserved a severe scowl for Will Fair. "I'll come back and let you out when it's safe. The people in here are asleep right now, so be quiet and all will be well." He closed the closet door, and exited the car through the back.

The gang around the Armory was on its way to the rail depot. Calo and Beeson were in the lead, although Howard Walters, not as able to run, was really in command. It wasn't long until they reached the corner at Wofford and Choice where Turbett was stationed.

"Jake, Jake," shouted Beeson. "Did you see anything?"

"Not a thing, Andrew," answered Turbett with as much assurance as he could muster, given that he had abandoned his duty not long before. Determined to counter any doubts, he put forth a question himself. "What was that shootin' all about?"

"Never mind that," said Calo. "Are you sure they didn't get that bastard out of there while you wasn't lookin'? We think he might be gittin' on that train."

"Didn't come by here if they did," responded Turbett, hoping no one had seen him near the Armory.

"No use arguing about this now," advised Howard Walters, who had caught up and joined the conversation. "Let's get down there and search that train before it leaves the station."

The crowd moved on with great determination, and Turbett followed, relieved that the interrogation was over.

John Chapman, loading two suitcases on a low cart, saw the conductor jump off the Pullman and make his way up toward the middle car. He went into the waiting room and summoned the two men waiting there.

"I'll put your luggage on, and the conductor will show you to your car," he said to the passengers. "Hurry along, for he's an impatient man and wants to get the train moving." From the window he could see the front edge of the mob coming down Choice Street, for one of them had managed to find a torch and was in the lead.

———•———

As they neared the station, Walters dispatched Calo and another man, both carrying rifles, to the front of the train. "Make sure that engineer keeps the engine where it is," he told Calo. "Threaten him if you must. We're gonna search every inch of that train. It's up to you to make sure they ain't hidin' somewhere on the engine or its coal car."

Walters and Fernandes marched into the waiting room where they were met by the stationmaster. "You're too late to get on now, gentlemen," said Chapman. "She's about to leave."

"I don't think so, John," barked Walters, who knew the stationmaster quite well. "We're here to search your train, and it's not leaving until we're done."

"Now, Howard," said Chapman calmly. "You're a fine man and an excellent undertaker, but you've got no authority over this train. I don't want any trouble, and I don't think you do either."

"No trouble, John. You just step aside and let us do what we came here to do."

"Why don't we see what the sheriff says about this," said Chapman.

"The sheriff has already caused this problem. He's protecting that nigger rapist brute, and we aim to make sure he isn't on that train and on his way out of town. He needs lynchin', and we're goin' to do it."

"Well, he's not here," protested Chapman.

"I've got thirty men with me, John, and we're not about to be stopped, so just step aside. There's nothing you can do about it."

At least half of the mob had joined Walters in the room, and they all went out onto the loading platform. The remainder of the men had gone around the building on either side. Chapman watched them go, then went into his office, where he used the telephone to inform James White of what was happening.

"Are you in danger, John?" asked the sheriff.

"Probably not, unless I try to stop them. Howard Walters is determined to search every car. They've got lots of guns."

"I could come down there if you want," said White. "But I think we have to rely on Hayes and Fair being well hidden. They ought to all be arrested, but I'm afraid that couldn't be achieved without bloodshed."

"I don't disagree," replied Chapman. "I don't know how Bernard may react. He's the conductor."

"Just stay out of the way, then, John. Let's hope the search fails."

As men continued to gather along the platform, Conductor Bernard made his way up the track, intending to talk with the locomotive crew. He was brought up short when he saw Jason Calo standing below the cab, his rifle cradled loosely in his arms.

"This is outrageous!" shouted Bernard as he moved back toward where Howard Walters was standing. "This is against the law. You can't interfere with the Southern Railway. This is Number 44, the Piedmont Limited. You cannot get on this train."

"We ain't goin' to interfere with your train, Mister Conductor. If that black brute's on there, we'll take him off and you can go on your way. If he isn't on there, then you can go on your way. It won't take long." He motioned to the men to begin. Bernard sputtered, but said no more, watching dejectedly.

Four men were detailed to search each car, and they boarded swiftly. Andrew Beeson led four men onto the front platform of the Pullman. The first man to open the door was a gentle farmer named Douglas Sloan. He immediately held up his hand, turning to the others as he placed a finger to his lips.

"It's a sleeper car, fellows, and there are women in there sleeping."

"No matter," argued Beeson. "We've got to search the car."

"We can't do it, men," persisted Sloan. "There are ladies in sleeping berths, and two others asleep in their seats. We can't wake them."

"They'll go back to sleep," said Beeson, becoming agitated.

"What kind of southern men are we to treat our ladies like this?" asked Sloan. "Two of them are nuns."

"I agree," said one of the others. "We've no right to do this—it ain't right."

The fourth man agreed. Sloan closed the door, took Beeson by the arm and led them all down the steps. "We'll report that the nigger ain't on here and be done with this."

Beeson started to protest, but Sloan shut him up. "It's much better this way. Even if he is on there, he'll be brought to trial. What white man's jury will ever find him innocent?"

"He's not here," shouted Sloan.

Every search group made the same report, and Walters shrugged in despair. He nodded to Bernard. "You can go ahead now."

Carrying a lantern, Bernard waved it at the engineer, who was relieved to see Calo moving away.

"All aboard," cried the conductor as he swung up onto the rear platform of the Pullman, and the train began to slowly pull away.

Howard Walters stood watching it. "This ain't over," he muttered to no one in particular.

## EIGHT

# Repercussions

Rosa Fair had spent a restless night. She had maintained her composure until the children had gone to bed, then she went to her bedroom and cried. She had been irritated with her man that morning, which was not unusual, and it occurred to her, even as the tears were flowing, that tender feelings about Will were actually quite rare. After Nathan Black and Isaiah Clowney had left, it began to dawn on her that very serious trouble had come to her family. Her husband did provide for her and he was good with the young ones. The likelihood that he would be returned to her was slim and she was filled with the sudden desire to go to him. That was not likely either, she realized, and as she sat crying in her room, the terrible weight of this tragedy overwhelmed her. The sight of her son, Tom, standing in the doorway caused her to cry even harder.

"Mama, what's wrong?" he asked timidly, slowly approaching her.

Rosa was moved by her son's serious concern and his tender words. She had not meant to share her troubles with him, but the words came flowing out before she could stop them. "Oh, Tom. Your Daddy's in jail and I don't know what will happen to him."

Tom, though not used to emotional displays, felt compelled to embrace his mother. Afterward, he stepped back and asked his question. "What did he do, Mama? Why did they arrest him."

Now that it was out, Rosa decided she needed to tell Tom the whole truth. "They said he raped a white woman, Tom. Do you know what that means?"

Tom nodded. "Yeah, I know what that means. Did he do it?"

"I don't think so, honey. Your daddy wouldn't do a thing like that, but they won't believe him. It'll be his word against that woman's, and we colored people don't do too well when it's like that." She sank down again on the edge of the bed.

Young Tom did not know what more to say. He stood looking down at his bare feet.

"Go to bed, honey," said Rosa. "I'll be all right now. We'll talk more in the morning." Tom left the room, and Rosa walked out to the kitchen, where she dipped a cup into the bucket that held the drinking water. As she drank, she thought about finding the jug that she knew Will kept in the lower cabinet and drowning her sorrows. Instead, she looked in on the other children, then returned to her bedroom and tried to sleep.

When morning came, she was glad of it, although the lack of sleep was nagging at her. She quickly arose and exchanged her nightshirt for a slip and a faded housedress. She slipped into her shoes and after a visit to the outhouse, started her daily chores that began with fixing some breakfast for her four children. She decided on oatmeal for this day, although she did have a box of Kellogg's Toasted Corn Flakes if someone balked at the oatmeal. She checked at the front door and was relieved to find two quarts of milk there. That would be the last until she figured out how to pay the bill. They would need some ice for the old icebox in order to keep the milk cool.

The children were happy with the oatmeal, and Rosa was relieved when they were fed and occupied outside. Tom had gone back to his room but he had said nothing more to her, smart enough to know that she did not want the other children to know what he did. The day was warm and bright, and she busied herself with sweeping and dusting. It was mid morning when she heard the car pull up outside. Maybe it's Nathan Black, she thought, although Nathan did not own a car. Her heart nearly stopped when she saw it was a police car. The driver stepped out first, dressed in his county police uniform. The other man was in civilian clothes and looked as if he was in charge. As Rosa came out on the porch, her three younger children all raced up and joined her, hanging on to her skirts as the two men approached.

"Are you Mrs. Fair?" asked Robert Gantt. When she nodded her agreement, he went on. "I am the county magistrate, Robert Gantt, and this is Officer Williams."

"How do you do?" said Rosa, a slight tremor in her voice. She put her arms around her young ones, pulling them in against her. William, who was 11, was on her left, while nine year-old John and six year-old Jenna, huddled against her on the right.

"We're here to talk about your husband, Will, Mrs. Fair," continued Gantt. "I assume you know that he was arrested."

"I know that," admitted Rosa, holding her children tighter. "But he didn't do it, I know that."

"And how do you know that, Mrs. Fair?" asked Gantt, his tone indicating his disbelief.

"'Cause I know my man," she replied, her voice rising and increasing in volume. "He'd never rape no woman!"

"When did you see him last?"

"Yesterday morning," Rosa answered quickly. "He took our boy Tom down to Thompson's Mill, then had to catch the train so he could get out to Wellford." She knew he had missed the train, but something told her not to mention that.

"How did you know he had been arrested?" continued Gantt with his questions. "And how did you know about a rape?"

Magistrate Gantt and Officer Williams had started out earlier that morning determined to discover the movements by Will Fair on Monday leading up to arrest. Williams had questioned the prisoner soon after taking him in, and then more a bit later in the day. The two men knew he had missed a train at White Stone and had eventually taken a streetcar in from Glendale. Beyond that they knew very little. It was also apparent that Mrs. Fair would not be of much help.

Rosa hesitated before answering the query from Gantt. She didn't want to get either Nathan Black or Isaiah Clowney involved with the police. Still, she had to explain herself in some way that made sense.

"A friend came by and told me that Will was in jail and that he was supposed to have raped somebody."

"What was the name of your friend?" asked Gantt, hoping this would give them another lead.

Rosa decided to give them Clowney's name since he was a preacher. "It was Reverend Clowney," she replied.

"And who is Reverend Clowney?"

"He preaches sometimes over at the colored church." Rosa was trying to be careful not to say too much. She couldn't see how there would be any trouble for Clowney, however. She was worried about that, for Clowney had been of help, especially when he sent his wife to comfort her the previous evening.

"There's a colored church just a bit west of the Glendale-White Stone Road," said Officer Williams, speaking for the first time. "That must be the one she means."

"Would we find him there?" Gantt looked also to Williams, hoping for an answer from one of them.

"No," said Rosa quickly. "He might be at home."

"So where does he live?"

Rosa realized she had never been to the Clowney house, though it was not far away, being part of the little neighborhood of colored people north of the tracks. "It's just up the road there a little ways."

Gantt was becoming sure that he would learn very little from this woman and probably nothing much from the preacher either. "How did Reverend Clowney know about what happened to your husband?"

"I don't know," answered Rosa after a short delay. "Maybe it was his daughter who told him."

"We'd better talk to the reverend and his daughter," declared Gantt, turning to Williams. The two men were walking to the door when Rosa called them back.

"Can I see my husband? Can I go to Will at the jailhouse?"

"I'm sorry ma'am," said Gantt. "That won't be possible."

"Why not? Surely I can see him now can't I?"

"Your husband isn't at the jail anymore, Mrs. Gantt."

"Oh God," cried Rosa, pulling her children tight against her. "Did they . . .?"

"No, no, ma'am," exclaimed the magistrate, realizing what she was thinking. "They took him to a jail in Columbia where he'll be safe until time for the trial."

"Thank God for that," she said bursting into tears. "Thank God."

"Yes," said Gantt, as he and Williams once again moved to the door. "Thank God, and Sheriff White."

———•———

Abigail Potter was home this morning, having returned from her in-laws' house with her husband and gone straight up to her bedroom. Jacob thought that it would be best if she went to bed for the day, but she was determined to get dressed and try to get back to some normalcy in her life. The miserable pain and discomfort that had plagued her for three days had departed.

Dr. Lancaster had attended her for over an hour on the previous afternoon. He had said very little to her after what seemed to her a very thorough examination. She had been thankful for the sleep potion he had given her, which helped her enjoy a deep slumber that had lasted for the rest of the day and most of the night. Jacob was greatly worried about his wife and he had cornered the doctor as soon as he emerged from the room where Abigail was resting.

"Dr. Lancaster, what can you tell me?" Jacob demanded. "Is she badly injured?"

Lancaster found it difficult to answer. He had found very little physical evidence of foul play. Still, he was well aware of the expectations of him, and he wanted to ease the mind of Jacob Potter.

"Mr. Potter, I don't believe your wife is badly hurt in a physical way," the doctor began, "although she has suffered a severe trauma."

"But what did you find? Did he ...?" Potter couldn't quite complete the question although Dr. Lancaster knew what was being asked.

"I didn't find absolutely positive evidence that he completed the act," the doctor replied after a brief pause. "That doesn't mean he didn't—I just can't say for sure." He watched as Jacob Potter shook his head, then covered his face with his hands.

"It's best that you not keep thinking about this," advised Lancaster. "Your wife will be fine, she just needs some time to heal. I've given her something to help her sleep."

Now, as Jacob thought back about the previous day, he felt unsatisfied about his own response. He had received several messages about the crowds gathered at the jail. Some even criticized him for not being there. His father had advised against it, and he had not really felt a strong desire to go there anyway. Did that mean there was something wrong with him? He should be furious with that black devil, yet that was not really what he was feeling even now. Maybe I should go to the jail this morning, he thought, and confront the man. But what would he say?

Still grappling with indecision, Jacob went upstairs to talk with Abigail. She had changed her clothes and was sitting on the bed. When her husband appeared in the doorway, she saw the pain on his face and wondered what he was thinking. She wondered if he was blaming her, and she could not stop herself from bursting into tears.

Jacob sat down next to his wife and pulled her close to him, kissing her on the forehead and brushing the tears from her eyes. "It's all right, darling," he whispered. "You will be all right."

"How can you still love me?" asked Abigail, choking back the tears. "I've been spoiled for you."

"Nonsense," exclaimed Jacob, squeezing her even tighter. "It's not your fault and I love you."

"Oh, Jake, do you? Do you?"

"You know it, Abby." Jacob stood up and pulled her up with him. "Can you stop crying now, darling? We will put this past us."

Abigail nodded, but said nothing. Her husband kissed her lightly on the lips then stood back. "Are you sure you want to stay up, Abby? Dr. Lancaster gave me some more of the sleeping medicine. It would help you sleep now if you want."

"What are you going to do?" she asked him.

"Well, I'm thinking I should go up to the jail, maybe. There are men in town wanting to get revenge for what that brute did to you."

"Don't go, Jake. Please stay here with me. That's what I want."

"Sure, darling, if that's what you want." Jacob was relieved to have the decision made for him. It was the decision he preferred all along, and now it gave him the excuse he needed.

———————

Howard Walters was in the back room at his mortuary when the four visitors entered. They were not unexpected, for Howard had suggested they visit his place around noon. This had been decided as they had departed the train station earlier that morning. "Sit down, men," was his greeting.

Jason Calo was the first to speak. "Do you think they've still got that nigger in the jail?" There were scattered knots of men throughout the downtown, and Jason had been talking with many of them. He had found plenty of sentiment to try to repeat the effort of the previous evening. "We can easily get a big gang together and storm that place again," Jason continued.

"He's right," chimed in Andrew Beeson. "I've got a cousin down in Laurens County and he says he can bring a bunch up here with him this afternoon. All we've gotta do is let him know."

There was more such talk and Walters let it go on for a few minutes. Finally, he held up his hand and the others grew quiet.

"It all sounds good," began Walters, "but it's of no use. The bastard ain't here anymore."

"I saw that in the paper this morning," said Henry Fernandes, "but I didn't believe it. The paper didn't seem to be sure about it either. How can you know about it, Howard?

"He's in the jail down in Columbia right now. They took him out on that damned train."

"How can that be?" persisted Fernandes "We searched the hell out of that train. He was not on there."

"Well, he was on there," said Walters. "We didn't search worth a damn."

"How in hell do you know this, Howard?" asked Beeson.

"Joe Waters came to see me a few minutes ago. He's an ex policeman and a good friend. He said that Officer Bobo told him they took the prisoner out on that train to Charlotte. "

"Maybe that's just a story they've planted to keep us away," offered Fernandes. "Who is Bobo anyway?"

"He's a city policeman, and he was one of the men at the jail last night."

"I know him," announced Jason Calo. "He's a good cop and he ain't no nigger lover. Waters is a good man, too." Calo knew that Waters had flirted with Klan membership in the past. It was one of the reasons that Waters had left the police force.

"Where was he on that train, then?" Fernandes wanted to know. "No way he could have been on the car I searched."

"Waters didn't know that," explained Howard. "I reckon we'll find out, though," he added, looking directly at Beeson.

Andrew Beeson looked away. He knew that the search of the Pullman Sleeper had been incomplete, but he wasn't about to mention that now. It hadn't been his fault anyway. He sensed that he needed to say something, however, so he put the question that was obvious. "So what do we do now?"

"We ain't about to let that damned sheriff get away with this" declared Calo. "There's got to be some way to make him pay for what he done."

"What if he decides to make us pay?" asked Jacob Turbett, speaking up for the first time. "He recognized some of us, and we blew up that gate. I reckon that must be against some law."

"He doesn't know who set those dynamite charges, and he won't go after any of us," declared Walters. "I know James White, and he won't go after us."

"No jury'd ever find us guilty," said Beeson. "The sheriff surely knows that."

"Hell, the damned paper is makin' him sound like a hero," remarked Fernandes. "He ain't no hero in my book."

"That's for sure," said Calo emphatically. "We've got to protect our women from them black brutes, and the sheriff ain't doin' that. He's a disgrace to the white race."

"I reckon we all agree with that," said Beeson, "but the question remains—what are we goin' to do?"

"I've got some ideas," said Walters, "but we need to think about it some more. Meet me here tomorrow night after supper and we'll make our plans."

"We'll be here, Howard, you can count on that," declared Beeson, looking at Turbett as he spoke.

Turbett nodded his agreement, but inside he wasn't feeling at all confident. He was wishing he'd gone home like Jordan Goode, but couldn't think of an excuse that would satisfy his friend Beeson. He followed the others out, hoping again that no one had seen him at the Armory.

---

The word was out that Will Fair had been taken out of the county, but many refused to believe it. A crowd of more than 100 men had gathered in the early afternoon just outside the jail yard where county policeman J. E. Vernon stood guard at the broken gate. Some were shouting and demanding for the accused to be brought out. Others were declaring that the reports about Fair's absence were false.

Sam Nicholls, standing near the front window of his law office on Magnolia Street, noticed the trickle of men passing into the court house and out into the jail yard beyond. Others turned down Wofford Street, and Nicholls began to wonder if the events of the previous night were about to be repeated. He checked with his secretary to see whether he had any impending appointments, and when he saw that the schedule was clear, he told her that he was going to step out for a few minutes.

"I'll be back shortly," he said. "I want to see if the sheriff is in his office."

Sam did enter the courthouse, and when he saw that Sheriff White was not in, he made his way on through and out to the rear of the crowd that had formed just back of the torn down gate. He could see that a man had emerged at the front of the men gathered there and was addressing them. He eased forward in order to better hear what the man was saying.

Douglas Sloan was protesting that the story of Will Fair's escape to Columbia was not true. "It's a hoax!' he exclaimed. "That nigger is still in this jail, and we will get him out. There's a mob comin' here tonight like none you've ever seen."

"How do you know that, Sloan?" came a question from the crowd.

"I know he's in there, because a friend of mine telephoned Coley Blease, and the governor told him that black thug was not in Columbia. If he was, the governor said, he would send him back on the first train. I know Coley will not protect a Negro who has wronged a white woman."

A roar went up from the crowd, and a chant began and grew loud. "Lynch the nigger. Lynch the nigger."

At this point Sam Nicholls pushed his way to the front and held up his right hand. The shouting quieted, and the mob became silent.

"Men, I am a friend of the governor, and I can assure you that the Negro suspect, William Fair, is not in the jail here in Spartanburg. He is in the state penitentiary in Columbia and there was nothing Governor Blease could do but protect him as requested by Sheriff White and Chief Hayes."

"This ain't right," said Sloan. "Are you sure?"

"I'm sure," answered Nicholls. "You men might as well go home now."

A few more protests were aired, but gradually, the men accepted what Nicholls was telling them and drifted away.

Sheriff White had intended to go to his main office in the courthouse, but seeing the assembly gathered between the jail and his destination, he went instead to his little room in the jail. He had heard some of the conversation, and again offered a quick thank you to the Heavenly Father that Will Fair was in Columbia. He had been to the residence for lunch and was relieved to find that his boys were doing a bit better. Dr. Blake had been there in the morning and determined that

William, Jr. no longer had any fever and could get out of bed. Dean was still feverish, but the doctor assured Mrs. White that the little boy was out of danger. It seemed to White that Viola was feeling a bit better, although he felt that she was still put out with him for what had been a horrendous night. He quickly ate the sandwich she had fixed for him, kissed her on the forehead, and left the room.

The sheriff had arranged for a construction crew to restore the jail yard gate to its former condition. They were supposed to begin the work this very afternoon, but he supposed they were being delayed because of the crowd in front of the jail. He had sent Officer Littlejohn out to relieve J. E. Vernon at the gate. Littlejohn was there under the orders of Chief Hayes, and Sheriff White was very glad to have his help. His musings were interrupted by the arrival of Robert Gantt and John Williams who had returned from their morning investigations of the movements of Will Fair. Gantt soon appeared at the door.

"Come in, Robert," invited White as he rose to greet the magistrate. "What did you learn?"

"Not much that you didn't already know, Jim. Things seem to be pretty much the way the prisoner told you in his own statement. He missed a train, went to Glendale and caught the electric. On the way several folks saw him."

"Was he near the victim's house do you think?" This question was of utmost importance to the sheriff.

"Yes, no question about that, but nobody seems to have seen him go in."

"Did you talk to the victim?"

"I went over to Tom Potter's house to see her, but Tom said she had gone back home with Jake. He thought it best not to bother her just now." Gantt's tone was a bit dismissive, and the sheriff understood that he was a bit annoyed with the elder Potter.

"Well, we may need to question her a bit deeper I suppose," admitted the sheriff, "but we've sure got enough reason for arresting Will Fair."

"Oh, yes," agreed Gantt. "I wouldn't have issued the warrant if that weren't true."

"Is the construction crew workin' on that gate yet? They promised to be there right after lunch, but that damned crowd was still out there."

"The crowd's gone, but I didn't see anybody working on the gate."

"I guess I'll have to call them again," replied White, feeling his irritation rising.

"Jim, I think we need to take Mrs. Potter to Columbia to see if she can identify Will Fair as her attacker." Gantt had been informed about her earlier false accusation.

"You're right, Robert. I need to set that up with the Potters and Solicitor Hill." White was hoping to do that on Friday.

"Jim, have you been following that case in Atlanta?" Gantt felt it was time to talk about something else. "I expect they'll find that fellow guilty, but I think he might be innocent."

"Haven't paid much attention, Robert," admitted the sheriff. "Is that the case where the shop owner killed a girl that worked for him?"

"I don't think he was the owner—maybe the shop manager. His name is Frank I believe."

A loud banging sound from the outside interrupted their conversation. "Maybe that's my construction guys finally, here to fix the gate," said White.

"Guess so," agreed Gantt. "Time for me to get back to my office. Hope you have a better night, Jim."

"I'll go along with that," laughed White. "We'll see, though. I've been told there are men comin' in from out in the county, maybe even from Laurens."

"Well, their target isn't here. Take them into the jail and show them he's gone. That should end this nonsense."

"That's good advice, Robert. Maybe I'll do just that!"

---

There was a constant stream of men gathering near the jail, hungry for information about the happenings of the previous night and for sorting out the truth of the various rumors. Some came from work at the mills, others from surrounding farms. Eventually, most were satisfied that Will Fair was no longer in Spartanburg and they drifted away. In the late afternoon, a contingent of men arrived from White Stone. Andrew Beeson was one of them, as was Jacob Potter.

Potter had spent the day stewing over whether he should go to the jail and confront Will Fair. Although he had decided not to do that, the idea kept returning. His wife tried to resume her normal duties, but she continued to break out in tears, and finally had gone back to bed. When his father brought his mother over to help take care of Abigail, Jacob began to think again about going to Spartanburg.

The choice became easier when Andrew Beeson came to the door asking to speak to Jacob. Beeson was known to Jacob, so he went to talk with him. He noted the two cars in the drive, both filled with men.

"What is it Andrew?" asked Jacob, stepping out onto the porch. "What is going on?"

"We're going to the jail in Spartanburg and demand to see that nigger that attacked your wife. We'd like you to go along. The sheriff might listen to you."

Tom Potter had followed his son to the door, and he now joined the two men on the porch. "The Negro isn't there," he declared. "Magistrate Gantt was at my house this morning, and he told me that they had taken him to Columbia."

"We heard that, too, but we don't believe it. We think that's a lie they're spreadin' to keep us away." Beeson had been brooding about this ever since leaving Howard Walters' office earlier in the day. He couldn't admit that they had failed to find Fair on that train, and as time went by he became more convinced that it was all a ruse being put forth by the sheriff and his friends. "We searched every inch of that train and that brute was not on there."

Tom Potter shook his head. "I'm afraid you're wrong about that."

Before Beeson could respond, Jacob Potter spoke up. "You may be right, Dad, but I've got to go with them. I've got to do something—it's eating me up. My wife has been violated and I can't just sit here and do nothing."

Tom Potter could see there was no use in continuing the argument. He supposed he would feel the same way if he were Jake. "All right then,

Jake. Go with them. You can drive my Ford. Your mother and I will look after Abigail."

Now the White Stone men stood by the partially repaired gate in the jail yard. Others had joined them, including Jordan Goode, who had left the mill early when he learned that men from White Stone and other out county areas had determined to make a second attempt at the jail. He stood next to Beeson as Andrew spoke to Officer Littlejohn, still at his post at the gate.

"We're from White Stone," began Beeson, thinking that in itself ought to gain special consideration. "We've got the victim's husband here and we demand again that you send that black bastard out here to face us."

"Men, it ain't no use," exclaimed Littlejohn. "The man ain't here, he's in the prison at Columbia. You just as well go home."

"We don't believe it," shouted Beeson. "We know he's in there and we mean to get him out."

Several of the men near the back began to yell. "Give us that nigger. We want justice."

Jacob Potter stepped to the front. "I'm Jake Potter," he said quietly to the officer. "Can you ask the sheriff to come out and talk to us?"

"What's goin' on Littlejohn?" The question came from J. E. Vernon who had just stepped out into the yard."

"It's the victim's husband," replied Littlejohn. "He wants to see the sheriff. I think it's all right."

Vernon walked back into the jail, and was soon joined by Sheriff White, who strode with determination straight out to the gate.

"I'm here, men." declared White. "What do you want?"

"These men seem to think that the suspect is still in your jail, Sheriff," answered Jake, who had assumed leadership of the group. "We need some proof if that is not the case."

"I can do that for you, Jacob," said White. "You and two of your friends can come in and I'll satisfy you that Will Fair is not in this jail. You must know by now that he is in prison in Columbia."

Beeson and Goode moved through the gate behind Jacob Potter, following Sheriff White into the jail. Beeson leaned over to whisper something to Goode. His confidence in what he had been saying about the whereabouts of Will Fair was waning.

"I bet they've got him hid somewhere in here, Jordan," Beeson said softly. "We'll never see him, but I don't believe what that sheriff is tellin' us."

Nothing more was said as they went up the stairs and walked along the hall, looking intently into each cell. White opened every door, including the restrooms. They went back to the ground level and repeated the process.

"Are you men satisfied now, or is there more you want to see?" asked White. "You can look anyplace you desire because I want there to be no more of this nonsense and I want you to tell all your friends that the Negro is not in this jail or anywhere else in Spartanburg."

"What about the residence?" demanded Beeson. "You could have him stashed in there for all we know."

"What about that, Jake?" The sheriff looked hard at Jacob Potter. "Do you want to go through the residence, too?"

Potter shook his head. "No, Sheriff. I'm satisfied. Come on men, the man isn't here. They're telling us he's in Columbia, and I'm convinced."

As the three men began to leave, Sheriff White called Jacob back.

"Jake, we need your wife to identify the prisoner as the one who attacked her. Can the two of you be ready to go to Columbia on Friday? The county will stand the expenses."

"We can do that, Sheriff. Abigail should be ready by then."

The White Stone men were waiting as the three men emerged through the gate. Several began to shout questions, and Jacob held up his hand.

"He's not there, fellows. Thanks for coming in, but it's time to go home now."

Those who had been expected to come in from other areas had not appeared, for the word was finally spreading that Will Fair was not in Spartanburg. Beeson wanted to argue, but he could see that it was useless.

"Let's go see Howard Walters," Beeson said to Goode. "I ain't ready to go home just yet."

It was evening and Sheriff White made his way to the residence. As he entered the kitchen, the phone rang and Viola quickly answered. White watched, as the color seemed to drain from her face. She tried to ask who it was, then slammed the phone and faced her husband.

"What was that about?" he asked.

"'Oh, God, James, it was a threat."

James went to his wife and she sagged against him as he took her in his arms. "What did he say."

"It wasn't a man," answered Viola. "It was a woman. She called us nigger lovers and said we'd better be careful, 'cause we ain't safe. James, I'm scared."

## NINE

# Confirmation

The Olympia Café was busy as usual on this Wednesday morning. It was a popular place for the merchants and professionals in the downtown area to enjoy a quick breakfast or a cup of coffee and a sweet roll. It was a regular part of Sheriff White's morning routine, his second stop after first checking at his office to make sure there was no emergency. The cafe was a few blocks from his office, but he enjoyed the walk. As he entered, he saw his friends gathered at a table near the back. He could not avoid meeting the scowl of Howard Walters, seated in a booth with Henry Fernandes. White put down the impulse to place Walters under arrest, and nodded instead. He knew Fernandes, too, but couldn't remember seeing him in the mob. The phone call that had upset his wife so much last night came to mind, and he wondered what Walters and Fernandes might know about it.

"Hey, men, better straighten up—the sheriff's in the house!" This shout came from John Story, rising up from the back table and pointing at Sheriff White. Story never tired of greeting White in that way, even though James found himself often annoyed with his friend for this routine banter. He laughed however, and pointed back at Story as he moved toward the table.

"And you ought to be under arrest for plain foolishness," exclaimed White. "However, you're excused since you were such a big help to me Monday night." The sheriff's tone had become quite serious as he sank into the chair that had been pushed out for him. "I'm mighty thankful for all the help I got that night."

Seriousness was not a normal component of this morning conclave, and Moss Hayes thought to lighten things a bit. "Hell, men, let's get to the important news. The Tigers lost yesterday." The Detroit Tigers were a favorite amongst many of the men in Spartanburg because of Ty Cobb, the big star from nearby Georgia.

"I'm surprised to see you, Moss," replied White. "I figured you might take a vacation day or two down at Columbia."

"He can loaf here as well as anywhere," observed Ed Bell with a chuckle. Bell was an auto dealer with a store on Magnolia Street. "Besides, who cares about the Tigers anymore, they're 27 games back of Philadelphia."

"Glad you're on top of that, Ed," remarked Hayes.

"You know, Ed, it isn't wise to be saying mean things about the Chief of Police." Sam Nicholls, the lawyer, was another regular of the coffee club, and the last to speak this morning.

"Free advice from a lawyer?" laughed Bell. "Now that's a first."

"I wonder what Walters and Fernandes are cooking up back there?" James White was not able to forget what was bothering him. "We got a threatening call last night. Viola is pretty upset."

This news put a damper on the light-hearted banter. "Really, Jim?" remarked John Story. "That's awful."

"Not a big surprise, though," said Nicholls. "There were lots of disappointed citizens out there Monday night. I doubt there'll be much follow through."

"What did they say, Jim?' asked Hayes.

"That we were nigger lovers, and we weren't safe."

Before anyone could reply, J. E. Vernon burst in and hurried to their table.

"Sheriff, you'd best come with me. Somebody threw a rock through a window in the residence."

"My God," shouted Nicholls as Sheriff White rushed to his feet, knocking his chair over with a loud crash. As he followed Vernon out, he stopped in front of Walters' booth.

"Are you responsible for this?" Not waiting for an answer, White dashed out with Chief Hayes right behind him.

Howard Walters watched as the other four men who had been at White's table walked out behind him.

"What was that all about, Howard?" asked Fernandes.

"I don't know, Henry, but something must have caused the sheriff to rush out of here just now. It's nothin' any of us have done, far as I know."

"Why did White stop and ask if you were responsible?"

"He knew I was leadin' the crowd at the gate Monday night. He ain't too happy with me."

"Are we still meeting tonight?" Henry was wondering now if that was wise.

"Yes, Henry. In the meantime, we need to find out what's goin' on with the sheriff."

———————

Viola White was waiting in the front room when the sheriff arrived. Magistrate Gantt was with her, having gone to the residence as soon as word had come to him in his office in the courthouse.

"Oh James," she cried, falling into his arms. "This is awful! What are we going to do?"

White hugged his wife tightly and kissed her on the forehead. He noted the splintered hole in the front window, with the cracks emanating out in all directions. The offending rock lay on the carpet where it had landed, shards of glass leading back toward the window.

"It's all right, Vi," he said quietly to his wife, who was crying, unable to stifle the tears. "There's lots of people very unhappy with me just now. I reckon this kind of stuff will end soon enough." He looked toward the magistrate and nodded toward the stone. "Was there a note or anything, Robert?"

"Not a thing, Jim. Vi assures me that she has touched nothing here."

White pushed back a step, his hands grasping his wife's arms, just below the shoulders. "Where were you, Love, when this happened?"

"In the kitchen," she replied, between sobs.

"You saw nothing, then? Just heard the crash?"

She nodded her agreement.

"They picked just the right time, Jim," said Gantt. "Nobody would have seen it. Coulda been some kid just lookin' for an excuse for some mischief."

"Could be, Robert," agreed the sheriff, walking away from his wife, "but it could be a lot more, too. I'm thinkin' I need to find a safer place for my family for a few days."

Viola White had mixed feelings about what her husband had just said. She was frightened, and could see wisdom in being someplace else for a while. On the other hand, she knew that James would not come with her, and she didn't like that thought. She wiped the tears away with the knuckles of her right hand.

"What are you thinking, James? I don't want to be separated from you. Maybe we should just send the children away."

"No, Vi, I want you and the children to all be away from here. This place is obviously a target for these idiots."

"I think he is right, Mrs. White," added Robert Gantt. "We don't know what these people, whoever they may be, are planning to do."

"My brother's farm at Glenn Springs would be just right. They have enough room, and you would be comfortable there." The sheriff was speaking of his brother Faber.

"I don't know," protested Viola. "Woodie has plenty to do with a seven month-old and a two year-old. She doesn't need five more people to look after."

"But you could be a help to her, Vi. I'm going to have to go to Columbia in the next day or two, and I would feel much better if you're with Faber and Woodie."

"We need to get them out there without anybody around here knowing where they are, Jim," said Gantt. "I'll keep an eye on things while you're gone."

After a bit more argument, the decision was made. Agreeing at last, Viola immediately contacted her sister-in-law, thankful that the family had recently installed a telephone. When the problem was explained, Woodie White was quick to extend the invitation, and plans were made for the sheriff's family to be moved to the farm as soon as darkness fell that very day.

The magistrate had another thought. "Have you made your plans for taking Mrs. Potter to Columbia, Jim?"

"Mostly," answered White. "Still a few things to be done. I haven't bought any train tickets yet."

"I'm wondering if we should arrange for Mrs. Fair to go along."

The sheriff was surprised at this suggestion, and amazed that his friend Gantt would think of such a thing. "I admire your empathy for the prisoner's wife," he admitted finally, "but I don't think the taxpayers would think we should be quite so courteous to the wife of an alleged rapist."

"Well, you are right, of course. I do think I will visit her to see if she might wish to send something to him."

"That's good," said White. "We can surely do that for her."

---

Rosa Fair was surprised and a bit dismayed to see the car pulling up outside her little house. She could see that it was the same one that had been there before, but she couldn't remember the name of the man who had talked with her. She could see now that he was alone. She went out onto the porch and waited as he walked up, stopping at the bottom of the stairs.

"Hello again, Mrs. Fair," said Magistrate Gantt. "I'm sorry to bother you again so soon, but I have something to ask you."

The two youngest children had joined their mother on the porch. The other boys were off fishing with some friends. John stood just behind his mother on her left, and little Jenna occupied the other side.

"I guess you can ask," replied Rosa, worried about what might be coming.

"The sheriff and some others are going to Columbia tomorrow to see your husband," explained Gantt, "and we wondered if there was something you might want to send to him." He thought it unnecessary to tell her the real purpose of the trip.

It was hard for Rosa to answer the question, since her mind was focused on the real reason for such a trip. Surely it wasn't because they were thinking about kindnesses toward her or Will. "I don't rightly know, sir," she said. "I can't write nothin' to him."

"Maybe something he likes to eat or a clean shirt, anything that would tell him you are thinking of him." Gantt was struck by the inconvenience brought on by illiteracy, as well as the hard realities of ordinary life suffered by families such as this.

"I don't have any food I could send," Rosa pointed out, "though I could find a shirt like you said." She whispered something to young John, who hurried back inside, returning after a short interval that had been filled with an awkward silence. He held a white undershirt that he gave to his mother.

"I guess he might be able to use this," Rosa said, handing it to Gantt.

"I'm sure he can, Ma'am," remarked the magistrate, "and I'll see that he gets it." Not sure what else he could say, and becoming eager to be on his way, Gantt turned and walked back to the driver's side of the car.

Rosa suddenly ran down the stairs and approached the car. "What's goin' to happen to him, my Will I mean?"

Gantt opened the car door and placed the shirt inside on the seat before turning to face Rosa. "There will be a trial, Mrs. Fair. It will be here in Spartanburg in two or three weeks, I suppose. Your husband will be brought back to the jail here just before the trial is to begin. He is charged with a very serious crime, and surely you know that."

"I'm real scared Mr. …"

The magistrate interrupted her. "My name is Gantt, ma'am. You can call me Mr. Gantt. And I know you are scared."

"I know he's not guilty, Mr. Gantt," Rosa was able to say, trying to stop the tears that were quickly forming. "But we can't afford no lawyer."

"We know that, Mrs. Fair. A lawyer will be provided for him at no cost to you." Gantt started to tell her not to worry, then realized how foolish that would be.

"He's a colored man. What chance does he have?" she asked.

Robert wondered what he could possibly say that would diminish her grief. "Justice is supposed to be color blind, Mrs. Fair. Let's hope that it is." He turned back and went to the front of the car, grasping the crank handle. It was then he felt her hand grabbing his left arm.

"Wait," she sobbed. "Tell him I love him!"

Driving back to town, Robert Gantt's thoughts turned to concerns about the safety of the Fair family. He concluded there was nothing that could likely be done about it. In that regard, he would have been very interested in the meeting held that evening at Howard Walters' place of business.

Although Walters had convened the meeting to consider plans to proceed against Sheriff White, the conversation quickly focused on what seemed to be happening to the sheriff without any help or knowledge from the little group gathered in the office at the mortuary.

"Howard, do you know any more about what caused the sheriff to dash out of the Olympia this morning?" asked Henry Fernandes.

"Somebody threw a rock through the window at the residence," noted Howard. "Nobody knows who it was."

Henry looked around at the men sitting so quietly. "Was it anybody in this room?"

The men looked at each other, some shaking their heads. "Well, it wasn't me," spoke Jason Calo emphatically.

"I don't think it was any of us, Henry," stated Walters, who looked at Calo, Turbett, Beeson, and Goode in turn. "I've learned that the family has also received threatening phone calls."

"So we have someone doing our work for us," said Calo. "That's a good thing, ain't it?"

"Maybe, but we need to stay out of it, I think," suggested Walters. "Jim White is already suspicious of us as you saw this morning, Henry."

"I agree for now, Howard," said Fernandes, "but I'm damned disgusted with the papers making Sheriff White a hero. It's a disgrace."

"I read the papers, too," remarked Calo, with a trace of anger. "It shows how they fooled us and got that nigger on the train."

"I was surprised about the help the sheriff got from the Hampton Guards," added Andrew Beeson. "That's a damned shame."

"What about the men who were supposed to search the Pullman car?" persisted Calo. "They didn't want to wake some sleeping ladies? Was that you, Andrew?"

"We didn't wake up the ladies, but we searched the car." Beeson was not willing to give in on this point, although he remembered his annoyance with Douglas Sloan. "He couldn't have been on there."

Calo started to press the issue, but Walters intervened. "No use of us fightin' and blamin' ourselves. The fact is, they fooled us and got the man out of town. Let's just wait now and see what happens. We can be glad that the sheriff is getting some grief out of this."

———◆———

Sheriff White walked quickly along Wheat Street in Columbia with the county solicitor, A.E. Hill, at his side. Jacob Potter and his wife, Abigail, along with Tom Potter, followed them, having just exited the Union Station after a train trip that had begun early that morning. There had been a change in Charlotte, and the sheriff was pleased at their arrival just before noon. He was hoping to be finished with their business in time to get the late afternoon train back to Spartanburg.

It hadn't been easy to organize this trip. Mrs. Potter had nearly backed out the previous evening. Her husband had pleaded with her to go, pointing out that it was important to have an identification of her attacker. Solicitor Hill had clinched the argument when he implied that they might not be able to keep Will Fair in jail without her help.

"I'm glad we're finally here, Jim," said Hill. "It was touch and go last night."

"Yes, I hope they are ready for us at the jail." Sheriff White was worried about delays that might cause them to miss the train.

"It's all set, Jim. Warden Atkins has assured me they will have a line-up all set for us before noon today."

Behind them, they could hear Abigail Potter questioning her husband. "What will I have to do, Jake? What if I make a mistake?"

Hill turned back to Abigail, assuring her there was nothing to worry about. "It will be easy, Mrs. Potter. They will have a line-up of five or six men and you just pick out the one who attacked you."

The little group had stopped at the corner of Wheat and Assembly streets, and Tom Potter took the opportunity to ask the sheriff a question.

"How much farther do we have to walk, Sheriff? I've never been to the penitentiary before."

James White laughed. "That's a good thing, Tom. The prison is over by the river, on Williams Street. It's still several blocks from here."

"We need to move on," urged Hill. "It's getting close to noon."

In a few minutes they had made their way to Williams Street where they had a view of the state prison.

"Wow," exclaimed Jacob Potter. "It's a lot bigger than I expected."

"It covers several acres," agreed A.E. Hill.

The boundary wall was made of granite and brick, and they could see the South Wing Cell Block rising above the wall in front of them. A taller building, at least five stories high could be seen against the north boundary, and very close to the Congaree River. They moved up to the front gate, which opened just behind a small guard building. Sheriff White, wearing his county police uniform, spoke to the officer in the small guardhouse.

"I am Sheriff White from Spartanburg. We are here to identify one of your inmates."

"Yes, Sir, we are expecting you. Go straight through to the administration building. It is just ahead. Warden Atkins will meet you there."

A uniformed guard led them through the gate and into the building where the warden awaited them.

"Greetings, A.E.," said the warden with a big smile. "It is great to see you."

"Thank you, Tom," replied Hill, the tone indicating that the two were old friends. "This is Sheriff White." The sheriff offered his hand to the warden who took it and shook it heartily.

"Nice to meet you, Sheriff. I've heard some pretty impressive things about you. Stopped a lynch mob they tell me."

"I had plenty of help," White assured him. "It is nice to meet you."

"And you must be Mrs. Potter," said Atkins, bowing slightly to Abigail.

"Yes," interjected Hill," and this is her husband, Jacob, and her father-in-law, Tom Potter."

"Pleased to meet you both," said Atkins, shaking their hands. 'I'm glad you could come."

"How is this going to work?" asked Hill. "We don't want to take up your time."

"We are all ready for you, A.E. You need to go on through to the North Wing and ask for Captain Sondley. He will take care of everything."

Captain Sondley greeted the Spartanburg party and invited them into the main hall of the North Wing Cell Block. Abigail was holding onto her husband's hand, and suddenly grabbed him by the arm, pulling him aside.

"Jake, I don't want to do this, I'm scared."

Shocked at this last minute confession, Jake took both her hands in his and spoke quietly, hoping the others couldn't hear. "Honey, we can't back out now. We have to go through this. What are you afraid of?"

"I don't know Jake, I just hate to face that man again."

"Abigail, we have no choice," Jake explained, now more sternly. The others had stopped and were staring at them. Jake signaled for Captain Sondley to come over to talk to them.

"Captain, would you explain to my wife exactly what will happen?" Jake asked as soon as Sondley came close. "She is a bit unnerved by all this."

The captain tried to reassure her. "It will be all right Mrs. Potter. I understand how you feel, but it will be real easy." He explained what would take place, and that she would be completely safe.

Jake Potter watched his wife with apprehension, concerned that she might suddenly burst into tears. He was relieved when she began to shake her head, nodding in agreement with what Sondley was saying. The officer smiled at Abigail and indicated to Jake that they could proceed.

The captain led the way to a small room off the main hall. They stopped just outside the door and Sondley gestured to a guard standing there.

"Go and bring them in Sergeant," he said to the man, whose name was Beachnow. Turning to the others, he said, "We'll wait here until they are ready for us."

In a few moments, Beachnow returned and led them into the room.

It was quite narrow, but divided by a short wall about waist high running the width of the room. The area behind the wall had a door on each side. A prison guard stood near each door and against the wall there were five black men seated in chairs. They were dressed in very similar citizen's garb, each wearing a hat. Solicitor Hill took Abigail by the arm and moved closer to the divider on the left side. Sheriff White moved up so that Mrs. Potter was between him and Hill. The two Potter men stayed back and out of the way. Captain Sondley stood against the side wall on the right.

The five prisoners had been sternly warned against making any sounds or facial expressions. Abigail Potter stared at them before turning back with a quizzical look at her husband. Tom Potter nodded to his wife, forcing a smile. She turned back as Solicitor Hill whispered to her.

"Take your time, Mrs. Potter," he advised. "You needn't worry, you are completely safe. Just look at each man carefully and let us know if you recognize one of them as your attacker."

Abigail knew immediately which one was Will Fair, for she had seen him clearly on the road going toward her house. She hesitated, however, because she realized she had not seen his face in the house. Of course, it was a fact that she had not seen anyone's face. She whispered something to White, who asked the men to stand up. Abigail indicated that she wanted them to turn their backs. Solicitor Hill moved closer and started to speak, when Abigail, suddenly filled with a blast of courage, commanded them to face about. She pointed to Will Fair, the second man in from the right. When he saw her pointing at him, Will began shaking his head violently, shouting "No, no!"

"Shut up," yelled the guard, rushing to stand in front of Fair.

Will tried to push the man aside, crying, "I ain't the man, it ain't me."

111

Abigail, speaking in a surprisingly bold and clear tone, pointed at Will Fair and said "There is the Negro who assaulted me." Sheriff White asked her to move closer and be certain in what she had said.

"He's the one," she asserted.

A.E. Hill had noted that Fair had appeared quite restless and unnerved as Abigail stood in front of him. "I can use that in the trial," he thought to himself.

"That's all we need Captain," said Hill to Sondley. "You'll sign as a witness that the victim has identified Will Fair as the man who raped her?"

"I will," agreed the captain. "There is no question, she knew the man immediately."

The guards were moving the five men out of the room, and Abigail, her boldness having fled, burst into tears. Her husband took her in his arms, while Tom Potter shook hands with Hill and pounded him on the back. "This is great," he said. "You did a wonderful job, A.E., helping Abigail keep her head." Sheriff White added his congratulations, although he had a curious feeling of discomfort. He couldn't understand it, but he seemed to be a little sorry for Will Fair. It was then he remembered the package in his pocket. He fished it out and handed it to Sergeant Beachnow.

"Please give this to the prisoner, Will Fair. It is from his wife."

"It ain't a hacksaw is it?" laughed Beachnow.

"I think it's quite safe," said the sheriff with a smile. "Thank you."

As they walked back to the train station, Hill had informed Sheriff White that he would not be returning with them on the same train.

"I have some business to attend to, Jim," he explained. "The special term of court will have to be postponed to the third Monday in September. I think that is September 15."

"Why is that, A.E.?" the sheriff wanted to know.

"The law requires at least 20 days must pass for the drawing of a jury," answered Hill. "It's no matter. This case should be real easy, especially now that we have this very positive identification."

Later, on the train back to Spartanburg, the sheriff was feeling better. Their plans had gone well, and he was satisfied to have made the afternoon train, for he was anxious to get home. His thoughts now turned to his family, settled at his brother's farm. Had their mysterious caller discovered that?

# TEN

# A Ball Game

Viola White sat at the kitchen table and watched her sister-in-law preparing supper. She and her four children had been at Faber and Woodie White's home since the previous Thursday, and she had heard very little from her husband, the sheriff. His secretary, Audrey Brown, had called earlier to tell her that he would be home on the train from Columbia later in the day. Viola was thinking that James could be arriving anytime, but she had finally advised Woodie that they shouldn't wait for him to arrive in time for supper. It was just then that the ringing telephone surprised them both.

After answering, Woodie turned and motioned for Viola to come over. "It's for you," she said, "but I don't know who it is."

"It's not James?" asked Viola. "Who else knows I'm here?" She took the earpiece from Woodie and stood up to the mouthpiece protruding from the wall mounting. "This is Viola."

"Do you really think you can hide out there in the country?" came the woman's voice. "You ain't safe anywhere, and neither is that nigger lovin' husband of yours. He ain't home yet is he? Maybe he's had an accident."

"Who is this?" shouted Viola, but the person had already hung up. She turned to her sister-in-law, visibly shaken.

"My God, Vi, what is it? You seem scared to death."

"It's the caller, the one I've been telling you about. She said James was in an accident."

114

"No!" exclaimed Woodie. "Are you sure? What kind of accident."

"She didn't say, but she knew he wasn't home yet."

"Well you didn't think he'd be home yet yourself. Are you sure you heard her right?" Woodie put her arm around Viola, who was fighting back tears.

Viola sank down in one of the kitchen chairs. "She might have said 'maybe'," Viola admitted.

"I think James will be here all right," said Woodie. "We have to stay calm. That woman is just trying to scare you."

"She's doin' an awful good job of it," sobbed Viola.

"What's wrong?" asked Faber White, having just come in from the evening chores. "What's Viola cryin' about?" he continued, directing his query to his wife as he tossed his work gloves into the corner near the coal bucket.

"She got another one of those calls," explained Woodie, "and it's scared her pretty bad."

"Damn, that's a surprise. How would they know she was here? Nobody should know about that except the folks at the jail." Faber walked over to where Viola was sitting, putting his hands on her shoulders. "It'll be all right, Vi."

"She's worried about James," said Woodie. "The caller said something about him having an accident."

"I never expected him to be home yet anyway," said Faber. "Do you think he's late Vi?"

Viola raised her head from the table and turned to look at her brother-in-law. "No, I guess not. We had decided to go ahead with supper. But I'm worried about him because of the way that horrid woman talks."

"Go and call the children, honey, and we'll eat," directed Woodie to her husband. "But don't talk about none of this to them," she added.

━━━◆━━━

The crowd was gathering near Morgan Square as Mayor Johnson sought out his chief of police, Moss Hayes. The occasion was a special remembrance for a civil war veteran, W. T. Shumate, the first Confederate enlistee from the area. The celebration was being tied in with an observance of the 50th anniversary of the Confederate victory at the Battle of Chickamauga in September of 1863. Shumate, who was actually from the nearby town of Greeneville, was a participant in that battle, a member of the 2nd Palmetto Regiment, a part of Longstreet's First Corps. Longstreet's Corps is given credit for providing the hard push that led to a Confederate victory on the second day of the battle.

The date for the ceremony had been put a month ahead of the actual 50th anniversary in order to accommodate Shumate, who was moving to Georgia.

"Hey, Moss," shouted the mayor when he saw the police chief. The two men met in the middle of Main Street just to the south of the monument to Daniel Morgan. "I hope you've got enough men here, Moss," said Mayor Johnson. "We could have a pretty good crowd today. There's homemade ice cream, you know."

"I don't expect any trouble, Mayor. I am down a man, though. You know that Lt. Alverson has resigned pending an investigation by the city council."

"Rightly so," emphasized the mayor. "He shot somebody didn't he?"

"He was doing his duty, Mr. Mayor, far as I know." Moss Hayes had not been happy with the mayor's actions during the Monday night disturbance. There had been several articles in the local papers that were critical of Mayor Johnson as well as Governor Blease, and Moss knew that Johnson was very sensitive about that.

"I don't suppose we can expect any help from our heroic sheriff, either," said Johnson with a smirk. "I hear he's been bragging about stopping that mob all by himself."

"What?" demanded Hayes, his face wrinkled in unbelief. "That doesn't sound like Jim White."

"Well, I received a letter telling me that White was bragging to people in the court house about what he'd done," explained the mayor. "Howard Walters said he'd heard the same thing from several people."

"Who was the letter from?" Moss Hayes couldn't believe what he was hearing.

"Don't know," admitted the mayor. "It wasn't signed, but I think it was someone who works in the courthouse."

"That's crazy," said Hayes.

"Watch what you say, now, Chief," admonished Johnson. "Remember who you work for." Taking advantage of the fact that someone was calling to him, the mayor turned away, leaving Hayes shaking his head.

"I work for the City of Spartanburg," muttered Hayes quietly.

Sheriff White was walking along Magnolia Street when he saw the mayor turn away from Chief Hayes. His gaze swept from side to side, for James White was mindful of his wife's last words to him as he left his brother's house.

"Watch out," was Viola's warning. "There's somebody out there who wants to kill you."

James had been greatly surprised when he had arrived at his brother's house the previous night to find his wife seriously disturbed.

"Oh, James," was her greeting, "I've been so worried." She went on to quickly explain about the phone call and the implied threat about an accident happening to the sheriff. Though he had tried to pass it off as nothing, White was taken aback that his family's location had been discovered by the wrong people. What was happening cried out for an investigation, and he did not know who could be trusted. Who had known about the move to his brother's farm? Robert Gantt, John Story, and the officers at the jail; Moss Hayes knew about it, but who else? He hadn't mentioned it to Hill or the Potters.

Viola had been even more distressed when he had told her that he must attend the festivities downtown this morning. "My God, James, you shouldn't go to that event. It would be the perfect place for these people to go after you."

"I have to be there, Vi, don't you see? I can't be seen as afraid to appear in public, and to ignore a celebration honoring the old Confederacy and one of its honorable soldiers."

Sheriff White came up to where the police chief was standing. "I see that you and the mayor were having a chat."

Hello, Jim," answered the chief. "Yeah, he's a bit sore about what the newspapers are saying. He also claimed you have been bragging about what you did last Monday night. Did you know that was being said?"

"No, but that's pretty ridiculous, Moss. You know me and that I wouldn't do that."

"Of course I know that," proclaimed Hayes emphatically. "So where is this comin' from?"

"You know that somebody is going after me and my family. We keep getting calls, a stone through the window. Somehow, they found out where my wife and kids were staying. It's got me baffled."

"Yes, I know about that. For that reason, I'm surprised you're even out here. You're exposed way too much, Jim."

"That's what Vi said, but I can't just hide, Moss. I need to do my job and I need to be here at a celebration like this. What would you do?"

"I guess I'd be just like you," agreed Hayes. "But we need to keep you protected just the same. Make sure you aren't standing out by yourself."

"I'm keeping a close watch, Moss. I appreciate your advice."

The crowd was beginning to gather, and the two policemen moved in among others, on the Magnolia Street side of the square. The speaker's stand was set up on West Main, west and a little south of the Morgan statue. Chief Moss had found Officer Claude Bobo and asked him to stay close to the sheriff while he determined to keep James White in sight himself.

The eleven o'clock hour came, the time set for the ceremonies to begin, and the 1st Regimental S. C. Band of Spartanburg provided a spirited rendition of *Dixie*. Mayor Johnson, who was the master of ceremonies, took the stand as the song was dying down. Fully aware of the oncoming election, the mayor delivered a lively opening address, emphasizing the glorious role of the home state in the late War of the Secession. There were several luminaries on the stage, including three other Civil War veterans plus the honored guest, W. T. Shumate.

The time interval between the speeches was occupied by the band, and when it broke into its version of the *Bonnie Blue Flag*, the audience began to applaud and cheer, for this old Confederate song was clearly its favorite. James White felt the swelling of pride in his own breast, for he was a loyal southerner, whose patriotism for the cause was as strong as the next man's. On the other hand, he also loved his country, the United States, and was troubled that his state had been on what he could sometimes see was the wrong side of that conflict. He found it hard to be a defender of the institution of slavery, so in his own mind, he retreated into the argument that the war was really about state's rights.

The crowd had pressed in toward the square and the ceremonial stage, leaving Sheriff White standing exposed at the back. Officer Bobo had immediately noticed this and moved closer when his eye caught sight of a flash of light reflecting off of what he thought was a rifle barrel. It seemed to be pushing forth above a trashcan standing in the alley next to the First National Bank building. The bank stood on the corner of West Main and Magnolia.

"Look out!" shouted Bobo, as he pushed the sheriff to the ground.

"What the hell?" screamed James White, looking up at Bobo, who was standing over him.

"I thought I saw a gun over by the bank," explained the officer. "I don't see it now."

Moss Hayes had joined them just in time to hear Officer Bobo say something about a gun. "Did you say you saw a gun?" he asked, addressing Bobo.

"Yes, but it ain't there now."

"Go take a look," commanded the chief. "I'll take over here."

Several men, who were close enough to hear what was going on behind them had gathered now watching as the sheriff got to his feet. The band was still playing, although it was near the end of the song.

Officer Bobo moved quickly across to the sidewalk in front of the bank, quite aware that he could be in real danger if there was an assassin lurking in the alley. He backed up against the corner of the bank building, then eased carefully around the corner. He pushed hard against the trash barrel, and it tumbled over. There was no one there, and Bobo began running down the alley. At the back he reached a cross alley that extended to his right toward Magnolia Street. There was nothing to see anywhere. He felt a bit foolish now, and turned back wondering what the sheriff and chief were going to say to him.

When Bobo returned he could see that Chief Hayes was questioning some of the bystanders, to find out if any of them had seen anything. Sheriff White watched as the officer rejoined them.

"Did you find anything, Claude?"

"I didn't, Sheriff," answered Bobo, a bit sheepishly. "I'm sorry I pushed you down."

"My God, don't apologize, Claude," said the sheriff, shaking Bobo's hand. "You acted with great haste, and you may well have prevented a shooting. I appreciate it."

Chief Hayes had ended his interrogations and rejoined the other two men. "Nobody saw anything. Maybe you didn't either, Claude."

"I'm sorry, Chief," began Bobo, expecting a reprimand.

"Don't be," said Hayes, slapping the officer softly on the shoulder. "You did the right thing. If there was somebody there, he had made sure he could get away quickly."

"That's right, Chief. I thank you both," said White. "Now maybe we should get in among the others. I know I'm stubborn, but I ain't completely stupid."

The festivities were nearly over. The guest of honor W. T. Shumate, now in his mid seventies, had little to say, for he wasn't a talker. Mayor Johnson made the appropriate fuss over him and presented him with a certificate and a plaque. Turning to the audience, he dismissed them with a reminder that homemade ice cream was being served on the sidewalk in front of the KWN Drug Store.

James White loved homemade ice cream above almost any food he could think of, but he knew that there was no chance of that under the circumstances. Nevertheless, he floated the idea to the chief.

"Hey, Moss, do you think we ought to sample that ice cream?"

Moss Hayes just shook his head and Claude Bobo laughed. Neither said anything.

"Well, I guess it wouldn't be fair to my kids.," observed James. "They love that stuff, but Vi wouldn't let them come."

"At least one member of your family has some sense," laughed Hayes. "Where's your car?"

"Over by the courthouse," answered White. "I do need to go home and get some rest. I've got a baseball game to play tomorrow."

"What?" exclaimed Hayes. "You can't be serious. That's just about the dumbest thing I've ever heard you say."

"May be, but I aim to do it," said the sheriff. "I can't let these people shut down my whole life. Besides, I'll have a couple of my deputies there to watch things."

"Come on Claude," said Chief Hayes. "We'd better walk this man over to the courthouse. Maybe the asylum would make even better sense."

"Whatever you do, don't tell Vi about what happened today," pleaded White.

Howard Walters welcomed Henry Fernandes to join him in the booth at the Olympia Café. "Glad to see you, Henry, and that you could join me for supper."

"The wife was glad to get out of cooking tonight, Howard, so it works out well."

"You should have brought her along," remarked Howard. "We could use some pleasant company," he added with a laugh.

"I wasn't sure what you had in mind, Howard, and didn't want to get her involved in any of our activities."

"I've got nothin' special in mind, Henry. Just wanted to congratulate you on your excellent letter to the editor in the morning paper."

"I was tired of reading all the damned flowery articles from all over praising Sheriff White. Especially when he defended a black brute guilty of the worst crime possible."

"I guess he thought it was his duty."

"Duty yes, but there's such a thing as common sense." Henry had not expected Walters to offer some kind of defense. "Besides, you were ready to do something about it yourself just the other day."

"I was and still am, but it seems that somebody is doing it for us."

"You mean the rock in the window of the sheriff's residence?"

"Yes, and the phone calls. But there is more than that."

"More? What do you know, Howard?"

"I received a letter yesterday saying that Sheriff White had been bragging around the courthouse about how he had stopped the lynch mob almost all by himself. That ain't goin' over too well. The mayor told me he got a letter like that, too."

Fernandes was surprised. "Who was the letter from?"

"Don't know, it wasn't signed." As much as he wanted to believe what the letter said, Howard had to admit that it didn't quite ring true. "It doesn't sound like White, however."

"I don't really know the man," said Fernandes, "but he did have a note in one of the papers thanking all the people who helped him."

"Yes, he did. There's more, though. Joe Waters told me that Claude Bobo thought he'd seen somebody pointin' a rifle at the sheriff at this morning's ceremony down at Morgan Square."

"My god," exclaimed Fernandes. "That's pretty serious. Did it really happen?"

"Bobo was pretty sure. He went after the guy, but couldn't find anything. He says that the sheriff and his family are pretty upset."

"Of course I wouldn't want to see the sheriff killed, but I can't say I'm too bothered by him being hounded like this. He deserves it."

The waitress arrived just then, and took their orders. Once she was out of earshot, Henry had another question.

"Do you have any idea who's doin' this, Howard?"

"I figured it was Jason," answered Walters almost in a whisper. "But he denies it and has no idea himself."

"Seems strange," said Fernandes. "Must be somebody who was with us that night."

"Could be, but it's best that we just leave it alone. It's a good thing for us, and we're in the clear."

"They said the victim had identified the brute, anyway," noted Henry. "That should make it easy for Hill to nail him at the trial."

"A. E. told me it should be open and shut." Walters extended his hand across the table and Fernandes shook it. "I'm feeling good," added Howard, "and so supper's on me."

———•———

Jason Calo arrived early at the ballpark in Glendale on Sunday afternoon, ready for the game against Beaumont. The opponent was the Mill League's best team, but Jason was hoping that a big surprise was in store for the day, because he knew that the Glendale manager had arranged to bring in a ringer to pitch against the league leaders. Few of his teammates had arrived as yet, although Jason was happy to see his friend Jordan Goode. It was always a worry as to whether all the team members would be present at a particular game. The players were volunteers, after all, and not usually paid anything, so other entertainments intervened. There was supposed to be some loyalty to the mill, of course, but that could be a tenuous affair, and often players were enlisted who had no connection to the mill team for whom they played.

Even though Jason was not the manager of the Glendale team, he seemed to be more concerned with its fortunes than anyone else associated. He loved to play baseball, and he hated it when games were called off because one of the teams did not have enough players. Jason was getting on a bit in years, and because of his physical stature, a bit too short for his weight, as he liked to put it, he knew that opponents were often surprised at his ability. His was not the typical build for a first baseman, and his foot speed was much better than expected.

"Hey Jordan," he called now to his friend. "Glad to see that you could make it today." Goode was an outfielder, and one of the team's better hitters.

"Wouldn't miss it for anything, Jason," he answered. The two men had discussed the upcoming game earlier in the week and they knew that Sheriff White sometimes played for Beaumont. Calo had assured Goode that if the sheriff did show up, Jason had some special plans for him.

"Did you see where Jess Willard killed a man in the boxing ring the other day?" asked Goode.

"Yeah, the champ knocked his brains out," said Jason. "The guy's name was Young, I think. Wish I could get White in a ring with me. I'd like to do the same."

In a few minutes most of the players had arrived and were warming up. Jason was relieved to see that there were at least a dozen Glendale Mill players, but there was one missing. It was the pitcher he had pinned his hopes on. He searched out the team's manager, Doug Snow, hoping to hear good news.

"Where is this hotshot pitcher you told me about, Doug? I don't see him anywhere."

"He'll be here, Calo, just calm down," replied the manager. "He promised me and he ain't about to turn down that 25 bucks I offered him."

"Are you sure he played at Charleston?" asked Jason. He could not quite be convinced that Snow would have enough influence to attract a man who had played in the South Atlantic League.

"He played in the Sally League for two years, Jason, I told you that at least five times by now." Snow turned and pointed across to the warm-up area beyond the first base dugout. "That's who we have to worry about."

The object of Snow's remark was a tall right-hander, tossing softly to a catcher who was already wearing shin guards and a chest protector. Snow needn't say anymore, for Jason knew all about Jack Mayberry, the Beaumont pitcher, who had recently struck out 28 batters in a 21-inning game against Inman Mill. This was the first time that Glendale had faced Beaumont in the current season, but Calo could remember striking out three times against Mayberry the previous season.

"Yeah," he admitted finally to Doug Snow. "But I think we're goin' to get to him today."

"By the way, Jason " said Snow. "I need you to catch today. The gear's over by the end of the dugout, there."

"Damn it, Doug," snarled Calo. "You know I don't like to catch. The 'tools of ignorance' they call 'em, and that's how I feel when I have to put on all that stuff."

"I suppose you could go without them, Jason, but I don't advise it."

Calo answered by reciting a poem. "We wear no mattress on our hands, no cage upon our face. We stand right up and catch the ball with courage and with grace."

"That's impressive, Calo," laughed Snow. "Where'd you hear that?"

"Don't remember, but I read it somewhere." [1]

"Well I hope you can hit as well as you recite poetry," said Snow, who strode over to speak with one of the umpires.

It was just a few minutes before three o'clock, the scheduled time for the game to start, when Manager Snow introduced Calo to the ringer, whose name was Mike Ingram. He was about six feet tall, and Jason guessed him at 180 pounds. He didn't look to Jason like somebody who could have played professional ball.

"This is Jason Calo, who will be your catcher today, Mike," Snow was saying. "He'll warm you up, but we don't have a lot of time."

"It'll be enough," said Ingram, who could not hide a look of disdain for his catcher. He turned and walked back just outside the third base line to where a warm-up rubber was located and begin to toss the ball Snow had given him to Calo, who had set up at a distance he thought to be about 60 feet. Jason had taken an instant dislike to this pitcher, who clearly considered himself much above this bunch of country bumpkins he had agreed to play with. Jason was unimpressed at first, but after a few throws, Ingram poured in some hard fastballs, and when he broke off two sharp curves, Calo was convinced that Doug Snow knew what he was talking about.

"I'm ready," indicated Ingram, and the home plate umpire shouted "Play Ball!"

---

[1] Harry Ellard, "The Reds of Sixty-Nine."

William James White loved baseball. He loved to play it, and he was quite good at it. At least, that was his own opinion, although he had to admit he wasn't great—not good enough to play at high levels. He did play some for Beaumont, which was certainly regarded as a good team. Of course that privilege was granted largely because the manager of the Beaumont team was David W. Henderson who was one of the sheriff's best friends. At 39 and almost 40, White was the oldest man on the team, but Henderson still let him play once in a while. Today was one of those days, and he was in the lineup, although batting eighth. It was the top of the third inning, and neither team had scored.

James was waiting on deck and he looked around the park. A good crowd had gathered. Many were family members of the players, but others had come because of Beaumont's reputation. White's family was not there, because the sheriff did not think it was safe. He had argued hard with Viola, who figured that if it wasn't safe for her and the children, it wasn't safe for him either. He had explained that if word got out that the county's sheriff was afraid to appear in public, he would be finished as the sheriff. She eventually gave in, but James knew that his homecoming would not be pleasant.

The Glendale ballpark was not the best in the league. It had a completely dirt infield containing pebbles that sometimes interfered with ground balls. There was an outfield fence made of wooden pickets, and James regarded this as one small positive thing about the park. Several of the teams had fields with no fences and this created a much different game.

The Glendale pitcher was tough. Henderson was grumbling about the fact that the home team had brought in a ringer, but there was nothing to be done about it. Although the league rules supposedly prevented bringing in non-roster players, no one ever enforced them, and so Beaumont was stuck with trying to hit this guy. The word was that he was a former professional, but not much else was known.

The batter was Jackson, who swung and missed for a third strike. James stepped up to the plate. There had been some scattered boos when he took the field in the first inning, but now there was a real chorus. Someone shouted, "Here comes the nigger lover." Similar barbs came

126

from the bleachers and a few from the opposing dugout. None of this was unexpected by the sheriff, for it was common for players and fans to rant and insult opponents. The epithet, nigger lover, bothered him though, and he tried to force it out of his mind.

"Well, if it ain't our brave, magnificent sheriff," hissed Jason Calo, who had been waiting patiently for this moment. "Most wonderful, honorable hero that ever lived—just ask him, he'll tell you."

White stepped back out of the batter's box, and the umpire called time. James glared at Calo, but said nothing. The umpire beckoned him back to the plate, and he stepped in again. "Better watch out, Sheriff. This guy's wild."

When the first pitch was on the way, White bailed out. Then the ball broke across the plate. Calo cackled with laughter and James White resolved not to step out of that box again. His resolve vanished when the second pitch came inside about chin high. He refused to look at the catcher who was again laughing. The next two pitches crossed the inside of the plate and White took them both. He walked back to the bench with Calo's stinging words stuck in his ears: "Our brave sheriff has struck out."

"Its all right, James," said Henderson. "This guy's really good." The other players said nothing. James knew that some of them probably agreed with Calo.

The game remained scoreless, and in the bottom of the fifth, Jason Calo managed to work a walk with one out. He stood on first and stared out at James White who was playing second. White glared back, and knew immediately that Calo intended to steal second on the very next pitch. He called time and trotted over to speak to Mayberry, the pitcher.

"He's going to try to steal on your first pitch. Be ready."

"Yeah?" was Mayberry's response. "That little fat man? Holcomb will throw him out."

"He's faster than you think," replied James, who patted the pitcher on the back and ran back to his position.

Mayberry took the stretch position, but gave only the barest glances at the runner, then delivered the pitch. Calo was running, and the catcher, Holcomb, fired the ball to second. White was covering and he fielded the ball on one hop, and held it in his glove down by the base, well in front of the runner. It appeared that Calo would be out easily, but Jason did not go into the usual slide. Instead he jumped feet first at the waiting second baseman. The spikes on his left foot came down with great force on White's left wrist. White gave out a cry of pain, and the ball trickled out of his glove.

"Safe," shouted the umpire as Calo fell to the left of the bag, before scrambling back to it. James White was sprawled on the ground holding his left arm.

"You son of a bitch," yelled Jim Soard, the shortstop, who had thrown down his glove from well behind the base where he had gone to back up the play. He was now running straight toward Jason Calo. "You did that on purpose."

The base umpire tried to get in the way of the angry shortstop as players emerged from both benches. The two managers ran to get ahead of the players, and Henderson was the first to reach the scene.

"This man's bad hurt," he screamed. "The rest of you get back. Get back now."

Doug Snow was there, too, and he added his voice in support of Henderson. "Get on back, men. There's no need for this. We need to get help for the injured man."

"Maybe he deserves it," argued Jordan Goode, who was just behind his manager.

"Shut up!" cried Snow, who could see how this could get out of hand very quickly. Calo was standing on the base, but seemed to know it was time for him to keep quiet. Shortstop Soard was still shouting at him, but the umpire had succeeded in keeping Soard away.

Sheriff White was on his feet, holding his left arm. "Damn, it hurts," he said, mostly to himself.

Henderson took him by the right arm and began to escort him from the field. "You're through for the day, Jim. How bad is it?" There were lacerations and some blood, but Henderson couldn't tell whether the arm was broken. White couldn't tell that either, although the pain was bad enough to support such a diagnosis. Several teammates came to pat him on the back as James made his way to the bench. He had looked back at Calo, who was clearly pleased with himself, but White said nothing. The shortstop was still jawing at Calo, but the umpire pushed him away, and he finally returned to his position.

There was polite applause from the crowd, although a few scattered boos could be heard as White sat down on the bench. The next batter, Jordan Goode, drove a single into center field, and Calo was able to score. Clearly proud of himself, he pointed at the sky with both hands, but avoided looking at the Beaumont bench. Even Calo could understand that they might be one unfortunate gesture away from a big brawl. Although he wouldn't have minded that, a victory in this game was probably more satisfying.

Robert Gantt had made his way from the bleachers into the dugout where he slipped in beside James White. Gantt had decided to attend after he learned that White was planning to play.

"James, why don't you let me take you to see Doc Lancaster? That arm could be broken."

"I don't think so, Robert. I don't want to bother Dr. Lancaster on a Sunday, nor Dr. Blake either."

"There's always my wife, James." Gantt's wife, Rosa, was the first woman doctor to practice in Spartanburg. "She's at home right now, and would be glad to take a look."

"Oh, no, Robert, I could not impose on Rosa like that." In spite of his usual positive outlook, White was not comfortable with being treated by a woman doctor. Besides, her specialty was with eyes, ears, nose and throat.

"Let me take you home then," persisted Gantt. "You need to do something with that arm before it swells up too much."

"I can probably drive myself, Robert." James White was not one to ask for help if he could avoid it.

"Nonsense," exclaimed Gantt. "Let me get you home so Vi can comfort you. I'll get someone to drive your car back for you."

"Well, it might be good to have you take me home at that. Vi may try to finish the job Calo started. She will not be too happy with this."

"Are you back at the residence, or still out at your brother's?" Gantt was thinking that someone told him the White family had moved back to town.

"We're back at home, Robert. I convinced Vi that we were probably safer there than out in the country. Whoever is doing this seems to know our every move anyway."

White went to tell his manager that Gantt was taking him home. On the way, the magistrate questioned White about the unknown stalker.

"What have you done to track down this person that keeps calling you, Jim?"

"Not much that's useful," admitted the sheriff.

"Have you checked with the telephone office? They might be able to tell you where these calls are coming from."

"I did talk to Shirley down there and she promised to keep a lookout. They could be using a pay phone. But it isn't just phones—they are writing letters, too, sayin' bad things about me."

"I heard about that, but nobody believes that stuff."

"Some people do. The mayor does, he told me so himself."

"I don't put much store in what the mayor says. What about today?" asked Gantt. "Did that guy hurt you on purpose?"

"Jason Calo? Yes, I think he did."

"Then why don't you go after him? Charge him with assault?"

"Come on, Robert," said James. "You know that wouldn't stick. It was a ball game and these things happen. That's the way Calo plays anyway, and there's nothing to be done about it."

"Do you think Calo is behind the phone calls?"

"It's a natural thought," admitted White, "but it's not really his style. Besides, most of the calls are from a woman. I don't know what woman Jason could get to make calls for him."

Gantt turned the car off of Magnolia and down Wofford, where he stopped in front of the sheriff's residence. Both men got out, and Gantt helped White up the walk. They were met at the door by Viola White, who saw immediately that her husband had been hurt.

"Oh," she cried. "What happened? I knew something would happen, James, I told you not to go."

"It's not so bad, Viola," said Gantt, hoping to take the edge off her wrath. "A runner slid into him and injured his arm."

"Is it broken, James," she asked now with a hint of sympathy.

"I don't think so, love," answered White.

"He didn't want to go to the doctor," added Gantt, "but you may want to clean it up and wrap it."

"Of course he didn't want to see the doctor, the stubborn fool. Thank you for your help, Robert." Viola helped James to sit down in a stuffed chair.

"Yes, thank you, Robert," he said. "She hasn't killed me right off, so I think I'll be all right. It's safe for you to go."

"Well, I guess I'll keep him after all," laughed Viola. "But it's not clear he deserves it. Good bye, Robert, and thanks again."

# ELEVEN

# Questions

The main hall in the courthouse was empty when Sheriff White made his entrance. He was pleased that it would not be necessary to explain to anyone why his arm was in a sling. He turned into his office and was surprised to find Audrey Brown already there.

"Good morning, Sheriff," she said cheerily. "What happened to you?"

"My, you're here early this morning, Audrey," responded James White, choosing to ignore her question.

"You are the one who is early, Sheriff," replied his secretary. "And you haven't answered my question."

"That's the reason I'm early," said White, with a sigh of annoyance. "I didn't want to have to explain myself to everybody."

Audrey laughed. "Do you plan to stay in your office until dark?"

White couldn't suppress a laugh himself. "I guess it is a bit silly," he admitted. "Suppose I tell you and then let you tell everybody else."

"I don't think it will be that easy," remarked Audrey, whose demeanor was suddenly much more serious. "But I'd like you to tell me what happened."

"Just a baseball game, Audrey. A runner slid into my arm while I was trying to tag him. An unfortunate accident."

A frown appeared on Audrey's face as she tried to understand what James White was saying. "I don't know much about baseball, I'm afraid. Are you sure it was an accident?"

"Not so unusual, really," explained White. "Viola didn't want me to play at all, and I guess she was right."

"Is your arm broken?"

"No Audrey, just a bad bruise and a few cuts. It feels better in this sling, though."

"Did you see a doctor?"

"Well, not one of the regulars. Dr. Viola White took care of me." James laughed at his own comment, but he was already tired of this conversation. "Any problems this morning, Audrey?"

"Nothing much," she answered. "Officer Williams brought in a drunk during the night, but that's it."

"I guess I'll go for coffee then," said James. "I was going to give that up today, but I've changed my mind."

Audrey watched him go, her pleasant facial expression turning to a frown. She shook her head, then rose and walked out slowly down the hall.

James White had thought about removing the sling during his walk to the Olympia Café, but decided against it. He nodded without speaking to a couple of acquaintances, but he couldn't avoid Asa Satterwhite, who was standing just outside the door to his barbershop.

"Hey, Sheriff, who did that to you?"

"Slept on it wrong, Asa," laughed James, pushing on past. Satterwhite tried to engage him further but gave up as White crossed the street and moved up toward Church Street. James was glad to reach the café, where he knew the questioning would be resumed full force, but it would be among friends.

The group was gathered, as usual, at the back, and John Story was once again the first to notice the arrival of the sheriff.

"Ah, here is Spartanburg's own Johnny Evers," laughed Story. "Best second baseman in the whole town!"

White was taken aback, for these men already knew the story. How could that be, he wondered. Then he saw Robert Gantt sitting quietly at the end of the table.

"Is it broken, James?" asked Ed Bell.

"No, it's not, Ed," answered White, all the while keeping his eyes on Robert Gantt. "It appears that Mr. Gantt has regaled you all with some big story about my prowess, or lack thereof, on the diamond yesterday. Let me explain it all right now and get it over with." James sat down in the chair that Story pushed toward him, and told them what had happened. He stuck to the bare facts without any accusations of wrongdoing, nor did he mention Jason Calo's name.

The men listened quietly, the lighthearted banter and demeanor having faded. The mood became serious.

"We know it was Calo," said Moss Hayes. "Did he do it on purpose, James?"

"Maybe, but there's no way to prove it."

"Well, I was there," pointed out Magistrate Gantt, entering the conversation for the first time. "He didn't slide, he just jumped right into James. He ought to be arrested, but I suppose James is right. There would be no way to prove anything."

"Is this related to the other stuff going on—the phone calls, I mean?" The questioner was not a regular member of the Olympia coffee club, but he showed up occasionally. It was Samuel T. McCravy, another lawyer, whose office was on Kennedy Place, a couple of blocks down on the other side of Main Street. He was a bit older than the others, and though his sense of humor fit in well, his advice was usually taken with great respect. James White was surprised that Sam knew anything about the phone calls he was asking about.

"I don't think so, Sam," replied White. "The phone calls have all been from a woman. Besides, Calo is well known to be a rough customer on the ball field."

Moss Hayes decided to get into the conversation. He and Claude Bobo had agreed to keep quiet about the events of Saturday morning, although Moss was tempted to bring it up. Instead, he took a different approach. "What have you done to find out about those phone calls, James?"

"The telephone office is cooperating, Moss. They're watching where the calls originate, but mostly they are from public phones."

"It's strange harassment," offered Sam Nicholls. "I got one of those letters talking about James bragging. Anybody else get one?"

"Not me, but I've talked to several people who did," said Hayes.

"But it's stupid," asserted Nicholls. "Everybody knows that's the last thing Jim White would do."

"The thing is, my wife is really upset by this stuff," said the sheriff. "And it's on my mind, too. So, you have to say it's working. I need to get it stopped."

"I doubt they plan anything physical," said McCravy.

"I'm not too sure about that," warned Hayes. "We need to find out who this is."

---

The bench was located in a wooded area near the northernmost part of Fairfield Park, and the two lovers who sat there were locked in a passionate embrace, oblivious to any observers. The kiss lasted for several seconds before they separated. The woman took a furtive glance toward the small opening between the two bushes lining the path across from her. Her companion pulled her back toward him and she kissed him again, looking into his eyes with pure affection. When his hand lifted up to cup her left breast, she pushed back.

"No, Joe, not here," she whispered.

"Why not, baby," he protested. "There's nobody around, and it's too dark for anybody to see us anyway."

"Because if you start undressing me, we'll never know if someone comes along, and we cannot be seen like this."

"Oh, nobody's gonna see us here. I want you, babe."

"I want you too, Joe, but I'm a married woman. I can't take chances like this."

"Then why did you agree to meet me out here?"

"Because I needed to talk to you about something."

Joe shook his head. "Well, let's talk then. What is so important?"

"It's this business with the sheriff, Joe. You said that nobody would get hurt, but I'm hearing that someone had a gun pointed at Sheriff White on Saturday down at Morgan Square."

"Just a scare tactic, honey. Never intended anything else."

"Doesn't seem like that to me. I agreed to help you with your plan because I love you. I think we've gone far enough, let's end it."

"Not yet, babe. That man ain't suffered enough yet to suit me."

"I don't know why you hate him so. He's not a bad man."

"I've got plenty of good reasons. Besides, he protected that damned Negro who raped a white woman. No good man does a thing like that."

"Some people say that was his job."

Joe took her by the hand. "You've got to trust me, baby. I know what I'm doin'."

"It's what I'm doing that has me bothered. They're paying attention to those calls down at the telephone office."

"Just keep usin' the public phones. Unless somebody sees you, there's no way for them to find out."

"I wish I didn't love you so much. Joe, we need to stop this."

They were both standing now, and Joe took her in his arms, holding her tight against his body. She pushed him away again. " I've got to be going. The last streetcar will be leaving from here very soon."

"I know, baby. Just give me a goodbye kiss."

She stepped back to him and planted a quick kiss on his cheek. Turning away, she started down the path.

"Make a call tonight, babe," pleaded Joe.

She did not turn back, but hurried over to the center path that led to the other side of the park and to the streetcar stop on Bishop Street. As happened every time after an encounter with Joe, she felt sick with guilt. She was on her way back to her house where her husband waited. She loved her husband, she supposed, but he was 20 years older and infirm. No longer a lover, he was instead her patient. In spite of her best intentions, she succumbed to Joe's seduction when it came, and now she could not seem to help herself.

The streetcar arrived shortly after she reached the stop. She boarded the car and took a seat, looking back wistfully toward the park, wondering if she would fulfill Joe's last request.

---

Will Fair was finished with his meal and he sat quietly in the cafeteria at the state penitentiary, awaiting the end of the allotted time for dinner along with his fellow colored inmates. The guards were tough against loud talk, but the prisoners could speak to each other if they kept their voices down. The black prisoners were kept in their own section of the hall. Although he knew the man sitting on his right, Will was not interested in talking. Depression had set in on the day that Mrs. Potter had identified him in the lineup.

As he took Will back to his cell that day, Sergeant Beachnow remarked, "Looks like your goose is cooked." It seemed that way to Will, too, and he couldn't shake the feeling of gloom that had been with him ever since.

The mealtime ended, and the prisoners were led single file back to their cells. Once inside, Will flopped onto his bed, which consisted of a mattress placed on top of a metal ledge attached to the wall. The room was small, about five feet by six, with a very low ceiling no more than six and a half feet high. The door was only 25 inches wide and contained a small barred window in the upper half. A single sink and toilet, plus a very small chest for personal possessions, completed the accommodations. Will was glad that it was a single cell for he had no desire to share it with anyone. Some of the older inmates told lurid tales of overcrowding and shared cells.

Tears came to his eyes as he thought of Rosa and the children. He wondered what she was thinking and what she knew. He went to the little chest sitting near the back wall and removed the undershirt that Beachnow had given him on the day of Mrs. Potter's visit. He held the undershirt against his face, thankful for this small remembrance of Rosa. It was her tiny gesture of concern for him, and it helped offset some of his despair. She was a good woman, he admitted, and he wished he had treated her better. He thought, too, of young Tom and how he had left him at Thompson's that fateful morning. He hated the idea that his children were thinking of their father as a jailbird—would they ever understand? He tried to picture William and John in his mind and imagine how this was affecting them. The most tender of his thoughts were of little Jenna, who liked to climb into his lap at night just before her bedtime. He closed his eyes and tried to feel her little arms around his neck. It was all in vain. He wondered if he would be allowed to see them ever again.

Will had been told that he would be returned to Spartanburg just before the trial, which was likely to be held within three weeks. He had escaped the terrible wrath of the lynch mob, but he figured the same fate was still in store. "No jury of white men will ever set me free," he said to himself. "They're goin' to hang me."

A knock on the wall across from his bed caught his attention. It was the inmate in the adjacent cell who wanted to talk. As with nearly everything else, this was something frowned upon by the guards. It was possible, however, although usually a bit hard to hear. Sometimes they went to the barred window in the door.

"Hey, Fair," came the call. "Are you all right."

Will knew the man only by the name Big Al. "Yes, Big Al, I'm fine."

"Do you want to talk?" asked Big Al.

"Not tonight, Al," answered Will. "I think I'll just try to sleep."

"You looked mighty unhappy."

"I ain't long for this world, Al."

"How do you know that? You told me you ain't guilty."

"What difference do that make? Who do you think them white jurors gonna believe—me or that white woman?"

"Don't borrow no trouble before it comes," advised Big Al. "That's my motto."

"Good night, Al," responded Will.

"Good night!"

———————

Viola White was huddled over the kitchen stove when her husband entered the residence.

"Hello dear," he said, walking over and kissing her on the cheek. "What's for dinner?"

"Fried chicken," was the immediate answer. "It isn't ready yet, though, so you might as well go in and sit down for a while. Anything happening today?"

The sheriff found his favorite chair and sat for a moment. He searched the little table by the chair arm, and then stood suddenly.

"Vi, where's the evening paper? Have you seen it?

"Oh, yes, James," she replied. "I have it in here—there's something I want to show you."

She came into the parlor carrying a section of newspaper. "You're famous, James, all over the country. There's an article in here from the Cleveland Plain Dealer. Listen to this." She pushed him back into his chair and began to read.

"A certain Spartan quality was evidenced by Sheriff White, of Spartanburg, South Carolina, when, with the assistance of one deputy, he protected a negro prisoner in the county jail and drove off a confident mob of would-be lynchers."

James tried to stop her from reading more, but she charged on. "There is a matter for thought in this deed of one southern sheriff. It tends to indicate that most lynchings could be prevented if the officers of the law were men of courage and fidelity to duty. The heroism of Sheriff White is all the more remarkable for having been displayed in South Carolina, a state whose executive has openly sanctioned and encouraged lynching."

"That's enough, Vi," exclaimed the sheriff. "That's just the kind of stuff my critics are complaining about. It doesn't tell the whole truth. There was more than one deputy involved. You know people have been getting letters saying I've been bragging about stopping the mob."

"Well, anybody that knows you, knows that isn't the truth," protested Viola.

"Besides that, the damned thing insults the whole state of South Carolina and the governor. That will not sit well in this town."

"I don't care, you are a hero and people all over this country know it. I'm proud of you James, even though I was scared the whole night." She handed him the paper and started back to the kitchen.

"Wait, Vi. This is the Herald, not the evening paper. Have you seen it?"

"No I haven't James. Maybe one of the boys had it."

"Have you had any of those calls today, Vi?"

139

"Not today," she said over her shoulder as she returned to the stove. "That's one good thing, anyway."

It was just then that the phone began to ring. White jumped to his feet and cried out. "Let me get that."

After the third ring, James pulled the receiver from the phone box on the wall.

"Hello," he said loudly. There was the sound of a person catching a breath, then silence. "Who is this?" shouted the sheriff. There was nothing but more silence.

"I don't know who you are, but we've had enough of these calls. Now…" Before he could finish the sentence, the caller hung up. James slammed the receiver onto its hook, and turned to his wife.

"Nothing but silence. What a coward. God, I wish I could find out who is doing this."

Glad that she had not had to deal with the call, Viola did not know what to say. "Maybe they won't try again, honey," she said finally. "Why don't you call the children, and let's eat."

---

Mayor Johnson stood and stepped around his desk as the three men entered his office in City Hall. Solicitor Hill remained seated as he watched Dr. O. L. Leonard, O. I. Gallman, and Larry Riebling come in. These men were city aldermen who comprised the Police Committee, and they were responding to an invitation by the mayor to come in for a chat.

"Welcome, gentlemen," was the mayor's greeting. "Find a seat and make yourselves comfortable."

"He's calling us gentlemen," laughed Gallman. "He must want somethin' from us." He nodded at Hill as he sat down. "Hello Solicitor Hill."

Hill acknowledged the men with a wave but said nothing.

"I always refer to you men as gentlemen," insisted the mayor with a smile. "A little fib at the right time never hurt any politician."

"You ought to know, Mr. Mayor," chuckled Gallman.

"Solicitor Hill and I were discussing the Fair case," said the mayor in a more serious tone as he sat down in his chair behind the big desk. "I'm thinking it should go well."

"Is the trial date set?" asked Dr. Leonard, a physician with an office on West Main.

"Set for the week of September 15th," answered Johnson. "Ain't that right, Albert?"

Hill nodded in agreement, but once again held his silence. It was unusual for him to be addressed by his first name.

"The victim identified the brute, didn't she?" noted Gallman. "That should make it pretty easy."

"That's what I think," said Mayor Johnson. "Justice will be served, even though our heroic sheriff made sure it came the right way." They all recognized the sarcasm in Johnson's voice, for they knew he had taken some criticism for his role in the events of that Monday night.

"It may not be quite as easy as we all think," Hill remarked, finally feeling compelled to speak. "There aren't any real witnesses to anything. It is her word against his."

"That shouldn't be much of a problem," observed Gallman. "A white woman's word against a black man should make it real easy for twelve honest white men."

"We'll see," sighed Hill.

"I want to know what you men are doing about that policeman, Alverson," said the mayor. "He shot two people during that fracas at the jail, didn't he?"

Dr. Leonard looked at the other two men on the police committee, and could see that they expected him to answer. "Lt. Alverson resigned, but asked for an investigation. That's our job, but we haven't finished it yet." Leonard could see that this answer was not pleasing to the mayor.

"Chief Hayes sent those city policemen down there against my advice," said Johnson. "I was afraid some people would get hurt like that."

"Those men were under a lot of pressure," said Leonard. "They have a right to defend themselves."

"From what I hear, the men injured were just bystanders," pointed out Johnson. " We need to keep in mind what the common people think about all this. We have an election coming up you know. The first primary is just two weeks away."

The city was putting in place a new city commission system of government. The first Democratic primary was scheduled for September 9. A mayoral candidate and four commissioners were to be chosen. A second primary would be held to select four from the top 8 candidates for commissioner, and a runoff between the top two in the mayoral race. Mayor Johnson had been an opponent of the new system at the time it was approved.

"I hear John Floyd is running for mayor again," said Riebling. "Anybody else?"

"Yes, Floyd and Ben Hill Brown are running," replied the mayor. "They're good opponents, although I think people will see that Floyd has lost his touch from when he served as mayor earlier. Brown is calling for a 'new deal', what ever that is. I think my chances are very good. What about you men? How do you see it?"

"I'm not running again, so this will be an easy election for me," said Riebling with a chuckle.

"Hell, Larry, you ought to run in the Republican primary," said Gallman with a wide smile.

"Maybe I should," agreed Riebling. "I might get all three votes."

"Didn't know there was that many Republicans in Spartanburg County," answered Gallman, breaking into loud laughter that was echoed by all the others.

Mayor Johnson stood, signaling that the meeting was ended. "Thanks for coming in, gentlemen. I'll see you at the council meeting on Friday."

———•———

Joe Waters lived in a second floor apartment in a house on Commerce Street just before its intersection with Liberty. His visitor didn't feel comfortable coming to Joe's apartment like this but she felt it was necessary. She knew he would not be pleased with what she had to tell him, but even without that, it just seemed to make her feel extra guilt. The other problem was that the house was the largest on its block, and there were many chances of being seen. Fortunately, there was a back stairway to the second floor, which helped considerably, but it was still visible to some of the neighbors.

Although it was nearly dark, she was extra cautious. Having come down North Dean Street from her own home, she turned on East Main and went all the way to Church Street. From there, she walked north to Commerce and then east again to the alley that passed just west of her destination. From the alley it was easy to access the back stairs. She was confident that no one had seen her.

Joe answered her knock and quickly ushered her inside. "What are you doing here?"

"There's something I need to tell you, Joe."

"Well, of course I am glad to see you, especially at my place." Joe took her in his arms and kissed her. She pushed away.

"We need to talk now, Joe. No lovemaking, at least not yet."

"So. what do we need to talk about?" Joe was annoyed by her announcement about lovemaking.

"I didn't make the call you wanted last night," she explained. "The sheriff answered and I couldn't make myself talk to him."

"Damn it, baby," exploded Waters. "You've got to make these calls and keep the pressure on."

"I don't see why," she argued, fighting back tears. "It's all over now anyway. What you wanted didn't happen."

"But they have to bring the son of a bitch back here again, and I want that sheriff to think twice before he interferes this time."

"I don't like your language, Joe. Besides, there's not going to be a lynch mob this time. The man is going to trial, and he's bound to be found guilty. Then you'll get the hanging you want."

Joe softened his tone and began pleading with her. "Baby, we don't really know what might happen. You agreed to help me, so don't go backing out on me."

"I can't talk if the sheriff answers, Joe. I'm afraid he might recognize my voice."

"No way, babe. You used the paper in front of your mouth like I taught you, didn't you?"

"Yes, but I don't think that is good enough." She was beginning to wish she had not come.

"It is, but it's all right. We can let it go for a day or two." Joe sat down in his stuffed chair and pulled her onto his lap. "I've got something planned that will really have an effect on them. Here's what I want you to say to them on the next call."

Joe gave her explicit instructions about what to say, although he withheld the details of his plan. He gave in to her fears and told her that she only needed to talk if the sheriff's wife answered.

"Just let me know when you do it," he said, "and I will go from there. Now come here and give me some love."

His caresses and kisses began to have their usual effect, and it wasn't long until they were in an intimate embrace. They made their way to his bedroom then, where her surrender was complete.

An hour had passed when she protested that she must get home. They dressed quietly and he escorted her to the door.

"Do you want me to walk you for a ways, baby?" he asked after they had kissed in the doorway.

"Oh no," she cried. "That would be far too dangerous. I'll be all right, but I must hurry. Alex will wonder where I am."

"I love you, baby," whispered Joe. "You are wonderful."

"I love you, too, Joe," she replied. 'In spite of the pain we're causing." With that she hurried down the stairs, thankful for the blackness of the night.

## TWELVE

# Found Out

Albert E. Hill was anticipating a busy day to begin the first week in September, but was not expecting the first visitor to enter his office that morning. It was two weeks ahead of the week in which a trial for Will Fair would begin and Hill's plan was to begin a thorough examination of potential witnesses. His first reaction, then, was annoyance when his long-time secretary, Mary Connolly, knocked gently on his door before poking her head in to make an announcement.

"Mr. Hill," she began, with some hesitation. "There is a man here named W. G. Querry. He says he needs to talk with you."

"Who did you say?' asked Hill, not recognizing the name at first.

"A Mr. Querry," she replied.

"Oh, yes," answered Hill, suddenly realizing who the visitor was. "He's the foreman of the grand jury. I'd better talk with him."

Miss Connolly closed the door for a moment before ushering in the visitor. "He'll see you right away, Mr. Querry. Please go on in."

Querry was a tall man, and rather handsome, noted Mary as he strode by her and went into Hill's private office. Hill stood and moved around his desk to shake Querry's hand.

"Welcome, Mr. Querry. It is good to see you." Hill thought it unusual for the grand jury foreman to be contacting him. Usually, it was the other way around.

"Good day to you, Solicitor Hill. " Querry sat down in the chair as indicated by the solicitor.

"What's on your mind, Mr. Querry? The general session is still a couple of weeks away."

"I've been talking with some others on the grand jury," he began, watching Hill closely for his reaction. "We're wondering about whether there should be a prosecution of the leaders of that mob that stormed the jail a couple of weeks ago."

Hill was taken aback, but he tried not to let it show. It was hardly the job of the grand jury to initiate a prosecution. "This is a bit surprising, Mr. Querry," said Hill, forcing a smile. "Are you anxious for some business?"

"It seems to us a serious offense," explained the foreman. "We've also heard that the sheriff is being harassed about the action he took."

"You are right on both counts, William. May I call you that?" Hill was struggling to maintain civility.

"William is fine," replied Querry.

"However, William, no one has brought any charges forward. No names have ever been given for leaders of that mob."

"Surely Sheriff White knows who they are," insisted Querry.

"Perhaps, but the sheriff has refused to bring any charges. We cannot act unless someone comes forward. Surely you know how this works, William." Solicitor Hill prided himself in his ability to stay calm and stifle his anger. It was very difficult just now.

"I do know, Sir, but surely something should be done here."

"Sheriff White's actions that night were strong and brave. He wants it left there, and I intend to respect his wishes."

Querry could see that he should back away at this point, but he could not quite give it up. "It is a shame, Mr. Hill, that people can incite violence and destroy public property and get away with it. I strongly urge you to reconsider."

"I have explained to you my decision and the sheriff's on this matter, and I ask you now to let it go. You and I will have business concerning the Will Fair case, along with others, to be dealt with on September 15th. I will see you then." Hill motioned with his hand, indicating that this conference was ended.

Querry frowned, but stood and nodded that he understood. "Thank you, Solicitor," he said, and left the room.

Hill was angry that the foreman had brought this to him, and that the manner was accusative. On the other hand, he could not deny that the man had some good reason on his side, and he couldn't completely squash a feeling of regret at his own inaction.

———•———

The sheriff was in his courthouse office, and Albert Hill was glad to find him there. His meeting with Querry had stayed on his mind and he resolved to get some advice from James White. He wondered if he had missed some indications that the sheriff might want to pursue some of the men that had caused such trouble at the jail.

"Can you spare me a couple of minutes, Jim?" asked Hill, pushing through the open door and past Audrey Brown, who had nodded that it was all right to go in.

"Certainly, Albert. You're always welcome. What's on your mind?" The sheriff nodded at an empty chair at the front corner of his desk, and Hill sank into it.

"I had a visit from William Querry this morning."

"The foreman of the grand jury? What did he want?"

"Well, it's a bit unusual, but he seems to think we should be prosecuting some of the members of the lynch mob from the other night. I told him that no one had come forward with any names, but he thinks you know them." Hill looked closely at the sheriff to see if this information might be striking a chord with him.

"I thought we'd decided to leave this alone," said James White, allowing a shred of annoyance to come out in his voice.

"I know, Jim, but Querry got me thinking about it some more. There was some damage that costs the county some money. Maybe we shouldn't be letting people get away with that."

"Feelings were high, Albert. People do things in a mob scene that they wouldn't normally do." In spite of his words, White couldn't prevent the images of Howard Walters and Jason Calo from coming to mind.

"It's more than that, Jim. I had a chat with John Chapman the other day, and he told me how Howard Walters and his men had acted down at the railroad station. They interfered with the operation of a Southern Railways train. John thought the railroad company might bring suit themselves."

"I get it, Albert, but the community is already worked up about this. I'm still concerned about what might happen when we bring Will Fair back for the trial."

"Yeah, that could be trouble. Still, there is plenty of good reason to do something." Hill could see that the sheriff was shaking his head. "I see you're saying no, Jim, but there's also this campaign against you and your wife. I can't help but think that Howard is behind that, too."

"We haven't had a call for several days now. I'm hoping that's over with."

"I'm thinking I might have a talk with Howard anyway, Jim. It can't hurt, and maybe we can head off some further action they may be planning."

"I'm not opposed to that, Albert. A visit from you might do some good, but we're going to be ready for anything when Fair comes back."

Hill stood and offered his right hand to the sheriff. "You've done a great job here, Jim, and I'm sorry for what you've had to put up with."

White took the proffered hand. "If Fair is found guilty, I reckon things will quiet down," he said. "You are confident about that aren't you?"

"I think so, Jim, but there isn't a lot of evidence. It's mostly the victim's word against his."

"Hard to imagine that won't be enough."

———•———

Howard Walters was in the back room at the mortuary when he heard the front door open. He hurried out to the reception hall to find Solicitor A. E. Hill standing just inside the door. He hoped the reaction he was feeling inside did not show, for this visit from the solicitor was not welcome. He recovered quickly, however, and offered his hand to the visitor.

"Hello, Mr. Solicitor," he managed to say with some firmness. "What can I do for you?" Walters' mind was scrambling in an attempt to discern what might be a reason for a visit from the county's prosecutor. He decided it might be in connection with the murder of the man named Cox that was coming to the court later in the month.

"Hello, Howard," replied Hill, dropping into one of the easy chairs that decorated the reception room. "I need to chat with you about something."

"Can I get you something to drink, Albert? It's mighty hot out there." Howard was not a real friend of Hill, but he thought it all right to address him by his first name.

"It is hot, Walter, but you're certainly cooler in here," the solicitor said, pointing to the electric ceiling fan turning lazily above. "Thanks for the offer, but I don't need anything right now."

"If you're sure. My receptionist is out today, but I think I could find something for you."

Hill smiled and indicated that Walters should sit in the chair just opposite.

As Howard sat, Hill came straight to the point. "Howard, you must know that the trial for the Negro man, Will Fair, is coming up in a couple of weeks, and he will be brought back to Spartanburg at that time."

"Why does that concern me, Albert?" Walters knew perfectly well why it concerned him, but he figured it was best to pretend innocence.

"Come on, Howard, you know how it concerns you. Sheriff White and I have discussed the action on the Monday night that Fair was arrested, and we have talked about whether I should bring charges against you."

Walters jumped to his feet with what he hoped was a clear expression of deserved indignation. "What are you saying. Why would anyone bring charges against me?"

"Because it is well known that you were the leader of that lynch mob, Howard. Not only were you threatening law enforcement officers, you caused physical damage to county buildings that is costing the taxpayers of this county. Furthermore, you threatened the railroad stationmaster, and disrupted a Southern Railways passenger train. These are felonies, Howard, and you well know it."

Walters sat down again, knowing the solicitor was right, but surprised that he would go this far with any legal action. His reply was feeble, but it was all he could do. "I don't see how you could prove any of that."

"Oh, I don't think it would be very difficult to prove."

"Even if that were correct, you'd have a pretty tough time getting a jury of my peers to find me guilty, especially in defense of some nigger." Howard saw the look on Hill's face, which he found perplexing.

"I think you might be surprised about that, Howard. However, Sheriff White has no desire to pursue those charges. He is concerned about what happens when we bring Fair back for trial, and so am I. Believe me, Howard, if there is any disturbance then and any attempt to take Fair and lynch him, I will bring charges against you."

Walters bristled. "I don't much like being threatened like that, Solicitor Hill."

"I don't suppose you do, but my words stand! Can you assure me now that you will not interfere?"

"I can, but I don't know why it's just me you're talkin' to about this."

"I've already explained that. There's something else. What do you know about the harassment of Sheriff White and his family that has been going on?"

"I don't know nothin' about that, and that's the God's truth," exclaimed Walters, glad to be on ground where he did not feel defensive.

"You do know that it's been happening, though, Howard. You do know that, don't you?"

"I've heard about it but I don't know who's doin' it."

"What about Jason Calo? We know he was one of the leaders of the mob the other night."

150

Walters was inclined to argue further about the mob and its leaders, but decided against it. Instead, he addressed the question. "I thought it might be Jason at first, but he denies it and I believe him."

"We've come to the same conclusion. Still, it would be a good idea for you to tell Jason about this conversation."

Howard nodded, but did not respond verbally. Hill rose and looked hard at Walters. "A word to the wise is sufficient. I believe it says that in the Bible. Good day, Howard."

A week had passed and Albert Hill had been very busy. He had spent some time interviewing Dr. Lancaster, who had attended the victim shortly after the attack. The interview was not quite what he had hoped for and he was determined to make a second visit. He had also met with the conductor of the streetcar that Will Fair had ridden to Spartanburg from Glendale. Still on his agenda were the arresting officer John Williams, and the victim Abigail Potter. However, just now he was on the way to see Sam Nicholls, who, he hoped, was to be his assistant at the trial of Fair.

Sam's office was on Magnolia Street, not far from the courthouse, and Albert was taking a chance that Sam would be available. He knew that he should have checked on that before making the trek from Main Street, but it was early enough that he didn't think Nicholls would be occupied with someone else. He was relieved when the receptionist waved him into the inner room.

"Hello, Sam," was the greeting. "Hope you don't mind me barging in on you like this. I know I should have called ahead."

"It's fine, Albert, although I was about to head over to the Olympia for coffee. Want to go along?"

"Can't do that this morning, Sam, but I won't hold you for long."

"So what is on your mind?"

"Sam, the trial for Will Fair is coming up in another week, and I need a good man as a second for me. I'd like it to be you."

Nicholls wasn't completely surprised by this request but was pleased that Hill thought highly of him. "Well, I've got the Parris trial and the Wofford trial going on then, but I'm certainly interested."

"It won't require too much of your time, Sam. I'd like you to visit a couple of my witnesses, and then provide some time next week to listen to my plans for the trial."

"I guess I could make that work," said Nicholls. "This prosecution should be pretty straightforward, shouldn't it?"

"There's not a lot to it, Sam," agreed Hill. "The main thing will be Abigail Potter's testimony. I need you to talk to her and make sure we know what she is going to say. She seems a bit put off by me, though I don't know why."

Nicholls laughed. "Well you scare us all now, Albert, so I'm not too surprised. Is her description of what happened a bit shaky?"

"No," said Albert, drawing out the word a bit. "Her story has remained pretty clear and the same every time she has repeated it. Still, I'm afraid she can become a bit flighty under pressure. We need her to be calm and collected."

"Did anybody see Will Fair go into the victim's house?"

"Not that I know about," sighed Hill. "That would be a clincher, but we don't have it."

"Well, you've got her word and her identification of Fair at the penitentiary. That should be enough in the end, Albert."

"I hope so, Sam. If we were to lose this case I wonder what the public reaction might be. Sheriff White is quite concerned about that."

Nicholls had no answer to that and so he changed the subject. "Today's election should be interesting. Have you voted yet?"

"Not yet," admitted the solicitor. "I suppose I'll try to do it later this afternoon. I expect the mayor to win by a wide margin, don't you?"

Nicholls knew that Albert Hill was a friend of Governor Blease and that the governor had expressed his support of Mayor Johnson. "I don't know, Albert. I think Floyd could have a chance. He and Brown together may force a runoff."

"Well, that's certainly a possibility. With so many candidates for commissioner, there will surely be a runoff for those spots."

"Democracy in action, Albert," laughed Nicholls. "I do appreciate your faith in me, and will be glad to assist you in the trial for Fair. I'll look in on Abigail Potter in the next day or two."

"Thank you, Sam," said Hill, rising and moving toward the door. "I'll get out of here and let you go for coffee. We'll talk later."

---

Election day had kept the sheriff busy, for it was desirable to have officers checking in at the various polling places. Interest in the races for city commissioners as well as for mayor was high, and larger than usual crowds gathered in the downtown area. James White was glad to return to his residence.

"Hello, Vi," was the greeting to his wife, who was bent over the kitchen stove. He kissed the back of her neck, which had startled her at first, before she turned and planted a kiss on his mouth.

"Hello, James, my love," she answered. "Rough day?"

"It was a little," he remarked, "but not really too bad. Still, it is nice to be home, and whatever it is you're fixing, it sure smells good."

"It's pork chops, dear," she said, turning back to the stove. "I thought we should have something you really like."

White settled into one of the chairs at the table. "How was your day?"

"It was pretty quiet. Today was a school day, you know." Viola turned and smiled at her husband. "Kind of nice for a mother."

"Yes, I guess so. No phone calls?"

"No, it's been quite a while since we had one of those calls. Maybe they've given up." Viola was not thinking of any other kind of phone calls.

"I hope so," sighed James. "I'm not convinced of that. I won't be satisfied until we get the trial over with."

"How is the election going?" asked Viola, knowing that had been another worry for her husband.

"Lots of interest and lots of people downtown. No problems, though, at least nothing serious." James arose from the chair and started toward the stairs, looking back to his wife. "Children upstairs?"

"They are," she affirmed. "The two older ones are supposed to be doing school work."

"I won't stop them. How long before supper?"

"Not long," said Viola. "No more than twenty minutes I would think."

The sheriff nodded, and started up the stairs. He was at the top step when the phone began to ring.

Viola had been hesitant to answer the phone for many days, but somehow that caution left her now, and she went to where the phone was attached to the wall and removed the handset. "Hello," she said. She couldn't react at first, the familiar woman's voice struck her dumb for several seconds. Finally she dropped the ear piece and began shrieking, "No, no."

James White had rushed back down the stairs and pushing past his wife, he grabbed the dangling earpiece and stepped up to the mouthpiece. "Who is this?" he demanded. He heard a startled "Oh!" from the speaker on the other end, then the click of the immediate hang-up. White looked back at his wife, who stood with her hands raised to either side of her face, framing a quizzical look.

"She hung up on me," he explained. "Did she say anything to you?"

Still extremely shaken, Viola White struggled to answer her husband's question. "Yes," she answered finally. "She said something like, 'You are snakes in the grass; beware of the snake.'"

"That's weird. I wonder what that is supposed to mean?" James went to his wife and pulled her close.

"I don't know, James," sobbed Viola, "but it scares me."

"I suppose it is a warning not to interfere with something that is being planned. I will have to make sure we have extra men on duty when Will Fair is brought back to town."

"I'm more worried about us, James. Some act against you or me or even the children."

"I doubt they'll do anything like that. They just want to scare me into taking no action."

"One thing I know," said Viola with emphasis. "I'm not answering that phone again!"

———•———

It wasn't his favorite thing to do, but when it was an important client, Sam McCravy was willing to make a visit to the hospital. Dr. George Heinitsh had been brought into the hospital on Dean Street after an accident with his car on West Main Street. There had been a mishap with the cranking of the doctor's Model-T, when the crank caught with the start of the engine, spinning quickly and striking Heinitsh's right arm. The arm was broken, and somehow the car lurched forward, knocking him down before running over a fire hydrant sending a geyser into the air. Sam had come to visit as soon as he heard what had happened, and could get away from his office.

In spite of the broken arm and some serious bruises, the doctor was recovering well, and he assured his lawyer that he would be able to go home the next day. Dr. Heinitsh, along with Dr. Hugh Black, had been a leader in the establishment of the hospital at 162 Dean Street back in 1907. McCravy had joked with the doctor that maybe they should think about suing the Ford Motor Company for causing his injuries. He chuckled now at that thought as he made his way down the main hall and toward the front door.

As he passed the nurse's station, Sam looked through the archway into the small waiting room to his left and noticed a woman speaking at the public telephone attached to the wall in the near corner of the room. He stopped for a moment, thinking there was something strange about her manner, and when she turned and gave him a furtive glance, he realized that he knew her. He nodded, then turned away, feeling somewhat awkward. He waved quickly to another acquaintance seated in the twin room on the opposite side of the hall, before pushing through the door and down the front steps.

McCravy stood for a moment on the sidewalk, trying to clear his mind about what he had seen. There was something unusual about the woman on the phone, but he couldn't figure out just what it was. He shook his head and began the trek back to his office. It would be the next morning before it came to him.

———•———

It was very dark and the man could barely see enough to make his way up Choice Street He struggled with the bag he was carrying, for although it was not heavy, its content was alive, and wriggling. It was also important, he thought, to not allow the bag to contact his leg. There was a dim streetlight at the corner of the intersection with Wofford Street, and across the way he could easily make out the large structure that was the sheriff's residence and the jail. He wondered if there might be a deputy around, acting as a night watchman, but the area seemed deserted. He stood for a moment, listening and watching, then crossed the street and moved up the walk toward the front porch.

He felt terribly exposed, suddenly afraid that someone might be looking out one of the windows of the house. He reminded himself that it was 2:30 in the morning, and no one in the house was likely to be awake. His goal was to find an open window, or at least one that was not locked. He would not try the two windows on the porch, but would instead try one of the four that lined the eastern side. He moved quickly now past the corner of the house and bypassed the first of the windows, thinking it would open into the parlor. He tried the second one, and found it closed but not locked.

It wasn't easy, but he managed to raise the window enough to get his hand under the bottom of the frame. He set the bag down and used both hands to push the window higher. It creaked more loudly than he expected, so he stopped and started several times until he had an opening that was a foot high.

"That should do it," he muttered to himself. The plan was to empty the contents of the bag through the open window. It would be somewhat tricky, he realized, since the bag was bunched together at the top and tied in a bow knot with a heavy string. He had to get the string untied while holding the bag upside down inside the window. He donned a pair of gloves that he had stuffed into a back pocket, and picked up the bag and its squirming contents. Grabbing the bottom end with his left hand, and the top with his right he pushed the bag through the open window and raised his left hand while struggling to release the tie with his right. He felt something bang against the bottom of the bag, and he almost dropped it. Finally, the bow came loose and the bag was open. The live contents spilled out but not without some difficulty, and when it was finally done, the man quickly removed the bag, and slammed the window down, no longer concerned about the noise it made. He rushed across the yard and back to Wofford, where he turned down to Choice, making his way toward the railroad station.

Once past Bobo Street, he slowed to a walk. He had purchased a train ticket earlier in the evening, and was on his way to Charlotte on the early morning train. It was not what he really wanted to do, but the anxious warning from his girl friend had convinced him that he would not be safe if he remained in Spartanburg.

Viola White was up early this morning and she had brought the baby, Mary Eloise, downstairs and placed her in the crib in the spare room next to the parlor. It was a convenient place to keep the child while she prepared breakfast and did her early morning chores. She was planning on bacon and eggs for the family this day, and she had begun mixing the dough for some fresh biscuits when she thought she heard the baby stirring. She had just stepped into the room, when she was brought short by the horrible sight lying on the floor next to the crib. "Oh my god," she screamed, backing out of the room. "James, James, come quick, there's a snake in the baby's room. Oh, god!"

She ran back to the stairs, hollering again for her husband to come quickly. The sheriff appeared only in pants and an undershirt, racing down the stairs to his wife who was continuing to scream. "God, James, there's a snake in there—I've heard that they can swallow a baby whole."

"Not unless it's a python, Vi," he said as he pushed past her. He started into the room, but stopped and shrank back, in spite of himself, at the sight of the big copperhead lying next to the crib. He had always been deathly afraid of snakes, and that fear held him in place for a moment. He knew that the child was probably not in danger, but still, the snake was no doubt aware of the heat source somewhere above him.

"It's a copperhead, Vi," he explained to his wife. "It won't swallow the child whole." Still, this was a danger to his household and he was not sure what to do. "Call the jail, Vi," he said finally, "and have Vernon come over here. Tell him there's a snake in the house. He'll know how to handle it, I think he's done it before."

James White knew that copperheads were poisonous and sometimes quick to strike when feeling threatened. This one looked to be more than three feet long, which was larger than average, he thought. His wife had stopped screaming and was on the phone. There was noise on the stairs, and the two oldest boys, John Earl and William, Jr., were at his side, trying to get past him and into the room.

"Stay back, boys," James said sternly. "This is no place for you. There's a deadly snake in there."

"What is it, Papa?" asked John Earl, trying to see past where his father was blocking the door.

"It's a copperhead, John," he replied.

"They're poisonous, aren't they?" John had learned about snakes the past year in school. "How did he get in our house?"

"You are right, they're poisonous, like a rattlesnake. I don't know how he got in here." James knew this was related to last night's phone call, but he didn't want to share that with the children.

Viola had completed the call and came over to where James and the two boys were standing. "J. E. said he will be here in a minute," she reported before grabbing the boys and moving them back into the kitchen. "James," she pleaded, "can you get the baby out of there?"

Somewhat embarrassed by his own inaction, White moved to the other side of the crib from where the snake was lying and picked up the child. As he started to move back toward the door, the snake suddenly slithered forward and blocked his path. The old adage was that "snakes are more afraid of you than you are of them," but James had never quite believed that. He knew that they should try to keep the snake in this room, but if they shut the door, then he and the baby were trapped in there with the snake. He could try to just jump over it, but what if the animal struck him as he was trying to get by. He knew that the strike

158

action could be very quick. "This is worse than facing that lynch mob," he thought.

He continued to think about simply moving past the snake and out of the room. The baby would be safe unless he was bitten and fell down as a result. This thought helped him make the decision to remain still. He watched as the snake moved into a coil with it's head slightly elevated, worried that it might decide to move out into the kitchen. He couldn't quite bring himself to call out to Viola to shut the door to prevent that. Mary Eloise was squirming in his arms and he was trying to think of a way to get her out of the room. He moved around behind the crib to distance himself from where the reptile was lying. He thought of trying to pass the child out through the window, but felt he could do nothing that might keep his focus off the snake. Also it would require coordination with Viola, and her state of mind might make that difficult. The best hope was that Officer Vernon would arrive before long.

It was a great relief for the sheriff when he heard J. E. Vernon's voice as he greeted Viola in the kitchen. Vernon appeared in the doorway with John Williams just behind him. Each man carried a long handled spade and wore heavy, high-topped boots.

"Never fear, Sheriff," Vernon said with a laugh. "The cavalry has arrived."

"You took your time," said White, trying to joke, but still unable to relax.

"Don't worry. John and I have done this before."

"I'm countin' on you to be knowin' what you're doin'." James moved back toward the wall, trying to comfort the baby, who had begun to cry.

Williams moved toward the back of where the snake was coiled, waving the spade. This action caused the snake to begin to crawl in the opposite direction, which allowed Vernon to slam the blade of the spade into the reptile's back just behind the head. The copperhead was pinned against the floor, and Williams now chopped down hard, just below where Vernon's spade was holding, severing the snake's body into two pieces.

"Get the bag, John," ordered Vernon, "and we'll put the head in there first. I ain't takin' any chances on gittin' bit by no dead snake."

Williams retrieved the heavy canvas bag the men had brought with them, and they managed to get the severed snakehead inside. Wearing leather gloves, John picked up the remaining body and dropped it into the bag. "He was a big one," he observed.

"Great work, men," exclaimed the sheriff. "What a relief. I'm not too brave when it comes to facing a poisonous snake."

"Wasn't much you could do without any weapon," observed Vernon.

The sheriff took the baby out and gave her to his wife, who had taken the two boys back up the stairs. "Oh God, James. Who could have done this to us?"

"I don't know, Vi, but we're going to find out." James went back to the little bedroom, where the two deputies were still waiting.

"What a great job," he said again to them. "You didn't even put a dent in the floor."

"No damage but a pool of blood," said Vernon, feeling quite proud of himself. "Want us to clean it up?"

"No, no. You guys have done enough good work for the day. I'll get the janitor at the jail to come over and take care of that. He's had plenty of practice."

"Sheriff, who would do such a thing to you?" asked John Williams. He knew that there had been some harassment of the sheriff and his family, but knew little of the details.

"We don't know yet," admitted James White. "He has a female partner, we know that much. She called us last night with a warning. We don't know if there are others involved."

"I think it is that bunch that was at the jail yard gate, leading that lynch mob," said Vernon, angrily.

"They deny it," explained White, "and we have no proof. Thanks again fellows. I need to go and comfort my wife."

---

It had taken a while for Viola White to calm down and get herself under control. It helped her to return to the task of making breakfast for her family. They ate together, with the parents trying to field the many questions raised by the three boys. Finally, their mother rose and addressed her husband.

"James, I'm all right now. I know you need to get to your office so you're excused."

"Thank you dear," he said gratefully, happy to get back to his normal routine. He left for the courthouse, determined to find out enough to prevent any repetition of what had just happened.

As he entered his courthouse office, his secretary, Audrey Brown rose immediately. "Sheriff," she said, "you have a visitor."

White wondered whether Audrey knew what had happened at his house. He didn't ask about that, but asked instead about the visitor. "Who is waiting for me?"

Audrey seemed a bit nervous. "It is Sam McCravy," she answered, moving toward the door to the inner room.

"Did he say what he wanted?" asked the sheriff.

"No, sir," was her muffled answer.

"Are you all right, Audrey? Something seems to be bothering you."

"Oh, no," she protested, as she opened the door. McCravy stood as White came in.

"Hello, Sam. 'What brings you out this morning? Did you hear what happened at the residence?"

When McCravy said that he knew nothing of what had happened, the sheriff explained it all to him.

"Good god," exclaimed the lawyer when White had finished his tale. "That's unbelievable. I knew you've been getting threatening phone calls, but didn't know stuff like this was happening."

"Well this was the worst," allowed White, indicating that McCravy should take a seat, as he sank into his own chair. "But what brings you in today?"

"I was at the hospital last night and on the way out I saw a woman talking on the public phone."

"Well, Sam, that doesn't seem too unusual," laughed James.

"I suppose not, but there was something unusual about it, and I couldn't figure out what that was until this morning." McCravy was not smiling, and the sheriff was suddenly keen to hear what was on the lawyer's mind.

"What was so unusual?" was the inquiry.

"She was holding something over her mouth as she spoke into the phone."

"What time was it when you saw her making this call?" The sheriff's excitement rose. This could lead to some answers he had been seeking for many days.

"I guess it was around six o'clock," said McCravy.

"My god," exclaimed White, rising to his feet. "We got one of those calls about that time. This could really be important, Sam."

"I thought it might."

"Who was the woman? Did you recognize her?" The sheriff had come around to the front of the desk. McCravy remained seated.

"I'm afraid I did recognize her," admitted Sam.

"What do you mean? Why are you afraid to tell me?"

"Because it is someone you know quite well, James."

"Are you going to tell me or not?"

"It was your secretary, James. It was Audrey Brown." Sam watched as the look of astonishment clouded the sheriff's face. White returned to his chair and slowly sank down into it.

"This is awful," White finally managed to say. "Are you sure? Of course you are."

"I'm sure, James, and she knows that I saw her." In fact, McCravy was wondering if Audrey might have already fled from the outer office. "What will you do?"

"I don't know, Sam, I don't know. It's hard to believe. She has been a wonderful secretary, and she has given no clue that she could do something like this. I've told her about all the things that have been happening." White bowed his head and was silent for what seemed to be several minutes.

Sam McCravy said nothing, remaining in his seat and wishing he had not had to deliver such terrible news.

"Sam," said the sheriff after a while. "Would you promise me something?"

"Anything," promised McCravy earnestly, glad for the awkward silence to have ended.

"I don't want you to tell anybody else what you have just told me. Not anybody, not ever. Do you promise?"

"Well, of course, James, but I don't understand why."

"I'm thinking of Audrey and her husband. Alex is an invalid, you know. If I press things with her, what will happen to him?"

"I'll do what you ask, James, but if you change your mind I will be glad to testify to what I saw."

"Thanks for your promise, Sam, and for telling me about this. At least I can bring all this stuff to an end now. I'm very grateful."

"I'll leave you to it, then," said McCravy. "You're a good man, James."

McCravy left the room and was somewhat surprised to see that Audrey was still there, standing beside her desk. He nodded toward her and went out. It was then that the sheriff beckoned Audrey into the inner office. "Shut the door, Audrey," he instructed.

Both took seats as Audrey burst into tears. James let her cry for a couple of minutes, before speaking to her in a quiet voice.

"Stop your crying now, Audrey, and tell me what's been going on. I suspect you know what Sam McCravy was here to tell me. Do you know what happened at my residence this morning?"

Audrey continued her sobbing, but she did manage to indicate that she didn't know what he was referring to regarding this morning. When he told her about the snake she began crying again, unable to say anything. White waited patiently until she finally stopped. "Nobody was supposed to get hurt," she finally managed to say.

"What was supposed to happen, and who was doing it?" demanded the sheriff.

Between sobs, Audrey managed to tell the sheriff everything she knew, revealing the name of Joe Waters and admitting that she had fallen in love with him.

"I hated what I was doing, but I'm in love with Joe, and he made me promise to make those calls. He always claimed that he never intended to hurt you or your wife, or anyone in your family. He never told me the things he was doing."

"My god, Audrey. You scared my wife to death with those terrible calls, especially the last one about the snake. Where is Joe Waters now?"

"I warned him that you might know and he left town on the morning train. I'm through with him, Mr. White. You have to believe that."

"I hope so, Audrey."

"What will you do with me. Am I going to jail?"

"Why didn't you leave town with Joe?"

"Because I couldn't hurt Alex like that. I'm so ashamed of what I did."

"Audrey, I am thinking of Alex, too. He doesn't deserve what you have been doing to him. To save him all this anguish, I'm going to let this go. You will remain here as my secretary, and no one will know about your part in it. I am going to name Joe Waters as the guilty party, but I won't go after him."

"But what about Mr. McCravy, he knows about me?"

"He has promised to keep the secret. No one need ever know unless you have let someone else know about it. Have you?"

"I don't think so, Sheriff. I don't deserve this, but you can count on me from now on. I'll always regret what I've done to you because you are the best man in all the world."

White rose and took Audrey into his arms. "I forgive you, Audrey, and I'm very glad this is over with."

She stood on her toes and kissed him on the cheek. "Thank you and God," she murmured.

"There is one last thing I have to say, Audrey," said White, with steely resolve. "If Joe Waters shows up in Spartanburg County again, he will be arrested and all these promises are out the window."

"I understand."

# THIRTEEN

# The Grand Jury

The story about the snake was all over town by noon, and by late afternoon it was known that Joe Waters was the culprit. Henry Fernandes brought the news to Howard Walters.

"Did you hear about the snake for the snake?" was the way Henry began the conversation.

"Yes, but I still don't know who is behind it. Was it you, Henry?" Howard asked with a laugh.

"No, didn't you know? It was Joe Waters."

"Joe Waters? Well I'll be damned. I knew he didn't like the sheriff, but I didn't think he would do something like that."

"That's the story, and White isn't denying it. I'm kind of surprised, too. I always thought Calo was behind that stuff."

"Jason convinced me he wasn't the one," said Howard. "I didn't like what White did, but he was doing what he thought was his job. I don't wish him harm." Walters was remembering his talk with Solicitor Hill.

"They're gonna bring that Negro back to town this weekend, Howard. What are we gonna do about it?" Henry had dropped into a soft chair in the receiving parlor. Walters sat down opposite him.

"Not a thing, Henry," exclaimed Howard. "Not a thing!"

"You can't mean that Howard. They have to bring him off that train. We need to get enough people together to take him away."

"You can leave me out," insisted Walters. "The sheriff knows what I did before, and he won't let us get away with anything like that again.

Even Hill has pointed that out to me." Howard couldn't quite bring himself to explain that he had been warned.

"We can't take a chance that bastard gets off," said Henry with some heat.

"The solicitor assures me that won't happen. That nigger is guilty and he'll be hanged for sure. The case is solid." Albert Hill had not quite said that, of course, but Howard preferred to believe it.

"Well, I'm a bit disappointed in you, Howard. Besides, we don't hang people anymore in South Carolina. It's the electric chair these days."

"Well, I knew that," said Walters, sheepishly. "But he'll get the chair."

"I wish I could be so sure as you are," said Fernandes. "I'll see what Calo has to say."

"Jason and I have had this conversation, too, Henry, and I think he'll agree with me."

"Damn!" exclaimed Fernandes. "You guys are big sissies."

---

Magistrate Robert Gantt had taken an unusual interest in Will Fair's family, in particular, his wife Rosa. Robert couldn't have explained it, except that he felt sorry that she had never had a chance to talk with her husband after he was arrested. He was at her place now because he wanted her to know that Will was being brought back to town to face trial.

Rosa Fair heard the car drive into her yard, and she recognized it as the one belonging to the man who had been there twice before. She tried to remember his name, but it escaped her. She thought about pretending she wasn't home, but she figured that one of the children, who were playing out back, would betray her. Instead, she moved out the door, standing on the porch as she watched Gantt approaching.

"Hello, Mrs. Fair," was his cheerful greeting. He stopped at the bottom of the porch stairs.

"Hello," was her quiet, hesitant reply. "What do you want?"

"I have some news for you. They will be bringing Will back this weekend."

"Oh," exclaimed Rosa with surprise. "Is it safe for him?"

"It has to be, Mrs. Fair, because he has to come back for the trial." Gantt could see the pain in her face. "We will make sure of it."

Rosa could not stop the tears that filled her eyes and trickled down her cheeks. "I'm afraid, Mr., uh . . ."

"Gantt," Robert said to finish her sentence. "My name is Mr. Gantt."

"I'm sorry," Rosa uttered through her tears. "I couldn't remember."

"It's all right," he assured her.

"They'll lynch him," she declared, finishing her earlier thought.

"They tried that before, but the sheriff didn't allow it," Robert reminded her. "We'll be ready for anything they try. We are keeping his arrival time a secret—no one knows when he is coming."

Rosa shook her head but said nothing more.

"I do want you to be ready, Mrs. Fair. We will try to arrange for you to see Will sometime before the trial." Gantt walked up and put his hands on Rosa's shoulders. "How does that sound?"

Rosa lifted her face and looked into Robert's eyes. "That would be nice, Mr. Gantt. You have been very good to me."

Just then, fourteen year-old Tom came around the corner of the house. "Mom," he cried. "What is it, what is this man doing here?

"It's all right, Tom, honey. He has news about your daddy."

The boy looked puzzled and angry. "What news? Is he coming home?"

"No, honey, but they're bringin' him back to town."

"It's time for me to go," said Gantt, retreating down the stairs and back to his car. "I'll be in touch when it's time," he remarked as he opened the car door.

"Thank you so much, Mr. Gantt," called Rosa, determined not to forget the name again.

She waved and pulled Tom to her side. "It'll be all right now, Tom. Don't you worry none."

The train from Columbia was scheduled to arrive just after 6:00 p.m. The day and time had been kept as a secret but Sheriff White knew that a determined person could easily check train schedules and figure out the possibilities. He had chosen this time on a Sunday evening, knowing that many of the churches held services at that time on Sundays. It struck White as strange that he was thinking that church services might reduce the chances of a lynch mob gathering. The church people would generally be opposed to mob action, but the circumstances were such that many of these good people were convinced that hanging Will Fair was the only path to sure justice. At least that was how White felt in excusing some of his acquaintances for their actions.

Officers Vernon and Williams had been sent to Columbia to retrieve the prisoner, and the sheriff along with five other deputies stood outside the station house awaiting their arrival. The whistle from the approaching locomotive signaled that Will Fair would soon be with them and Sheriff White sent a deputy along the track in each direction. Officer Claude Bobo came out of the waiting room and hurried to where White was standing.

"I took a look all around, Sheriff," stated Bobo. "It is pretty quiet. There are a few men scattered between here and the jail, but they don't seem threatening."

"Thanks, Claude," responded White. "We need to keep an eye out, though. These damned mobs can gather pretty fast." He waved at the other men, calling them together. "Stay close, men. We'll keep a ring around the prisoner all the way to the jail."

The train soon pulled into the station. Vernon and Williams stepped down from the first car with Will Fair between them. Fair was dressed in a suit that was a bit too large for him, and was handcuffed to Vernon. The look on the prisoner's face was one of fear and confusion. Fair and Vernon were surrounded by the deputies and they all began a brisk walk toward the jail, led by Sheriff White.

"We'll go down Choice Street, men," he said. White was surprised to see that a number of people were lining up along the edge of the street. There were several women in the crowd.

Officer Bobo moved up beside the sheriff. "These folks weren't here just a few minutes ago," he explained, concerned about what the sheriff was thinking about his earlier report.

"It's all right, Claude," the sheriff assured him. "I told you they could gather in a hurry. So far they seem peaceful enough." White briefly contemplated taking them through his private residence, thinking there might be a more determined group at the jail-yard gate. He decided against it.

"We'll go down the near side of the yard and then through the main gate," he declared.

There was another small crowd of men near the gate, the same gate that had been blown down by dynamite on the night of Will Fair's arrest. When the sheriff's cohort approached, the crowd was mostly quiet, although there were a few shouts aimed at Will.

"There's the nigger," hollered one.

"Hang him," yelled another.

The jailer, E. L. Wilson, had been instructed to be ready to unlock the gate and he was there to do that as soon as the sheriff appeared. Sheriff White, Will Fair, and the eight officers slipped quickly through the gate, across the yard, and into the jailhouse. Robert Gantt was waiting for them and he took Will Fair by the arm.

"Sheriff," said Gantt, "let's get these cuffs off the prisoner. There is someone here to see him."

"Yeah, I'll be glad to get these cuffs off myself," remarked Officer Vernon. He led Fair over to the side and fished a key from his pocket to unlock the cuffs, removing them from his own arm first.

"Who's here to see him, Robert?" asked Sheriff White quietly, moving out of earshot of Vernon and the prisoner.

"I've brought his wife in, James. She hasn't seen him since before his arrest."

"You've taken a real interest in her haven't you, Robert? It is very nice of you, but I wonder if it is safe." White was fearful that someone might abuse the woman once it was known who she was.

Gantt was surprised at the comment. "Surely no one is that crass. How could anyone blame her?"

169

"Logic ain't one of the driving forces when people get riled up," answered White. "Where is she?"

Gantt nodded at the open door across the hall, and White led Will into the little room he used as an office. Rosa Fair was seated in one of the two chairs sitting in front of the desk, and she jumped up, rushing to meet her husband as he entered the room.

"Oh, Will," she cried. "I'm so glad to see you, honey. I thought I might never see you again." Will took her in his arms and kissed her, holding the embrace for several seconds.

"I'm mighty glad to see you, too darlin'," he said softly. They sat down in the two chairs and faced each other, both reaching out to hold the other's hands.

"How did you get here?" Will wanted to know.

"Mr. Gantt brought me in. He's been very nice to me."

Will's joyous mood darkened. "They goin' to hang me Rosa. You know that, don't you?"

"Mr. Gantt says you will have a trial."

"Yes, Rosa. And then they'll hang me." Will had heard the talk about the electric chair, but he still thought in terms of hanging. "Can you and the children go and live with your Mama?"

"Oh, Will. I wish you wouldn't talk like that." Rosa could not stop the tears.

"You have to make some plans, Rosa. I ain't goin' to be around."

"Preacher Clowney and his wife have been a big help."

"I'm glad, but you can't count on that for very long. I'm hopin' your Mama can take you in."

They stood, holding each other. Will reached out and put his hand under her chin, raising her face toward his. "You ain't asked me, but I'm innocent, Rosa. I didn't do the things they's chargin' me with."

She looked down, staring at the floor for a moment, then looked her husband in the eye and spoke. "I know that, Will. I know you wouldn't rape no woman."

"I'm glad of that, at least," he murmured. "And thank you for sendin' me the shirt. It meant a lot to me."

Sheriff White had pulled the door shut when Will went in. Now Jailer Wilson knocked lightly, and pushed the door open.

"Sorry folks, but I've got to take the prisoner up stairs now."

Will took his wife into his arms and kissed her again. "I wish I could see the kids one more time," he whispered. Rosa burst into tears, crying loudly.

"Surely they'll allow it," she managed to say. "I'll ask Mr. Gantt."

———•———

William Querry sat in the front row of the courtroom, on the right side of the aisle. He was joined by the remainder of the 18-man grand jury serving the seventh circuit and assembled for this special session of the court of general sessions. William knew that the special session had been ordered by Governor Blease in response to the Will Fair case. There were a few other new cases requiring action by the grand jury as well as some regular court cases held over from the last session.

The public was well aware of the purpose of the court session, and every seat available to spectators was already occupied and people were jammed into the aisles. It was shortly past 10 a.m. when the bailiff asked everyone to rise as he announced the entrance of Judge George W. Gage.

The newspapers had announced earlier the appointment of Gage, who came from the sixth circuit. Querry had not encountered Judge Gage before, and he liked to know something about judges involved with his own cases. His research had brought some conflicting opinions. Governor Blease was known to be no friend of the Negro race, and the fact that Gage was his appointee led some to think Gage would be especially hard on Fair. Others, however, insisted that Gage had a good reputation in the sixth circuit as strict but just.

Querry watched expectantly as the judge took his seat, greeted the crowd and began with the first business of the day, that of giving a charge to the grand jury.

"Gentlemen of the grand jury," began the judge, with a broad smile, "welcome to this special session of the court of general sessions. As you

171

can easily see from the packed house around you, these proceedings are of great interest to your fellow citizens."

The judge paused for a moment, and surveyed the scene in front of him. Querry's impression of Gage was a positive one. He liked the broad face with its handsome features, and the dignified way that the judge handled himself. "He'll do," Querry thought, turning to Joe Clayton, who was sitting next to him. The two men nodded at each other, signifying their approval.

Gage turned his attention back to the grand jury members seated just slightly to his left. "As you know, this term of court was ordered by the governor of South Carolina for the prime purpose of trying a Negro, Will Fair, for one of the most heinous crimes that the human mind can conceive of."

"Yes," shouted someone from the back of the room, and a low noise began to erupt from all sides. The judge raised his hand, and quiet returned.

"There is a grave responsibility resting upon the shoulders of those men who must pass on the guilt or innocence of the accused, and they must needs do what they think to be right whether it coincides with the views of the public or not. The duties of this grand jury are rendered doubly important because of the fact that a mob of white citizens attempted to overthrow the majesty of the law and lynch the man."

Judge Gage paused again, before recalling an incident that had happened in Spartanburg County thirty-four years earlier, upsetting what had long been a reputation of the county for abiding by the United States Constitution.

"A mob surrounded my old friend and classmate, Wash Thompson," he told the crowd, "the sheriff of this county. They took a prisoner from him, tried him outside the courthouse, convicted, and executed him. Not since that time have the citizens of Spartanburg County flouted the law of their native land. To the sheriff who did his duty is due the commendation of every law abiding citizen." A low murmur of discontent with the judge's words began again, but Gage commanded the audience to be quiet. Addressing the grand jury members directly, he gave them their charge.

"Gentlemen, take these indictments into your room; weigh the evidence well, and if it seems to you that those charged with crime are guilty, write 'true bill' across the back of the indictment. If it seems to you that the evidence is insufficient or that all the allegations set forth in the indictments are not correct, write 'no bill' across the back of these indictments. Good day to you."

The bailiff led the eighteen men out of the general courtroom and up the stairs to the room used by the grand jury.

"Solicitor Hill will be with you shortly," he informed them as they took seats facing the front podium.

Querry was seated in the aisle seat on the first row, and Joe Clayton sat in the seat next to him. "So, William, how many cases do we have to deal with today?" asked Clayton.

"I think there are at least four, Joe."

"Anything interesting, other than the one with the nigger?"

"Careful with your language, Joe. Hill ain't goin' to like that."

"Well he ain't in here yet."

Querry laughed. "That's true, but you need to keep it in mind anyway. I think there's at least one murder case besides the one about rape."

At least fifteen minutes had passed before Solicitor Hill entered the room, with Sheriff White right behind him. Considerable conversation was underway, but the noise quickly died down as Hill took his place at the front.

"Good morning, gentlemen," was his greeting. "We have some business to take care of, but I think it should not take you too long. The public seems to think there is only one case here, but there are actually four." He waited for the room to become silent, then continued.

There were four cases altogether for the grand jury to consider, and Hill brought them forward in what he thought might be the order of less difficult and controversial to the more difficult. Thus the cases of John Gillespie for assault with intent to kill, and Isaiah Macker for housebreaking and larceny were heard and dispatched with brevity, true bills sent forward in each case. The case against Will Hughes and Lula

Huff for murder was more complicated, and was not decided until after a break for lunch, when a true bill was delivered.

"Our last case," explained Solicitor Hill, "is the one for which you know there is great public interest. You heard what Judge Gage had to say about this and I know you will give it your utmost attention and concentration."

Hill spent some time explaining the law then got to the point.

"This case involves the State of South Carolina versus Will Fair, of White Stone, a Negro laborer. Fair is charged with entering the home of Mrs. Abigail Marie Potter, assaulting her and raping her on the morning of Monday, August 18, 1913. The facts of the case are simple and straightforward, and clearly show that the grand jury should report out a true bill of indictment."

Hill paused for a moment, consulting a folder he has holding in his right hand. He now looked directly at Querry as he resumed his speech.

"I am going to ask Sheriff White to witness to you the details surrounding the arrest and charges against Will Fair, who is the defendant in this case."

Sheriff White exchanged places with Hill, and addressed the jury.

"Mr. Foreman and members of the grand jury: here are the facts in this case. The accused, Will Fair, was seen by many witnesses on the road that passes by the home of Mrs. Potter. Mrs. Potter observed Mr. Fair walking down the road ahead of her. Just a few minutes later, she was in her house when she was attacked, being struck on the head and also taken advantage of in a sexual way. She became unconscious, but when revived she knew what had happened. She called for help and was aided by two men, Ed Bolton and Alan Wright, both of White Stone, who called a doctor and also my office. Her husband, who had been out of town, arrived shortly after."

White continued to describe the activity that led to the arrest of Will Fair at the railroad station. When he had finished he asked for questions.

William Querry, feeling it vital to his role as jury foreman, was the first to ask.

"Sheriff White, did anyone see Mr. Fair go into the Potter house?"

A smile crossed the sheriff's face as he shared a quick glance with Albert Hill. Querry had immediately hit on the weak point of the state's case, and White was hoping his smile would take away some of the effect of the question. "No, Mr. Querry, we have no such witness. The victim, however, is quite sure it was Mr. Fair, she positively identified him as the one who attacked her."

"Did she see him in the house?" asked Joe Clayton, who had chatted with Querry about this very point.

White knew that Abigail's testimony might not state this directly, for he and Solicitor Hill had discussed it. Still, it was certainly an inference easily drawn. Right now Hill needed a true bill, and so the sheriff's answer was a bit stronger than he actually could justify. "Yes, I believe she did."

"How can we not report out a true bill?" The question came from the back row. "They'll string us up if we don't." This remark from Harvey Caldwell brought a quick buzz in the room, then quiet. What Caldwell implied was on everyone's mind, but most would have thought it couldn't be spoken so plainly. Querry was quick to reply.

"We can't think that way, men. You heard what the judge said."

"Mr. Querry is right," interjected Solicitor Hill. "Even though I very much want you to return a true bill, I don't want it to be because you fear public reaction."

"We don't need to worry about that," said Robert Hancock. "We've got the word of a good citizen, a white woman, against that of a black man. Which one is likely to be the truth? I don't think we have any choice."

A number of voices erupted, and the discussion continued for several minutes before Hill again intervened.

"I'm hearing lots of opinions. Are there any more questions of me or Sheriff White? If not, I will leave you to talk and take a vote."

The prosecutor and the sheriff left the room and Querry went to the podium, taking control of the conversation. Urging the men to be quiet, he recognized E. M, Watson who had remained silent throughout the previous discussions. Watson had earned the respect of the other jurors, and they were ready to listen to what he had to say.

"I wonder why no one saw the accused enter the woman's house," he said. "The sheriff mentioned that there were several people who saw him on the road."

"It's a country road," said Hancock, with an inflection indicating that he thought the answer was obvious. "There are plenty of times when no one is around."

"There's a back door, too," noted Harvey Caldwell. "You wouldn't see that from the road."

"Then maybe we should go out to the scene and have a look," suggested Watson.

This remark brought an eruption of comment. Foreman Querry fought to gain control again.

"Men, we need to keep some order here. We'd need permission from the solicitor before we could take an excursion to the scene. I suggest that we first take a vote to see where we stand."

The vote was taken on the proposition that a true bill be reported, and surprisingly, the count was 9-9. Twelve votes were needed for the proposition to pass. The result was a bit of a surprise to Querry, who had voted yes, even though he had some doubts. It was decided that a short recess be held, after which they would vote again.

Querry sought out Joe Clayton and W. M. Watson in the hallway. Both men had voted no. "What are you men thinking?" he asked. "Surely there's enough evidence here for an indictment."

"But William," protested Clayton. "No one saw the man go in the house. You told me you had your own doubts."

"But Will Fair was seen near the house, and the victim has identified him with no hesitation. That seems enough to me that a trial should be held."

"You know what's goin' to happen, William," asserted Watson. "If this goes to trial, that black man will be found guilty and go to the electric chair. You know that."

"I don't know that," protested Querry. "It's not our job to decide whether the man is innocent or guilty—just whether there's enough to justify a trial."

Back in the room there was more talk about visiting the crime scene. After another vote that stayed at 9-9, it was decided to ask the solicitor to take them out to White Stone. It was just after five o'clock when Hill came in. Querry informed him of the voting results and of their request.

"That would be very unusual, men, and not really necessary. Let us stop for the day and we will resume tomorrow afternoon. You are free to go home, but don't discuss the proceedings with anyone."

"You are refusing our request?" asked Querry.

"We'll talk about it tomorrow," replied Hill. "Go home and get a good night's sleep."

———

Sam Nicholls was waiting for Solicitor Hill when he came out of the grand jury room. "Albert, may I have a word with you?"

Hill led Nicholls to a bench in the hallway and they both sat down. "What can I do for you, Sam?"

"I know I promised to help you on the Fair case," he began, "but I'd like to beg off if I could. I'm helping Sims with the Parris trial, which isn't over yet, and then defending Harvey Wofford starting tomorrow. I don't think it would be fair to you when the Fair trial is so important."

"Hell," exclaimed Hill. "It's not clear there will even be a trial of Fair. The grand jury is locked up on that one."

"I gathered something strange was going on in there."

"It seems pretty obvious to me that they should return an indictment, but they are resisting it. Anyway, I understand what you are saying, so I'm glad to release you from your promise. Maybe I can get Sims to help me."

"Thanks, Albert," remarked Nicholls, feeling relieved. "I'd be glad to help you with the Hughes-Huff case if you'd like. That will be later in the week won't it, and pretty straightforward?"

"You would think so all right," answered Hill with a chuckle. "At least there aren't many witness to be interviewed in that case, which is much different than the one with Fair."

The two men stood and shook hands before Nicholls went on his way. Hill waited for William Querry to emerge from the grand jury room. He was the last to come out and was surprised to see Hill waiting for him.

"William," exclaimed the solicitor. "I need you to guide your men into making the right decision here. We can't have an important case like this die in the grand jury. What can I do to help you?"

"I think you need to emphasize to them that it isn't their job to decide guilt or innocence. I've tried to tell them that." Querry felt that Hill was blaming him somehow, and it annoyed him.

"You're absolutely right, William, that is exactly the point. I'll have a chat about that at the beginning of tomorrow's session. And we can't take time to visit the scene. You need to talk them out of that."

"I'll do my best," responded Querry, "but I'm no dictator, Solicitor Hill, and neither are you."

"I take your point, William. We need to do this gently but it is important that we get it right. Good evening."

Querry nodded and walked away.

Solicitor Hill made his way down the stairs and entered the sheriff's office. He was surprised to find Audrey Brown still at her desk.

"Hello, Audrey. You still here. Your boss is working you way too hard." He smiled at Audrey and then nodded toward the sheriff's inner office. "Is he in there?"

"Yes, Mr. Hill, he is. I'll tell him you're here."

Audrey knocked on the door before pushing it open. "Sheriff White, Solicitor Hill is here and would like to see you."

"Send him in," was the answer.

"There's no true bill yet on the Fair case," announced Hill as he slid into a chair facing the sheriff. "I thought you might be waiting here until you heard something."

"I was, Albert. I thought you might want him arraigned right away. What kind of crowd is there in the courtroom?"

"Most have gone home by now I think."

"I kept some deputies around in case we needed to bring Fair in. I'll let them go now."

"James, I have to admit I am worried about what this grand jury might do. What will the public do if there is no trial for Will Fair?"

"Surely that won't happen, Albert. There is plenty of evidence to warrant having a trial." White felt very confident in that statement, although he had come to have some doubts as to whether Fair was really guilty,

"The vote was 9 to 9, James," exclaimed Hill. "I know we aren't supposed to let public opinion have any sway in these things, but for practical reasons, I think the grand jury needs to think about it. I can't suggest that to them, of course."

"I hear you, Albert. If this case is dismissed, Fair and his family won't be safe. We'd have to get him out of town."

"You're right about that, James. I've got to convince William Querry and his boys to bring a true bill." Hill got up and turned to go.

"Good luck to you, Albert," said the sheriff. "I'll do all I can to keep the peace."

Hill turned back to face White. "I know you will, James, and we can't let your heroic work of last month be wasted. See you tomorrow."

———•———

Audrey Brown remained in the office long after Solicitor Hill and Sheriff White had departed. It had been 5 days since her secret about aiding Joe Waters had come out. She was extremely thankful to the sheriff for forgiving her and keeping her on the job. She tried to put in extra hours and make sure she was helping the sheriff as much as possible. Tonight, however, she was reluctant to go home. She had tried hard to show extra attention to her husband, Alex, but lately it had become more difficult. He seemed unusually cranky and impatient with her. She wondered if somehow he knew what she had done.

The jangling ring of the phone interrupted her reverie. It was a mystery to her as to who would be calling this number at this hour. Any general call to the sheriff rang at the station at the jail, not in the sheriff's courthouse office. Her heart quickened as she suddenly thought of who it might be. Should she even answer?

After the sixth ring, she lifted the receiver. She felt the old thrill when she heard the voice, then her reason returned and with it a cold fear.

"Joe," she whispered, "you shouldn't call here, I'm going to hang up."

"No, No, baby," pleaded Waters. "I have to talk to you. Don't hang up on me."

"It's too dangerous, Joe. I promised to have no more contact with you."

"I miss you, darlin'," said Joe. "I want you to come here to Charlotte and be with me."

"You're crazy!" exclaimed Audrey. "You know I can't leave Alex. He is completely dependent on me."

"Then maybe we should eliminate him," suggested Joe.

"Oh," shouted Audrey, astonished at such a thought.

"I'm just teasin', honey," said Joe with a laugh. "You know I wouldn't do nothin' like that."

"I don't know anything, Joe. I didn't think you would dare call me like this either."

"Suppose I come to Spartanburg and meet you in the park like we used to do. I need you babe."

"You are crazy. If you show up in Spartanburg you will be arrested."

"And you might be found out yourself," said Joe, his tone having changed to one of accusation. "That's all you care about."

"I do care about that, but I don't want you to go to jail either."

"I could out you from here, you know, babe. You best think about that before saying no to me all the time." After a few seconds, Joe spoke again. "I'm callin' you again two nights from now. You need to have a different answer."

Before she could answer, Joe had hung up. "Oh, my god," Audrey said aloud. "What shall I do?"

———•———

Sheriff White stopped in at the jail on his way back to the residence. Jailer Wilson was waiting to talk with him.

"Hello, E. L.," said White. "There is no indictment for Will Fair yet. You need to inform him about that."

"He's been askin' about seein' his family. What should I tell him about that?"

"The magistrate thinks we should accommodate that request, and we will if necessary. If the grand jury doesn't indict, we will be letting him go, so no need to bring his family in."

Wilson gave the sheriff a quizzical look. "Is that possible?"

"The way it's goin' right now it is," responded White, shaking his head. "They'll meet again tomorrow to decide it."

"I ain't sure how the public would take to letting Fair go with no trial. Would he be safe if we just released him?"

"Probably not, E. L. We'd have to get him out of town I reckon." White picked up a paper from the counter and read it carefully. He was aware that Wilson was watching him. "Anything else I need to know?"

"I guess not," answered Wilson. "Been pretty quiet this afternoon. I'll go up and tell Fair what's happenin'."

"Good. I'll see you tomorrow. I'm goin' to see what Viola's got for supper."

Wilson climbed the stairs and walked down the hallway to Will Fair's cell. The other inmates became quiet, straining to hear what the jailer had to say.

Will sat on his cot and did not rise as Wilson appeared at his cell door. It was not common for jailers and guards to speak kindly to the inmates, but Wilson had come to feel some sympathy for Fair.

"The grand jury ain't made a decision yet, Will," he explained.

"What does that mean?" asked Will, who stood now, and walked over to face the jailer.

"It means they haven't returned a true bill on you," explained Wilson. "Do you understand what I'm talkin' about?"

"Can't say I do, boss," replied Will. "What's a true bill?"

"If the grand jury returns a true bill, it means you will go to trial. If they don't indict, there is no trial and we let you go."

Fair was astounded at this news. "You mean I might not have a trial at all?"

181

"Possible but not likely," responded Wilson. "If that happened there's no way to know what the public will think and do."

Fair nodded and went back to sit on his cot, bending down and holding his head in his hands. After a moment, he stood again and spoke to Wilson. "That's it, ain't it. Hell, the mob would get me and string me up sure as anything."

"I ain't denyin' that could happen. We'd try to get you out of town, though, Will, before the mob gets formed."

"What about my family—can I see them? Mr. Gantt said he thought I could."

"We'll wait to see what the grand jury does, Will. If you're held over for trial, we'll try to get them here. The sheriff is in favor of it."

"Don't look too good for me either way, does it, even without no true bill?"

"Can't really say, Will," answered Wilson. "I'll talk to you tomorrow."

———•———

The grand jury re-convened in mid-afternoon on Tuesday, September 16. Solicitor Hill, at the time involved in the courtroom prosecuting the case of Harvey Wofford, who was accused of assault and battery with intent to kill, ducked into the grand jury room during a brief recess in Wofford's trial. William Querry had addressed the group and listened as the rather lazy discussion proceeded. It was evident to him that the men of the grand jury were concerned about the large crowds in the courthouse, especially the ones gathered in the hallway outside the very room in which they were meeting.

Querry was happy to see Hill when he entered and he motioned for the solicitor to take over at the podium.

"Well, men," Hill began. "Have you made any progress?"

"We've been talkin', Mr. Solicitor," observed Querry, "but have come to no conclusions."

"I haven't much time," said Hill, "so I need to impress upon you the importance of your bringing an indictment against Will Fair and allowing his case to go to trial. Your vote does not have to be unanimous, two-thirds in favor of a true bill is enough. Also, let me say again, that your decision should be based on whether there is enough evidence to have a trial in which there is a real chance for conviction. You do not have to decide on guilt or innocence yourselves."

"What about that mob out there, Solicitor?" asked Harvey Caldwell. "What are they going to do?"

"They will do nothing," said Hill emphatically. "There is great interest, it is true, but there will be no violence. You can't let that interfere with your actions in this room." Hill wanted to add that the likelihood of violence would be much higher if they refuse to indict. He held his peace, for he knew Judge Gage would disapprove mightily if he heard that such a thing had been said.

The room was silent, and Hill put in one last argument. "Men, I want to point out again very clearly that the defendant was on the road in front of the victim's house just prior to the attack, that she was attacked, and that she identified Will Fair as the attacker in a lineup four days later. That is powerful evidence and definitely indicates that he should be brought to trial. Please men, do your duty."

Hill left the room, and talk erupted throughout the room, as small groups of men discussed their opinions with each other. Querry let this go on for quite some time, before taking control of the discussion for himself.

"Men, we need to settle this thing. I can see that some of you might think they've arrested the wrong man, but I believe that Solicitor Hill is right. There is plenty of evidence for us to indict Will Fair for this crime."

"There's still the problem that nobody saw that Negro go into the house," said W. M. Watson, with some fire in his voice. "It's clear to me that Mr. Hill is worried about the public response if we refuse to indict. That isn't right."

Robert Hancock returned to his argument of the previous day. "The victim identified the man as her attacker. She is the wife of a prominent farmer and I see no reason not to believe her. It's as simple as that."

The vote was called for and the result was 10-8, a slight movement. Feeling encouraged, Querry urged more discussion. After several more votes and late in the afternoon, a vote of 14-4 decided the issue. Feeling relieved, Querry informed the guard, and sent him to report the news to Albert Hill.

It was after five o'clock, and the large crowd had mostly gone home. A few men remained in the second floor hallway as the grand jury members filed out and went down to the main courtroom. They took seats in the back and waited as the Wofford trial continued.

Sam Nicholls was making his closing argument as the defense attorney for Harvey Wofford, when the door to the courtroom suddenly opened and Sheriff White, along with eight deputies entered bringing Will Fair, who was heavily shackled, into court to be arraigned. The spectators, though not numerous by this time, craned their necks for a view of the accused Negro. Will Fair, thoroughly frightened, glanced about the room, watching for some sign that the spectators might try to attack him. The guards kept a very close watch.

Nicholls finished his plea in behalf of Wofford, and Judge Gage, after delivering a short charge, dismissed the jury to consider its verdict. He waved at the sheriff to bring the prisoner forward. Sheriff White removed the shackles, and led Fair to the front where he was directed to sit at the defendant's table to the far right of the judge. As Will Fair sat down, Attorney C .P. Sanders slid in and sat next to him. This was a surprise to Will, but Sanders placed a hand on his arm and smiled, before indicating that they pay attention to the judge.

Sanders had assisted Hill in the prosecution of Roland Parris. Judge Gage, in anticipation of the fact that Will Fair would need a court appointed attorney, had asked Sanders at the conclusion of that trial if he would attend the arraignment of Will Fair. Sanders had agreed and had also put in a word with Ralph Carson, a fellow attorney, friend, and current president of the South Carolina Bar Association.

"Ralph, I think Judge Gage is going to appoint me as the defense attorney for the Negro, Will Fair," Sanders had mentioned. "I'd really appreciate having your help on that."

"Misery loves company, eh, C .P.," Carson had replied. "Glad to help out with that. It ought to be interesting."

Judge Gage now called on the Clerk of Court, James Bennett, to read the indictment against Fair, who had been asked to stand. When this was concluded, the judge asked Will to enter a plea. Somewhat confused, and gripped with fear, Fair tried to talk, but the words would not come out as he wished. He turned to Sanders, the look in his eyes pleading for help. Sanders stood immediately.

"Mr. Fair pleads not guilty, your Honor. Not guilty!"

The judge smiled. "Not a surprise. I don't suppose you're ready for trial."

"No, Sir," said Fair, finally able to get some words out.

"Mr. Sanders," said Gage. "I would like to appoint you as the defense attorney for Mr. Fair. Will you accept that appointment?"

"I will," replied Sanders.

"It is an important job, especially considering the circumstance surrounding this case," admonished Judge Gage. "I think it best in a case of this kind to appoint a man who has years of experience in the practice of his profession."

"I have never shirked a duty, Judge Gage," noted Sanders, "and I will protect the interests of this client to the best of my ability. I wish to state also, that I have asked Mr. Ralph Carson to assist me in this case." He nodded toward Carson who was seated on the aisle a couple of rows back in the spectators' section.

"Excellent," exclaimed the judge. "I declare this session of court to be adjourned."

# FOURTEEN

# The Trial

It was a post-election Wednesday at the Olympia Cafe. The topic dominating the conversation at most of the tables in the room was the squeaker of a victory in the mayoral election by John Floyd over O. L. Johnson, the current mayor. The usual crowd was at the table with Sheriff White, and Ed Bell was bragging that he had predicted Floyd's win.

"Yeah, Ed, you predicted a landslide, didn't you?" laughed John Story.

"Forty-five votes looks like a landslide to me," chuckled Bell.

"How is Mayor Johnson takin' this?" asked Story.

"Not good," asserted Moss Hayes. "He plans to contest it I think. He says a bunch of registered voters were prevented from voting."

"And naturally, they would have all voted for him I suppose." John Story was not a fan of the current mayor.

"Who are the new commissioners?" asked Albert Hill, not one of the regulars at this table.

"Fielder and Waller got the four year term," said Hayes. "Gallman and Hudson were the other two."

"Hey Mr. Solicitor," said Bell, acting as if he had noticed Hill's presence for the first time. "What's happening in your big rape case?"

"Why Mr. Bell," responded Hill with a grin. "Don't you read the newspaper?"

"He never gets past the front page," noted Story, with a loud laugh. "And even then, it better be a picture."

This brought laughter from everyone, including Ed Bell. "The grand jury brought a true bill out yesterday, Ed," said Hill. "The trial is Friday."

"Who is defending the nigger?" asked Bell, noting the disapproval on the solicitor's face. Hill's feelings about the Negro race were not much different than most of his neighbors in the south, but he had never liked the word "nigger."

"The judge appointed C. P. Sanders to the job," answered Hill, after a short delay. "Ralph Carson will assist."

"That's probably the reason for C. P. to be joining us," said Moss Hayes, pointing to the tall man striding purposefully toward them. "We don't usually see him in here at this time of day."

"They told me I might find you here, Albert," announced Sanders, walking directly to where Albert Hill was seated.

"You've found me all right, C.P.," acknowledged Hill. "Pull up a chair and join us."

"I'm short of time," laughed Sanders, "as you well know. I've got to figure out a way to beat you, and only two days to do it."

"You're getting no sympathy from me, you know," was Hill's response, adding a chuckle of his own. "What did you want to see me about?"

Sanders pointed to a nearby table and Hill got up to join him there. He waved at the others with a smile.

"Oh, oh," exclaimed Ed Bell. "We've got trouble now fellows. Two lawyers talkin' together in secret."

Sanders, trying to ignore the hoots and laughter following Bell's comment, spoke quietly to Hill. "I'm sorry for taking you away from your friends, Albert, but there's something I want to ask of you."

"Not sure they're all friends, C. P., but I'm listening."

"I'd like to speak to the lady, Albert, to Mrs. Potter. Is that all right with you?"

"It's all right with me, C. P., but it may not be with her. She doesn't have to talk to you if she'd rather not."

187

"I know that, Albert. I didn't want to approach her without talking to you first. I've read the reports, but I would like to talk to her directly."

"I'm sure you would, but I've explained to her and her husband that she needn't talk to you or any of your assistants. I will say that most of what she will say has been in the newspapers in one form or another. You know she identified your client as the man who attacked her in a lineup at the penitentiary in Columbia."

"Yes, but I don't know much about her description of the alleged attack."

"I'm afraid you're going to have to wait on her testimony. My best advice is to talk to Robert Gantt. He has talked to many of the witnesses."

"Thank you, Albert. I'll take that advice." Sanders stood, and after waving to the others, strode quickly out to the street.

---

Ralph Carson and C. P. Sanders were on the way to Abigail Potter's house. They were riding in Sanders' new Buick Touring Car.

"This is a mighty fancy car, C. P.," remarked Carson. "Where did you get it? I didn't know anybody in Spartanburg was selling Buicks."

"I got it in Columbia, Ralph. I saw it in a dealership there while visiting. Couldn't resist, even though I spent more than I intended."

"I bet Ed Bell didn't approve at all."

Sanders broke out laughing. "No, Ed wasn't pleased with me. He wanted me to buy one of those Overlanders."

"What kind of chance have we got, C. P.?" asked Carson, changing the subject. "Can we get this fellow off?"

"Well, my first thought is probably not," admitted Sanders. "Still, I promised to do my best, Ralph, and I intend to do that."

"Of course, and that's our duty. But, do you think he's guilty or not?"

"I try not to wonder about that too much. I talked with him a couple of hours last night. He insists that he's not the man, but I don't know how convincing he would be to a jury, especially one that is already inclined to convict."

"Do we know whether the woman was actually raped, or was the act not quite completed?"

"I don't really know the answer to that, Ralph. We need to talk to the doctor who attended her. As I understand it, Dr. Lancaster is who we need to question."

"You know, C.P., I don't really think this is such a good idea for us to do this. You should have sent an investigator, someone we could have questioned at trial."

"I know you're right, Ralph," admitted Sanders, "but there wasn't time for me to get someone lined up."

They had arrived at the Potter residence, pulling into the driveway and stopping just behind Jacob Potter's Model T. The two men looked at each other, betraying their lack of confidence, then got out and approached the front door. Before either could knock, the door opened and they were facing Jacob Potter.

"I saw you drive in," explained Potter with an edge to his voice. "You're the lawyers for that Negro brute, I reckon."

"Yes, we are the lawyers for Will Fair," responded Sanders. "We understand your feelings toward our client, but every person is entitled to representation in our country."

"I suppose that's so, but it is hard to see how anyone could defend someone who committed such a horrible crime against a woman." Jacob Potter held the door open for another moment, before stepping outside. "I'm sorry but I don't feel like inviting you in just now."

Sanders glanced at his partner, who spoke up quickly. "We are sorry to hear that Mr. Potter," said Carson. "I know your father, and I assumed you would be willing to talk with us."

"Yes, Mr. Carson, I know who you are and my dad thinks you are a good lawyer. Even so, I have nothing to say to you."

"We came here to see if we might talk with Mrs. Potter," said Sanders, realizing that was not likely to happen.

"No way, gentlemen," said Potter firmly. "Mr. Hill told me that she did not have to talk with the defense lawyers if she didn't want to, and I'm telling you she doesn't want to."

"Mr. Potter," began Sanders. "Do you know for sure that your wife was actually raped?"

Potter exploded. "What kind of question is that? Everybody knows she was raped. I think you men had best be on your way."

Sanders started to reply, but Carson grabbed his arm. "Let it go, C. P. We may as well leave them alone here." Turning to Potter, Carson said, "We are sorry to have bothered you, but we are only doing our job, you know."

"Well, you've done it," growled Jacob, "and good day to you." Potter stepped back inside, closing the door behind him. He was somewhat ashamed of his unusual and rude behavior, but he felt he must be protective of his wife and her honor.

The two lawyers, surprised at being brushed off so quickly, stood in silence briefly, before returning to the car.

"I didn't expect Mrs. Potter to want to answer our questions," said Sanders, "but I didn't quite expect quite such a cold reception."

"The Potters are reasonable people, I think," said Ralph, "but feelings are running high. I can't say I'd be much different if I thought my wife had been violated."

"We really need to talk to Dr. Lancaster. Would you do that for me, Ralph?"

"Consider it done," replied Carson.

———

Jailer Wilson was grumbling as he made his way up to the second floor cell of Will Fair. Magistrate Robert Gantt had appeared at the jail with Rosa Fair and her four children. Sheriff White had directed Wilson to bring the prisoner down to meet his family. Wilson argued that it would be hard to keep the proper security. Normally, visitors were taken to the inmate's cell and conversed through the bars. Both Gantt and White felt this would not be good for the children.

"You've got visitors," Wilson growled at Fair as he unlocked the cell door. "Come with me and don't get any ideas about trying to escape."

"Don't worry 'bout that, Cap'n. I ain't feelin' too safe in here, let alone on the outside. Who's visitin' me anyway?"

Wilson didn't answer but delivered Fair to one of the interrogation rooms on the first floor. His face lit up when he saw the children. Little Jenna came running, shouting "Daddy, Daddy!" He gathered her into his arms and lifted her up, kissing her forehead and both cheeks. The three boys gathered around him and he spoke to each in turn, finishing with Tom, his oldest. Rosa stood back and watched, unable to stop the tears streaming down her face.

In the midst of the gayety, Tom became serious. "Poppa, what is going to happen, are you coming home?"

Will put his little girl down and put his hands on Tom's shoulders. "I don't know, son," he said after a delay. "You know they say I committed a crime."

"I know, Dad," sighed Tom. "But Mom says you're not guilty."

"And she's right, Tom. I didn't do nothin' wrong, but there's goin' to be a trial, and the jury might find me guilty." Will decided not to mention that there was little chance of a jury of white men to find him innocent.

"But that ain't fair," cried Tom. "It ain't fair."

"Sometimes life ain't fair, Tom. You'll be alright, just listen to your momma."

Robert Gantt knocked on the door and stuck his head in. "Would the kids like some soda?" he asked. "We have some root beer out here."

The children's reaction was immediate. "Come with me," said Gantt, and then as an afterthought, "if it's alright with your mother."

Rosa smiled and indicated her approval, watching as all four of her children followed Gantt from the room. She went at once to her husband and fell into his arms. They kissed and caressed each other for several minutes before Will pulled himself away. Rosa sat down in the chair.

"Rosa, have you talked to your mother? You must go and live with her."

"Oh, Will, I don't want to do that."

"It's the only way, Rosa. I'm not going to be around."

"But you ain't guilty. Maybe they'll let you go."

"No chance, darlin'. Even if I was let go, I wouldn't be safe, nor would you and the kids. My lawyer tells me that I have to get out of town if they get me off." Will knelt in front of her and continued to plead with her. "You have to go to your mother's. We've got no money nor nothin' to keep you all alive."

Rosa broke into tears, and stood, pulling her husband into her arms.

"Honey, the children will be back and you don't want them seein' you like this." Will kissed her and tried to wipe the teardrops away with his rough hands. He felt his own eyes watering, and he began to wish that he could just go back to his cell.

The children came back into the room, the younger ones jabbering about how good the soda had tasted. They quieted when they saw their mother.

"Momma, you crying?" asked Jenna, rushing to hold onto Rosa's skirt. "Please don't cry."

Tom glared at his father. "Poppa, did you make her cry?"

"I'm afraid I did, Tom, because we're havin' to say goodbye," said Will in a voice barely above a whisper. He nodded to Gantt and Wilson who had both entered. "These men have come to take me back upstairs now, so we have to all say goodbye to each other."

Will hugged each child. "I love you all, never forget that. I want you to be brave and help your mother." Taking Tom by the hand, he shook it and said, "I'm countin' on you now, Tom. Do you understand?'

"Yes," answered Tom quietly. He turned abruptly and left the room.

His final words were to Rosa. "Goodbye, Rosa. Remember I love you and I'm innocent. Thanks for bringing the kids in to see me." He bent to kiss her one last time.

"I love you, Will, but this isn't goodbye for us. Mr. Gantt says he will see that I can come to the trial."

"I wish you wouldn't, Rosa. I'd rather remember us like this."

"Wild horses couldn't keep me away, Will. I'll see you again." She kissed him, squeezed his hands and bounded away.

He watched her go as he whispered, "Goodbye my Rosa."

—•—

Audrey Brown was still at the office, though it was well past closing time. Joe Waters had threatened to call her on this day, and she had been stewing about it for two days. She could have gone home but she was worried about what he might do if she weren't there to answer. His demands of her before were unreasonable and impossible for her to meet, yet his threats could result in dire consequences. She had thought hard about reaching out to Sheriff White, although this could endanger the shaky agreement she had with him. She was pretty sure she was over any love she had for Joe Waters, but the thought that what she had done would become known to the community, and, most of all, to her husband, was unbearable.

"Maybe he won't call," she muttered aloud. She sat quietly at her desk, the phone within easy reach. When the office door opened unexpectedly, she jumped to her feet, half expecting it to be Waters, himself. Instead it was the sheriff, which was not much less comforting to Audrey.

"Audrey, what are you doing here so late?" was his greeting.

"Oh, Sheriff, I was . . ." She stopped in midsentence and burst into tears, sitting down with her head in her hands.

"My god, Audrey," exclaimed Sheriff White. "What has happened now?"

It took her a few moments to get her crying under control, but she had made a decision and she stood to face the sheriff.

"Oh, Sheriff White. I hope you will forgive me for I haven't known what to do. Joe Waters called me on Monday night."

"Audrey, you know I told you to have no more contact with him," replied James White sternly."

"I know, I know," cried Audrey. "He called me and made threats if I didn't agree to join him in Charlotte."

"What did you tell him?"

193

"I refused him and said he mustn't contact me again. He said he could tell on me anytime and I had better do what he wanted. He said he would call me again in two days and I'd better have the right answers."

"So you expect him to call you here tonight?"

"That's what he said."

"All right. I'll stay here with you. If the phone rings, answer it, but then leave the rest to me." White patted her on the back, and went into his private office. "I'll call Viola first and let her know I may be late," he called out to Audrey.

Fifteen minutes passed and it felt like hours to Audrey as she paced the floor of her office. She began to think it would be better to just not answer the phone and let Joe do whatever he wanted. "What did the sheriff plan?" she wondered. Perhaps he was ready to end it all and bring Joe Waters to justice. She didn't blame him, but it would be the end of her job and her reputation in the town. Before she could act on this thinking, the telephone rang. She sank into the chair, and with shaking hand, picked up the earpiece.

"Hello," she said, fighting to keep her voice steady. James White was quickly at her side and took the over the phone.

The caller responded immediately. "Audrey, I'm so glad you answered. You know how much I love you and need you. I want you to come to Charlotte as soon as you can. You know I'll take very good care of you. I love you."

"Your love talk doesn't impress me much, Joe," said the sheriff quietly.

"What the hell is this?" sputtered Joe. "Who is this?"

"This is your friend, William James White, Joe. Are you pleased to speak to me?"

There was silence for a moment, but Joe finally recovered from the shock. "I wasn't callin' you Sheriff, I was talking to Audrey."

"Well, we have the same phone number here, Joe, surely you remember that."

Feeling brave, Joe now voiced his threat. "You'd better put Audrey back on, Sheriff. She knows what will happen if she doesn't do what I want."

"You listen to me, Joe Waters. If we have one more contact from you, I will begin the process of arresting you and putting you in jail. It can and will be done, no matter where you try to hide. You're through here and through with Audrey. You may think we will bow to your threats, but it isn't so. Believe me, it won't be worth it to you, Joe. Now go on with your miserable life and leave Audrey alone. Goodbye, you son of a bitch!"

After replacing the receiver on its hanger, James White faced Audrey, whose face had drained of all color. "I apologize for the profanity, Audrey, but that describes what he is."

"What's going to happen to me, Sheriff, if he calls again or shows up here telling his story."

"Believe me, Audrey, it won't happen. If somehow it does, we'll get through it together. I'll be with you all the way, and we will protect Alex. It is entirely up to you Audrey, not Joe Waters."

"I hope you're right," sighed Audrey. "I could resign if you want me to."

"That wasn't our agreement, Audrey. Go home now and take care of your husband. I'll see you tomorrow."

———•———

Joseph Lee arrived at the courthouse well before the ten o'clock hour, the time at which he had been directed to appear. His selection to the pool of jurors for the special court session had occurred all the way back on September 3, when 36 names had been drawn. He lived in Landrum, more than ten miles from Spartanburg, and he had left home early because he possessed a phobia about being late. He was surprised at the size of the crowd already in the room. He knew there was great interest in the last of the week's trials, the one involving a black man accused of assaulting a woman. Since he wasn't chosen for any of the trials earlier in the week, he was confident he would be selected today, and was looking forward to it. He took a seat near the back of the room and watched as the trial of Hughes and Huff was drawing to a close.

A. F. Burton came in at the back and was stopped by one of the guards. After discerning that Burton was a prospective juror, the guard informed him that he should go to a holding room down the hall. Burton pointed at Joe Lee.

"That man is a prospective juror just like me," said Burton.

"You go on," insisted the guard. I'll send him down to join you." Getting Lee's attention, the guard indicated he should come out with him. Lee was annoyed for he was enjoying the closing remarks by the defense lawyer, Alvin Dean of Greenville, speaking on behalf of Hughes and Huff.

"That was one of the most eloquent speeches I've heard in our courthouse," remarked Lee to Burton as they sat down to wait in the holding room. "I'm sorry I've missed the end of it."

"I'm surprised that trial is still ongoing," said Burton. "The next one is scheduled for eleven, I thought."

"Well, it will be delayed no doubt," asserted Lee. "I'm sure hopin' to get chosen for that one."

"Really?" asked Burton, in disbelief. "I'd rather just go home."

Others began to drift in until more than twenty men were in the room. The subject of most of the discussions was Will Fair and what the evidence would show. Prospects of being called to serve were questioned. One man declared he would not be selected because he already knew "that damned nigger is guilty."

It was past eleven when Judge Gage delivered the charge to the Hughes-Huff jury. While this was happening, Sheriff White and four deputies escorted Will Fair into the room. He was heavily shackled, and after the restraints were removed, he took a seat just inside the bar. The judge was interrupted, before he had finished, by people trying to enter the courtroom. Those already present became visibly excited, sure that a mob was coming in to seize the prisoner. Gage quieted the crowd, and directed that the doors be closed during the remainder of the proceedings. He finished his charge and the jury filed out to be taken to their jury room. The judge retired to his chambers for a short break, but he informed the bailiff that the Fair trial would begin within fifteen minutes.

The courtroom had filled to the point that Sheriff White and his deputies determined that no more observers could be allowed in. The halls outside the room were also packed, and people were searching for any way to get into the courtroom. There were two doors at the front of the room to the left of the bench. It was through these doors that some of the officers of the court were admitted. A few spectators had tried to get in that way, but were prevented by sheriff's deputies on guard. The crowd had spilled into the yard surrounding the courthouse, and some had climbed onto windowsills, hoping for a view of the proceedings.

Albert Hill was exhausted. He had been in the courtroom all week, and had just finished his closing arguments in the Hughes-Huff case. He sought refuge in a small conference room adjacent to the judge's chambers, and was joined there by C. P. Sims, who was assisting him in the Will Fair prosecution. The two men had discussed their plans the previous evening after Sims had spent the day with a final interview of their intended witnesses. They had closed the day with a stop for a drink at the New York Restaurant on Magnolia, and were surprised to encounter Judge Gage, there for the same purpose. Their conversation with the judge had been very pleasant.

"It's been a busy week, Mr. Solicitor," was Gage's greeting to Hill. "The big one is tomorrow. I hope you are ready."

"It certainly has, Your Honor," agreed Hill. "I'm a little shaken, though, by your last remark. Is there some special meaning that I am missing."

"Oh no," laughed Gage. "Nothing intended like that." Then, in a more serious tone, he added, "I do expect this to be a very fair trial, if you understand my meaning, and no pun intended."

"I do, sir," replied Albert, "and you must know that my principal evidence will be the testimony of the victim."

"Yes, but we should not be discussing the facts of the case here. We need some more lighthearted conversation. Do you know any good lawyer jokes?"

As he recalled this discussion, Hill felt conflicted, and a bit uneasy. "This judge is going to be tough, C. P.," he said to his assisting counsel. "We can't count on the jury believing Mrs. Potter just because she is white."

"I know that Albert," responded Sims. "But her testimony will be solid. I don't think we have anything to worry about."

Cotesworth P. Sanders was feeling differently about the jury's reactions as he and Ralph Carson entered the courtroom and made their way to the defense table. He, too, had met briefly with the judge in the lobby of the Gresham Hotel where the judge was staying. It was clear to Sanders that the judge was concerned that there was a vigorous defense of Will Fair, but expectations for a successful defense were not high. Sanders and Carson had interrogated a large number of witnesses, and many would be asked to testify, but would they be believed? He took a seat at the table, and Carson escorted Will Fair to the table where he took a seat at the end of the table furthest from the jury box.

Sanders turned and surveyed the crowd packed into the room. It was entirely white, there were no Negroes anywhere inside. Normally, the defendant's wife would be seated close behind the defendant's table, but Rosa Fair was not in attendance. Sanders and Carson had talked about getting her there, but there was no place for her. After consultation with White and Gantt, it was decided, for safety reasons, to leave Rosa at home. This was unfortunate for the defense, thought Sanders, because it was usually helpful to have the jury see a faithful and supportive wife.

Shortly after the prosecutors had entered and taken their seats, the bailiff announced the beginning of the session and all stood as Judge Gage came in and took his seat at the bench. He asked that everyone sit down before briefly addressing the audience.

"I am asking that everyone in this room remain quiet during the trial so that everything might move along smoothly. This is a solemn occasion for all concerned. The court does not belong to any one man but to the sovereign people of South Carolina. It behooves those people to remain orderly while justice is being meted out to the accused."

The first item of business was to seat a jury. Several were challenged by the defense because of an inclination to believe that the defendant was guilty, while others were rejected by both sides because they lived in the White Stone region. Twelve men were finally seated in the jury box and Joseph Lee, destined to be named the foreman, was one of them.

"Mr. Hill," announced Judge Gage, after quieting the audience, "you may make your opening statement."

Albert Hill arose from the table, which was the closest to the jury, and walked around toward the bench. "Thank you, your Honor," he said, before moving over until he stood just in front of the jury box. He let his gaze shift from left to right along the entire jury, seated in two rows slightly elevated above the well of the courtroom.

"Gentlemen," began the solicitor. "This is a very simple case. We will show that the defendant, Mr. Will Fair, committed sexual assault against a young white woman in her home on the 18th of August. We will hear from several witnesses who saw the defendant near the house around the time of the assault. We will establish that the victim in this case clearly identified her attacker and we will hear her detailed description of the attack. She will tell you how the defendant walked ahead of her on the road past her house, and then came back to attack her after she had gone inside. You will hear how he grabbed her from behind, struck her in the head with a board, threw her down and took carnal advantage of her. It will be clear to you that the crime was committed and by the accused. I don't need to explain to you the seriousness of this crime and how important it is that such a crime be punished. Simple justice demands it. This is all I need to say at this time."

Hill returned to his seat and the judge indicated to Sanders that it was his turn to make a statement. Sanders patted Will Fair on the shoulder, then stood and made his way to a spot very close to the jury box. He stood quietly for a moment, looking from one end of the seated jurors to the other. He smiled.

"Perhaps you will note that there were a couple of things our distinguished solicitor did not say to you. He did not promise to bring before you one single witness who would be able to claim that he or she actually saw my client go into the house of the alleged victim. Furthermore, Mr. Hill will not produce any physical or medical evidence that the alleged victim was actually assaulted. Neither of these things can be shown to have happened because they did not happen. They will not show you any torn or bloody clothes worn by the defendant because they do not exist. There is no actual evidence that Mr. Fair committed this or any crime, and it will be your duty to acquit him. Thank you for listening so attentively to what I have said." With a nod of his head, Sanders turned and said, "Thank you, your Honor."

As Sanders returned to his seat, the crowd stirred, and a low murmur spread throughout the room. Judge Gage pounded his gavel.

"Ladies and gentlemen in the audience. You must remain silent, I will not tolerate discussion and expression of favor or disfavor from you during these proceedings." The room became very quiet. Nodding his head in satisfaction, Gage directed Albert Hill to begin his case.

---

Because of the heavy press of people, both in the courtroom and in the adjoining halls, the prospective witnesses were being sequestered in a room across from the judge's chambers, so that they could be brought in through the door to the judge's right. Albert Hill stood at his desk and spoke the words that initiated the trial proper.

"The state calls Miss Ruth Foster."

The bailiff opened the door and called to Ruth to come in. The young 14 year-old girl had been alerted that she would be the first called, and she was waiting just outside when the door opened. She walked in slowly with eyes down and straight ahead. She was clearly nervous, although she was actually glad to be out the room where the witnesses were gathered. She had felt the tension in the room between those testifying for the state, and the others, mostly colored, who would be on the side of Will Fair. The bailiff led her to the witness chair, just to the judge's left and close to the jury. He instructed her to stand as the clerk of the court, James Bennett, held out a Bible and instructed her to place her right hand on it.

"State your name," ordered Bennett.

"Ruth Foster," was the answer in a voice barely audible.

"Speak up, Miss," said Bennett, with a bit more tenderness. "The Court needs to hear you."

Ruth repeated her name a bit more loudly.

"Do you swear to tell the truth, the whole truth, and nothing but the truth, so help you God?" asked Bennett.

"Yes, sir," replied Ruth, still trying to talk louder.

"Be seated," said Bennett with a little smile, before retreating to his desk.

Albert Hill approached the witness stand with a wide smile. "Now Ruth, do you know the victim in this case?" Hill wanted to avoid using Abigail's name as long as he could.

"Objection," cried Sanders, immediately on his feet. "There is no established victim in this case."

"Sustained," said the judge. "You need to be careful with your language, Mr. Hill."

"I'm sorry, your Honor," replied Hill. "That was not intentional." Addressing Ruth again, he asked, "Do you know the alleged victim, Ruth?"

"Yes, sir. She's our neighbor."

"Did you see her on Monday, August 18, the day she was allegedly attacked?"

"Yes, sir. She came to our house and had coffee and cinnamon rolls with my mother and me."

"This was before the alleged assault?"

"Yes."

"Thank you, Miss Foster, you are doing very well." Hill looked over at the jurors, before returning to face the girl. "Can you tell us, in your own words, anything more about the visit of your neighbor that morning? Was she upset in any way?"

"Not at first, but she did tell us she'd had a bad night." Ruth remembered Abigail's comment about her monthly period, but she didn't want to talk about that and Mr. Hill had said she didn't have to mention it. "Her husband was not home, and she said something about being followed by a Negro man the night before. I think it was about ten o'clock when she said she needed to go back home. She went down the

201

path to the street, but I didn't see her after that. The path goes through a patch of woods."

Sanders thought about objecting, as what Mrs. Potter said to Ruth would be hearsay. However, the story of Abigail Potter being followed the night before might actually cast doubt in the minds of the jurors, and the defense attorney let it stand.

"Now Ruth, did you see a Negro man walking in the street?" asked the prosecutor.

"I did see a Negro man on the street walking toward my neighbor's house, but then he was out of sight behind the wooded path."

"Ruth, you've been very patient with me and I appreciate it very much," said Hill, again with a slight smile. "I have just one more question. Could you tell if the Negro man you saw was the defendant, the man right over there?" Hill was pointing at Will Fair, who sat quietly with his hands clasped, but unable to keep from looking down at the table.

Ruth Foster bowed her head and shook it slightly from side to side. "It could be, but I didn't really see him very good. I can't say."

"Thank you, Ruth," said Hill. "That's all I have of this witness, your Honor."

Ruth stood and began to leave the stand when she was stopped by Judge Gage. "Just a minute, honey," he whispered. "The defense lawyer may have something to ask you." He nodded at the defense table. "Mr. Sanders?"

Sanders stood quickly on his feet and approached the witness who sat down again. "Miss Foster," he began. "Can you tell us what Mrs. Potter said about being followed by a Negro?" This was the first time the alleged victim's name had been mentioned in public, and there was a noticeable reaction from the audience. Young Ruth went ahead with her answer.

"Well, she said he followed her and went into her house."

"Did she see him in the house?"

"I don't know. She said that she locked herself into her bedroom, and he couldn't get in, so he left."

"When was this?"

"On Sunday night, I think."

Sanders stole a glance at the jury, trying to gauge their reaction. He turned back to Ruth Foster, trying to be as pleasant as possible. "Miss Foster, did you see a Negro man go into your neighbor's house at any time?"

This was a question that Ruth could answer with great confidence. "No, sir, I did not."

"That's all, your Honor," Sanders said and returned to his seat.

"You are excused, Miss Foster," said Gage. "Thank you very much."

Solicitor Hill next called Ruth's mother to the stand. She reinforced her daughter's testimony and explained that the two of them had gone over to the alleged victim's house after finding out about the attack where they took care of her until her husband came in.

Cotesworth Sanders pursued a new line when he had his chance. "Mrs. Foster, did the alleged victim say anything about having trouble in connection with her monthly menstrual period?"

"Yes, she talked of being terribly uncomfortable because of that."

"Is it common for her to have this complaint?"

"Well, she has mentioned it before, but I wouldn't know if it was common."

"When you saw her after the alleged attack, did she show physical signs of a struggle or of being hit by something?"

Mary Foster had been warned by Solicitor Hill that she might face such questions. She was ready with her answer. "She had blood on her dress and her hair was disheveled, but I am not really qualified to say much about this. She was very upset, I can say that."

"Could the blood have been because of the time of the month for her rather than a result of some blow or attack?"

"I suppose so, but I don't really know."

Sanders hoped he had defused any strong feelings about the presence of blood. "Thank you, Mrs. Foster." To the judge he said, "I'm finished with this witness."

Ed Bolton and Alan Wright were the next witnesses, Bolton telling of finding the woman shouting that she had been raped, and Wright testifying that he had called the police and Dr. Lancaster. Sanders did not question either man.

Albert Hill knew that it would be the natural thing for him now to call on Dr. Lancaster, who was the attending physician. He and Sims had held a long discussion about Lancaster and it was decided that there was no real advantage for them to question him on the stand. He was likely to be a defense witness, not a good thing for their case. Sims had argued that they should have him on the stand first as their own witness, but Hill had decided otherwise. Just now he wondered about that decision, but instead he called J. L. Williams, the arresting officer.

After the preliminaries, Hill asked about the actual arrest.

Williams explained how he had first seen the defendant on the streetcar, and after departing the car at Pine Street had learned of the crime and a description of the alleged assailant. He realized that he had seen the man on the electric car, and went immediately to the Union Station where he took him into custody.

"What, if anything, did the defendant say to you when you arrested him?" asked Hill.

"He said, 'you've got the wrong man.' Of course they all say that."

"Objection," interjected Sanders. "Officer Williams' opinion was not requested."

"Sustained," answered Judge Gage. "Just answer the question asked, Mr. Williams."

"Officer Williams," responded the solicitor. "Did you believe the defendant when he claimed he was not the man?"

Sanders objected again. "What Officer Williams believes is completely irrelevant," he noted.

"Sustained," said the judge. "Do not answer that question, Mr. Williams."

Hill turned and smiled at Sanders, who couldn't quite suppress his own smile.     Facing the witness again, Hill asked Williams to explain why he had decided to arrest Will Fair.

"I heard a description of the assailant and realized that it was a description of the man I had seen on the electric car. I figured he would be at the train station, so I went there and arrested him."

"What was the description of the man that you received?"

"I was told that he was stout and of medium height, wearing a hat, a white shirt, and black pants with suspenders. That definitely described the man I saw on the car."

Will Fair stiffened as he heard the testimony. He realized that he was dressed in a similar way at this very instant, and he wondered how that might affect the jury. His lawyers had first thought they would dress him in a suit, but later decided it was best to have him dress in his usual way. The clothes he was currently wearing had been provided by his wife. He supposed it didn't matter anyway, for things did not seem to be going well.

"Did the defendant appear to be nervous when you saw him on the streetcar?"

"He wouldn't look me in the eye, but I can't say he was especially nervous." Williams hated questions like that, but he also thought that Will Fair was guilty, and wanted his testimony to be helpful to the prosecution.

Hill finished his interrogation of John Williams and Sanders began his cross-examination.

"Officer Williams, did the defendant have anything else to say when you arrested him?"

"Well, he said he could name witnesses that saw him on the road who could prove that he never went into the house. He said that he saw a young woman at the edge of the woods and she was tying the strings of one of her shoes."

Sanders walked over and faced the jury for a moment, then turned to the witness. "Did you examine his clothes at the time of the arrest or later? Were they clean or did they have any bloodstains on them?"

Williams hesitated for a brief time before giving his answer. "No, his clothes were clean, there was no blood on them. I examined them after we had put him in a cell."

"I see," said Sanders, now walking over to stand in front of Williams. "Could he have changed his clothes before you examined them thoroughly?"

"I don't see how," admitted Williams.

"Did the defendant tell you that he had heard about the assault while in Glendale?"

"I guess he did," said Williams. "He claimed a man on a gray horse had ridden into town and reported it."

"Thank you, Officer Williams," said Sanders. "That's all I have for this witness, your Honor."

As Sanders returned to his desk, Albert Hill rose and approached the bench.

"Your Honor, I have one more question."

"Proceed," directed the judge.

"Officer Williams, is it possible that the defendant could have changed his clothes sometime after he committed the alleged crime? Just a yes or no will suffice."

"I object, your Honor," shouted Sanders. "The witness already gave his answer to this question and now he is being asked to speculate."

Once again, the objection was sustained.

Cotesworth Sanders could not let this stand without further challenge. He asked the judge for permission to ask a follow up question. Judge Gage agreed.

"Officer Williams, is it true that at the time of the arrest, Mr. Fair was wearing the clothes as described by the alleged victim?"

"Yes."

"And is it true that the clothes you examined were the same clothes the defendant was wearing at the time of the arrest?"

"Yes."

"Thank you. I am finished, your Honor."

The next witness for the state was the conductor on the Glendale car line, Earl Holcomb. Holcomb identified Will Fair by pointing him out at the defense table, then testified that Fair had boarded his car at Glendale sometime shortly after 11:00 a.m. on the 18th of August. He declared that Fair appeared to be extremely apprehensive. The defense had no questions for Holcomb.

At this point, Albert Hill called Abigail Potter as the next witness for the prosecution. There was a noticeable moan from the audience as Abigail was brought into the courtroom and took the oath. Her name had never appeared in the press, nor, in the court proceedings until Sanders had mentioned it in his examination of Ruth Foster. Many in the crowd were aware of who the victim had to be, but her appearance came as a bit of a shock nonetheless. A pretty woman, she was dressed in black, with a long skirt that reached the floor, and a top with a high neck that nearly hid a pearl necklace. Her dark hair emerged below a small hat.

Jacob Potter had come in with his wife, and was allowed to take a seat at the table with the state attorneys.

Judge Gage directed that the witness chair be moved so that when seated, Mrs. Potter faced the jury. "I do not want her to be subject to the gaze of the multitude," he explained to the bailiff. Once she was in place, the judge bade Hill to proceed.

Hill moved to a place on the right side of her chair and facing the jury. His position mostly blocked a view of the witness from the audience. "Mrs. Potter, I know this is a question a man is not supposed to ask a woman, but I wonder if you would mind telling us your age and your marital state."

"I am 21," said Abigail in a strong, clear voice. "I was married to Jacob Potter on December 5, 1912."

"And you live in White Stone, on Union Road?"

"I do."

"Mrs. Potter, I know it is a difficult thing for you to have to relive the horrible events that happened on the morning of August 18. However, we need for the jury to hear the story straight from you." Hill looked quickly at Jacob Potter, who nodded his assent.

"I understand, Mr. Hill, and am quite ready to testify." She, too, stole a short glance at her husband, who smiled at her.

"We have heard testimony from Mrs. Foster and her daughter, Ruth, that you paid them a visit that morning," said Solicitor Hill. "Can you tell us about that visit, when it was and how it came about?"

"Yes," answered Abigail. "I was not feeling well when I woke up and was feeling a bit scared, so I thought it would be good to have coffee at the Foster's. She makes great cinnamon rolls."

This remark brought scattered laughter from the audience. Albert Hill knew about Abigail's fears of the night before, but he and his co-counsel, Carl Sims, had decided it best not to emphasize that too much. He wished she hadn't said that she was scared.

"So you had coffee and cinnamon rolls, and an enjoyable time with young Ruth and her mother?"

"Yes," responded Abigail quickly. "It was a very nice time."

"What time did you leave to go back home?"

"It was around 10 o'clock, I think," said Abigail. "I remember the clock striking ten. I needed to get home because I expected my husband home any time. He had been in Henderson."

"Thank you, Abigail," said Hill. "Could you tell us in your own words all the circumstances surrounding the alleged criminal assault?"

Abigail began with a description of her walk down the wooded path where she saw a Negro going by on the road in front of her. Albert Hill interrupted her at this point.

"Excuse me, Mrs. Potter, but could you identify for us the Negro that you saw on the road?"

"Yes," replied Abigail, turning slightly to point back at the defense table, indicating that she was identifying Will Fair. "He is the one I identified in the penitentiary in Columbia."

Hill had not expected the last statement, wishing she had waited for him to ask about directly about that. Since it was out, he thought it best to follow up on it right now.

"Could you explain how that was done, Mrs. Potter?"

Abigail had been schooled carefully on how to answer that question.

"Yes, there were five Negro men all lined up and dressed alike. I was asked to point out my attacker from among them, and I pointed to the defendant, the man at the table over there."

"You had no doubt about which one it was?"

"No, sir."

"Thank you," exclaimed Albert Hill. "Please continue to tell us about the attack."

Abigail explained how she had stopped at the end of the path to tie the strings of her shoes, and let the Negro go on ahead of her. He wasn't very far ahead, and kept looking back at her. She went to the front door of her house, unlocked it, went in and relocked it. "I went on to the back and unlocked the rear door. Then I went to the small dresser to comb my hair, which was a mess. My little dog came over and was playing at my feet."

She stopped talking for a moment, gathering herself before going on with her story. The room had become completely silent. Someone coughed in the back, and there was silence again, as if everyone realized that the next words from Abigail Potter might settle the case on the spot. Will Fair sat with his hands clasped, and his gaze fixed on the floor in front of the table.

Abigail took up her story again, saying that she did not hear the man come in, but first saw his feet and then felt his hand clamped over her mouth. "He grabbed my hands like a vice in his other hand, then threatened me not to holler."

"Did he say anything to you, Mrs. Potter?" asked the solicitor.

"Yes, 'don't you holler, or damn you, I'll kill you,' he said."

This statement brought a howl from the crowd, causing Judge Gage to bang his gavel. When the room was quiet, he directed Abigail to continue her testimony.

In a strong voice, Abigail told how the Negro grabbed a lath from the windowsill and struck her in the head with it before throwing her to the floor and accomplishing his purpose. She testified that she had resisted with all her might, but that he was too strong for her. She lost her senses and was unconscious. When she awoke, she said that she thought of going for her husband's gun, but it was much too late for that, and she had gone on the porch, calling for help.

"That's when Mr. Bolton and Mr. Wright found you?" asked Hill.

"Yes. My husband came home right after that." As Hill turned toward the judge, Abigail suddenly added something. "Oh, and the Fosters had come over by then to help me inside."

Deciding that this was a good place to end Abigail's testimony, Hill indicated to Judge Gage that he was finished.

"Thank you, Solicitor Hill," said the judge. "You may proceed if you wish, Mr. Sanders."

"Thank you, your Honor. If it pleases the court, my associate, Mr. Ralph Carson will conduct the questioning of Mrs. Potter."

The two Sams, Nicholls and McCravy, were standing in the back, having used their positions as well known lawyers to persuade the guard at the door to let them in.

"Ralph better be at his best," observed Nicholls. "That testimony from Mrs. Potter was quite strong."

"Yes, she did a nice job, kept her composure and spoke with a strong voice," agreed McCravy. "Hard to see how a jury can disregard any of it, even if the accused were white."

Ralph Carson had slipped out from behind the defense table and moved to a position where he could question the witness, who remained seated, facing the jury. Carson was a contrast to the tall, handsome Sanders, his stature much shorter and his body bordering on the corpulent. His face was round and his jowls a bit heavy, yet there was gentleness to his manner and pleasantness to his features that put people at ease. His hair was gray, with streaks of white, and altogether, a word that seemed to associate itself with him was the word, wisdom. He was, of course, the president of the South Carolina State Bar Association.

"Good afternoon, Mrs. Potter," he said quietly. "I have only a few questions for you."

Abigail nodded but said nothing. Solicitor Hill had told her that he expected Mr. Carson to conduct her cross-examination, and that he would be kind to her. "Don't worry," he had said. "Just tell the truth."

"Now, Mrs. Potter, in her testimony, Ruth Foster told us that you had said you had been followed by a Negro man on Sunday night, and that he got into your house. Did you see the man following you, and did you see him in the house?"

Abigail was ready for this question. "I didn't directly see him, but I could hear him."

"And you definitely heard him inside the house?"

"I did, and I locked myself in my bedroom, and shoved a dresser against the door. He couldn't get in, so I reckon he left."

"So you cannot say that it was the defendant, Mr. Fair, who was in the house."

"I suppose not."

"I have to ask you some rather delicate questions now, Mrs. Potter." Carson looked up at the jurors, then back to the witness. "Was it that time of the month for you, Mrs. Potter?"

"Yes."

"And do you have a difficult time with this?"

"Yes, sometimes," admitted Abigail softly. "Most times, I guess."

"And do you take any medications to help you feel better?"

At this point, Albert Hill thought he should say something. "Objection, your Honor. What is the purpose of this line of questioning?"

"Mr. Carson?" asked Judge Gage.

"Strong medicines could affect memory and state of mind, your Honor. I believe it is important."

"I'll allow it," said the judge. "Objection overruled."

"Would you answer my question, Mrs. Potter? Do you take medicines for your monthly problems?"

"Yes."

"Which one is the most effective?"

Abigail wondered what Carson knew about her medicines. How could he know about the Laudanum? She supposed she had better answer truthfully. She stole a quick glance at Jake Potter, then replied. "Laudanum."

"How does the Laudanum affect you, ma'am?"

"I guess it makes me sleepy sometimes." Abigail thought it best not to mention that she often felt drunk as a result.

"Do you ever suffer from fainting spells, Mrs. Potter?"

"Sometimes," was the answer.

Carson smiled, then said. "Thank you. I only have a couple more questions. You testified that you had gone to the back door and unlocked it. Why did you do that, I wonder?"

"I thought I was locking it, but I was flustered and unlocked it instead."

"And you believe your alleged attacker came in through that back door?"

"Yes, for the front door was locked."

"Did you hear the door open or slam?"

"No."

"With all that was happening, with him holding a hand over your mouth, holding your hands, hitting you with a stick, and throwing you down, how were you able to see him clearly, see his face, tell what he was wearing?"

" I don't know, but I did." Abigail uttered a small cry, but fought against tears. Carson did not want her to cry, but he wanted to establish one thing. He waited a moment before continuing.

"Was your description made possible because you saw him in the road? Was that how you knew what he was wearing?"

"I suppose so," she admitted, then thought better of it. "But I saw him in the house."

Carson smiled and thanked Abigail for answering his questions. "I just have to ask about one more thing, ma'am. You have told us about your trip to the penitentiary, and how you identified the defendant. Were you helped in any way by the sheriff or the solicitor in making this choice?"

"No sir," replied Abigail confidently. "They told me to identify the man only if I was sure."

"And you were sure?"

"I was."

"Because you saw him in the road." Without waiting for her response, Carson indicated to the judge that he was finished, and returned to his seat.

Albert Hill stood wanting to complain about Carson's last remark, but thought better of it. He led Abigail from the witness chair over to where she was met by her husband. The two of them left the room as a murmur arose from the audience. Hill then called his next witness, R.C. Hall, a captain of the city police.

Hall was called to tell about his interrogation of the defendant shortly after his arrest. There was little he could say except that Will Fair had admitted passing the Potter house and that he had seen Mrs. Potter at the end of the path down from the Foster house. The defense, however, had several questions for Hall.

"Captain Hall," began Sanders, "did you examine the defendant's clothing and his person after his arrest? Did you find any blood on his clothes or any other thing that might have indicated he was in some kind of scrape?"

"Yes, I did examine him and found no blood nor any tears or anything of interest about his clothes."

"Any scratches or bruises on his person?"

"No, sir."

"Did the defendant say anything about going inside the house?"

"No, Mr. Sanders." Hall looked briefly toward the jury, then back to his interrogator. "He said very emphatically that he did not go in the house and did not attack the woman."

"Captain Hall, did the alleged victim identify a different Negro as her assailant earlier and prior to her identification of Mr. Fair?"

"Yes, she did. A man was brought to her home, in her bedroom, and she asked him to turn so that she could see his back."

"Then what happened?"

"She stated that he was the man, but he protested and started taking off surplus clothing. He was wearing two shirts and two pairs of pants. When she saw him without the extra clothes, she said he was the wrong man."

Sanders indicated that he was finished with Hall, when Albert Hill stood at his desk.

"Captain Hall, were you there during this episode with the other Negro man? Were you in the room?"

"No, I was not," replied Hall.

The police captain was dismissed, and the state called Chief of Police, Moss Hayes.

Hayes was asked to tell about his part in the investigation of the crime and also his part in taking Will Fair to Columbia for safekeeping. When his turn came, Cotesworth Sanders wanted to revisit some earlier testimony.

"Chief Hayes," began Sanders, "were you present when the alleged victim identified a different Negro as her attacker?"

"Yes, I was," answered Hayes. Sanders turned and walked a few steps toward the center of the room before facing the witness again. As he did so, he gave a quick smile at the prosecution table.

"Could you tell us how that came about?" was his question.

Hayes told the story, very much the same as Hall had given it earlier.

"When you heard that she had identified Will Fair in Columbia, Chief, did you wonder if she had made a mistake again?"

Hill was on his feet before Hayes could respond. "Objection, your Honor, Chief Hayes' opinion is of no consequence."

"Sustained," said Judge Gage. "Do not answer that question, Chief Hayes."

"No more questions," said Sanders, returning to the defense table.

As its final witness, the prosecution called James White to the stand.

"Sheriff White," began Hill. "Did you accompany Mrs. Potter to Columbia at the time she identified Will Fair as her assailant?"

"Yes, sir, I did."

"Would you tell us how this was done?"

Sheriff White gave a detailed explanation of the process of setting up the lineup of men from which Mrs. Potter picked out Fair as the attacker. When he had finished, Solicitor Hill had another question.

"Sheriff did you notice anything about the defendant as he stood in the lineup while Mrs. Potter was making her choice?"

"Well, he was very nervous and that was apparent. He tried not to look at her."

"Did you and I discuss this later, that we had both noticed it."

"Yes, that's true," agreed White. He wondered about this line of questioning, for he could have pointed out that one or two of the others were uneasy as well.

Hill indicated he had no more questions, and Sanders rose immediately.

"Sheriff White, of the men in that lineup, was Mr. Fair the only one from Spartanburg?"

"I suppose so," answered White, "but I don't really know."

"Since Will Fair was the only person in the lineup who Mrs. Potter had previously seen, isn't it pretty natural that he is the one she would have picked out?"

"I suppose so, but I can't know that for sure."

"No more questions," announced Sanders. Albert Hill quickly put in one more.

"Sheriff White, in your experience was there anything unusual about that lineup procedure?"

"No, sir, it was done in the usual way."

"Thank you Sheriff," said Hill. "The state rests, your Honor."

The audience, anticipating a recess, broke into a flurry of private conversations, raising the noise level in the room. Sam McCravy was interrupted in his comment to Sam Nicholls by the violent pounding of his gavel by the judge. "I'll have quiet in this room," he said evenly, "we are not in recess just yet."

Judge Gage waited as the room slowly became quiet. He struck the gavel one more time, then nodded to Sanders.

"Mr. Sanders," he said. "You may begin."

The first witness called by the defense was A. G. Kennedy, a white man who stated that he was from Jonesville.

"Mr. Kennedy, do you know the defendant, Will Fair?"

"I do," exclaimed Kennedy. "I've known him for at least 15 years."

"What is your opinion of Mr. Fair?"

"He is a very humble Negro and always respectful to white people."

"Do you know him as a man who is truthful and dependable?"

"Yes, he has a very good reputation with those who know him."

The prosecution had no questions and Sanders next called Dr. W. B. Lancaster to the stand.

"Dr. Lancaster, were you called to examine Mrs. Potter on the day of the alleged assault?"

"Yes, I spent quite some time with her. She was quite distraught."

"I'm sure she was," agreed Sanders. "What did you find in your examination? Did she show any signs of being assaulted?"

"She had no marks on her body that I could see, no abrasions."

"Was there any indication that she had been struck in the head with a stick?"

Dr. Lancaster was slow to answer, for he knew that there had probably been testimony to that effect. "I could see no real sign of that," he said finally.

"Dr. Lancaster, this is a delicate question, but was the alleged victim having her monthly period?"

"Yes, she was. She informed me that it had begun a few days earlier, and there were evidences of this on her clothing."

"Could you determine, Doctor, whether she had been assaulted fully, sexually, I mean?" This question brought a reaction from the crowd.

"To be sure of that I would have needed a microscopic examination, which I did not do."

"Dr. Lancaster, do you think that if the defendant had committed this assault, there would have been bloodstains on his clothes?"

Lancaster looked down and rubbed his left hand on his forehead, before looking up at Sanders and replying. "Yes, I believe there would have been stains on his clothing."

Albert Hill leaned over and whispered in the ear of his associate, C. P. Sims. "Do you think we need to question the doctor?"

"Yes," replied Sims. "Would you like me to do it?" Hill nodded his assent.

Judge Gage, observing the conversation between the two prosecutors, and after Sanders indicated he was finished, spoke to Hill.

"Mr. Hill, do you have any questions of this witness?"

"Yes, your Honor. Mr. Sims has some questions."

Sims was on his feet and approaching the witness stand. "I have just two questions," he said. "Dr. Lancaster, is it a fact that there would have been blood on the attacker's clothes, or is that just your opinion?"

"Well, of course, it is just my opinion." Lancaster had no grudge against Mrs. Potter, and was glad to be able to say something more in her favor.

"My last question is this: considering her behavior and state of mind, would you agree that something had frightened the alleged victim in a very severe way?"

"Yes, I would agree with that."

Two more witnesses were called by the defense, J. H. Pickens and Sam Brewington. Pickens asserted that he had seen Will Fair at White Stone as the train passed the station. Brewington testified that he had seen Fair seated on a rock wall in Glendale, and that Fair told him he was on the way to Spartanburg. The news of the criminal assault had reached Glendale, according to Brewington, and was being discussed in the town.

Judge Gage noted that it was nearly two o'clock, and that the trial would be in recess for dinner until 3:00. The court officials filed out of the room, but most of the audience stayed put, the people worried about losing their seats.

———•———

Sam Nicholls and Sam McCravy made their way out of the courthouse and across the street to the New York Restaurant. Both men had closed their offices for the day, knowing they would want to be present at perhaps the most interesting trial of the year. They found a booth in the fast filling room, and gave their orders.

"Well, what do you think, Sam?' asked Nicholls. "Mrs. Potter's testimony was strong and she stood up well under Ralph's cross."

"No doubt about that, although Ralph may have scored with his emphasis on her identification of Fair because of seeing him on the road. Sheriff White's testimony may have shed some doubt on the Columbia identification as well."

"Yes, but did the jury pick up on those things? I watched them pretty close and saw no indication that they were impressed."

"Didn't know you were a champion reader of juries, Sam," chuckled McCravy.

Nicholls added his own laugh. "Clearly you don't know me well."

217

The defense team, Sanders and Carson, deciding to forego dinner, found a quiet room instead.

"You did a nice job on Mrs. Potter, Ralph," observed Sanders. "How do you think we stand?"

Carson shook his head from side to side before answering. "I don't know, Cotesworth. Her testimony was solid and her identification of him from a lineup in Columbia will weigh heavily, I'm afraid."

"We will put Will Fair on the stand. I think he will do well. He's never wavered in his declaration that he did not go into that house."

"The problem is whether he will be believed. If he was a white man, then we might have a chance."

Sanders shook his head. "Listen to us, Ralph. We like to deny this reality, but the fact is, having a Negro client facing a white accuser makes it really difficult."

"Well, we knew that going in. What else do we have?"

"We have the medical stuff." Sanders gave Carson a quizzical look, searching for some assurance.

"Is Dr. Blake solid on that, do you think?"

"I've talked with him twice. He gave me some written material, and he's ready to testify about menstrual problems."

"Enter the written evidence, Cotesworth. Stuff like that impresses juries, even if you don't read any of it."

Sanders nodded his agreement. "Think there's time for us to get something to eat?"

Eating was definitely on the minds of the jurors. The bailiff and another guard led them out of the courtyard, through the jail yard gate and into the dining room at the jail. Joseph Lee found a seat next to A. F. Burton and S. E. Brian, who were both from the village of Inman.

"What do you think so far, Burton?" asked Lee.

As Burton began his answer, he was interrupted by the bailiff, who was standing near them. "Save that talk for the jury room, gentlemen. You ain't supposed to discuss the trial 'til it's over."

Burton shrugged and leaned back as a server placed a plate in front of him filled with Irish potatoes, some bacon, and a piece of corn bread. This was the same as was on the menu for the prisoners, who had eaten earlier. The meals were prepared by a female Negro prisoner, who received a small payment for performing this service. The servers were also inmates, two young white men who had been sentenced for public drunkenness.

"Not bad," commented Burton after eating for a few moments in silence.

"A little skimpy, I'd say," replied Lee. "I suppose it's what they give the inmates, so I reckon we shouldn't expect too much. I don't see why we can't talk about this case. It is our job after all."

"It's too public here," said Brian, injecting himself into the conversation for the first time. "I was on one of these juries a few years ago, and they got real mad at us for talkin' outside the jury room."

"Well, I just hope we get this over with this afternoon," said Burton. "I don't want to be kept all night, that's for sure."

"What'll they do with us if we ain't done by bed time?" wondered Lee.

"I reckon they'll put us up over at that new hotel," suggested Brian.

"You mean the Gresham?" questioned Lee. "Hell, it ain't exactly new anymore, it's a couple of years old by now. Still, that wouldn't be too bad, I guess."

It wasn't long until the bailiff let them know it was time to return to the court room. "If you need a stop at the rest room, you'd better do it quick," he announced.

At three o'clock, all had returned to their places in the courtroom, and Judge Gage took his spot again at the bench. "Mr. Sanders," he pronounced, "you may resume your defense."

———•———

The first witness called after the recess was C. C. Lawson, whose purpose was to testify as to the character of Will Fair. He described Fair as being a quiet, inoffensive Negro. He was followed on the stand by a civil engineer named W. M. Willis, who had made a map of the Potter house and the surrounding area. He had also taken some photographs of the premises, and he swore to the correctness of this material. It was placed in evidence.

John Suber was next to the stand, testifying that he had seen Will Fair on the day of the assault.

"Did you speak to the defendant that day?' asked Attorney Sanders.

"Yes, sir, I did," asserted Suber. "I gave him a drink of my root beer, and we talked for a while. He was in a hurry, though."

"Did he tell you why he was in a hurry, John?"

"Why, yes, sir. He said he was goin' to Glendale to catch the electric car. Had to catch a train in Spartanburg to Wellford where he had a job."

Albert Hill had some questions for this witness. "Mr. Suber, did the defendant actually tell you he was trying to get to Wellford?"

"Yes, sir, I think he did."

"Aren't you a bit confused, Mr. Suber? Didn't he tell you about the Wellford job a couple of days earlier?"

This question was surprising to Suber. "Well, I guess it could have been." Suber was remembering being with Fair and some friends on Saturday night.

"Are you sure it was on Monday, August 18, when you saw Will Fair on the road?"

Thoroughly confused now, Suber hung his head. "I suppose it could have been a day or two before." Suddenly realizing what he had said, Suber shouted. "But I don't think so."

Hill was already returning to his seat. "No more questions, your Honor," he said to the judge.

There followed a string of witnesses who had seen the defendant on the day of the assault. Nathan Black testified that Fair had told him on Saturday that he had a job in Wellford and wanted to catch the train in White Stone on Monday morning. "He missed that train, though, and stopped at my house right after," explained Black.

Will Glenn followed, noting that he was at Black's house when Will Fair stopped. "I was the one that said he should catch the electric in Glendale. He took off in a hurry right after that."

At this point, Sanders called for Vergie Moore. "Miss Moore, did you see the alleged victim on the road on the Monday morning of the supposed assault?"

"Yes, Will Fair was ahead of her on the road, and I saw her go into the house."

"Now, Miss Moore, this is very important," said Sanders slowly and with emphasis. "Did Mr. Fair go into that house?"

"No," exclaimed Vergie with conviction. "He did not, he went right past. Annie Clowney was with me, and she saw that too."

"Objection," cried Albert Hill. "Miss Moore cannot say what someone else saw."

"Sustained," said the judge. "The jury will disregard the statement about Miss Clowney."

Unperturbed, Sanders had one last question for Vergie Moore. "Miss Moore did you know about the alleged attack?"

"Yes, we found out about it when we came by on our way back from the store."

When Sanders returned to his seat, the assistant to the prosecutor, C. P. Sims, rose to question Vergie. "Miss Moore, you say that Will Fair did not go in the house. Do you know for sure that he did not return and go in after you were gone?"

Vergie shook her head. "Well, I'm pretty sure." This remark brought laughter from the audience and a pounding of the gavel by Judge Gage.

Sims was regretting having asked the question, but he tried to recover. "And how can you be 'pretty sure'?"

"'Cause he was ahead of us, and we never saw him turn around."

Sims sat down and Vergie was dismissed. Several others testified to having seen Will Fair on the way to Glendale, that he had missed the train in White Stone, and was trying to get to Wellford.

Becoming tired of this, Hill announced that the prosecution was willing to agree that Will Fair had missed a train and walked to Glendale to catch the electric car. Judge Gage agreed and asked the defense to move on with its case.

"We call Mr. Will Fair to the stand," responded Sanders.

Will walked slowly to the front and was sworn in by the clerk. He sat with his eyes to the floor and his hands clasped in front of him. Cotesworth Sanders' first question surprised everyone.

"Will, are you guilty of the alleged criminal assault?"

221

"I ain't the man, captain," replied the defendant. "I didn't go into that house."

Sanders smiled. "Now that we've got that out of the way, would you tell us a little about yourself?"

"Well, sir, I was born at Bishop in Union County, about four miles from Jonesville. I've been a farmer most of my life."

"Do you have a family, Will?" Sanders knew about Rosa and the children, and he had instructed Fair on how to answer the question. He didn't want Albert Hill to be able to question Will's truthfulness.

"My wife's name is Rosa, and we have four children. We don't have a marriage license, but we've been together for fourteen years."

"So Rosa is what we call a common law wife?"

"I guess so," agreed Fair.

"Will, can you tell us about your actions on the morning of August 18?"

Will recounted his movements, most of which had already been mentioned by other witnesses. He told how he had intended to catch a train at White Stone, and then take another train from Spartanburg to Wellford, where he had a construction job. He'd taken his son to a job at Thompson's, which caused him to miss the train. He described his stop at Nathan Black's and the suggestion by Glenn to go to Glendale to catch the electric car to Spartanburg, advice he had followed. He gave names of people he had met on the way.

"Did you see the alleged victim on the road that morning?" asked Sanders.

"Yes, captain, I did." This remark brought a low moan from some in the audience.

"Tell us about what you saw, Will. What was the alleged victim doing?"

"I saw her coming down the path to the road, and she stopped while I went on by. I think she was tying her shoe."

"Did you know the woman, Will? Did you know who she was?"

Will was slow to answer this question, although his lawyers had told him it was important that he tell the truth. "I thought she was maybe the wife of Mr. Potter."

"Had you met her before, Will?"

"No, sir, but I knew a little about the Potters. I worked as a hired man on one of their farms a couple of times."

"Will, after you passed by and were walking ahead of the woman, did you ever look back at her?

Fair looked down, then back up, facing his lawyer. "I don't rightly remember, sir. I guess I did notice that she'd gone into the house."

"You mean her house, the one you never went in."

"Yes, sir."

"Then what happened, Will?"

"I got to Glendale, but the electric hadn't come along just yet, so I bought myself a watermelon at the grocery." Fair was silent for a moment, then remembered something else. "I gave some of the melon to a man working in the yard of the house next to the grocery. His name is Morse, Arthur Morse."

Fair went on to tell about a man riding in on a horse and shouting about the rape in White Stone "by a big nigger."

"Did you think the man might have been talking about you?" inquired Sanders.

"No. No. No reason for me to think that. Not 'till they arrested me at the train station."

"Is it true that you had bought a train ticket for Wellford?"

"Yes, sir, Mr. Sanders. I was waitin' for that train when the policeman arrested me."

"Thank you, Will," said Sanders. "That's all I have for this witness, your Honor."

Albert Hill was invited to begin his cross-examination, and he stood in front of the defense table as he began his interrogation. "Now Will," he said and stopped. "Is it all right if I call you Will?"

"It's all right with me," answered Will, although he couldn't help but wonder if the prosecutor could simply not bring himself to say Mr. Fair.

"Thank you, Will. Now you say that you saw Mrs. Potter on the path from the Foster house. What did you think, did you say to yourself, now ain't that a pretty woman?"

"No, sir. I just noticed that she had stooped to tie her shoe." Will figured he probably had thought such a thing, but there was no way that lawyer could know that.

"And you went by the house did you, Will?"

"I did."

"But Will, didn't you turn around and come back through the woods to the back door of that house? Were you surprised to find it unlocked?"

Will refused to fall into that trap. "No, I did not. I don't know 'bout that door or whether it was unlocked or not. I was nowhere near it, I was just goin' on up that road, scared I'd be late to catch that electric."

"Aren't you lying to us, Will. The alleged victim explained carefully to us how she was attacked, and she identified you as the attacker. Are you calling her a liar?"

"I'm not callin' her nothin'," Will said loudly, almost shouting. "I just know I ain't the man who did it."

"But she identified you," insisted Hill. "She described you perfectly on the day of the attack, and she picked you out of a lineup four days later."

"I reckon she saw me in the road," admitted Fair, "but she never saw me in that house, 'cause I was never in there."

Albert Hill sighed and shook his head. "I have no more questions."

Arthur Morse was the next witness, and he told of talking with Will Fair, and that Fair had shared his watermelon with him. Fair was quite anxious about whether the electric car had come along or not, he remarked. Albert Hill had one question for him.

"Mr. Morse, when you heard about the rape, did you think that Will Fair might be the one who did it?"

"Well, I knew he come from that direction, so I did wonder a bit. We were both aware of the looks we were gittin' from the white folks."

After Hill had sat down again, the defense called for Dr. L. J. Blake. A short middle-aged man strode up to the witness stand. A local physician, he carried about himself an air of authority. Attorney Sanders followed him and waited while the clerk swore him in. After a

224

few warm-up questions about his background and his practice, Sanders asked him a critical question.

"Dr. Blake. In your medical opinion, could a woman who had difficulties with her monthly period be subject to unusual reactions, even hallucinations?"

"Yes, there have been such cases. Women, during the time of their menstruation, can have what is called menstrual psychosis. In such a state it has been reported that patients can have delusions, hallucinations, confusion, depersonalization, insomnia, emotional instability, and unexpected behaviors."

"Is it possible, Doctor, that such a patient might believe she had been attacked, even raped."

"Yes, I believe it is possible."

"Thank you, Dr. Blake. That is all I have."

"Dr. Blake," said Albert Hill, trying to keep calm, but eager to refute this testimony. "Are you a specialist in the new field of psychiatry?"

"No, I am not," admitted Blake.

"Did you examine Mrs. Potter yourself?"

"No."

"Then how can you give such a statement as you gave to Mr. Sanders a few moments ago?"

"With all due respect, sir, my response was general information concerning menstrual distress. It is based on reading and study I have done on this subject." Blake knew his testimony would be attacked in this way. He had wanted to justify his opinions up front, but the defense team thought it better to bring it out under questioning by the prosecution.

Albert Hill was surprised that Blake would have knowledge on this subject, and though he suspected he might have been led into an uncomfortable situation, he plunged ahead. "Can you enlighten us Dr. Blake on how you happen to be an expert on women's monthly difficulties."

"I do not claim to be an expert, but I have read the two volumes written by the famous German psychologist, R. V. Krafft-Ebing. One is entitled *Psychopathia Sexualis,* and the other is called *Psychosis*

*Menstrualis.* Both have been translated into English, and I have personal copies."

Attorney Sanders was on his feet, approaching the bench and holding a volume in each hand. "Excuse me, your Honor, but if it please the court, I would like to enter these two volumes into evidence at this time."

There was a noticeable stir in the crowd, and a momentary annoyance in the judge's manner. "You might have picked a better method than to interrupt the prosecution's examination of this witness, Mr. Sanders. However, it appears to be relevant evidence and perhaps appropriate at this time. Your evidence is so entered. Please continue, Mr. Hill."

"So, Dr. Blake, the opinion you expressed earlier is based, we are to believe, on your reading and interpretation of the material in these books." Hill glanced at his co-counsel, whose return gaze was one of puzzlement. Neither of them had expected this testimony.

"Yes, that is true. There are many cases described in these books, and the possible behaviors I mentioned are carefully laid out in the case histories." Blake was feeling very confident.

"Have you personally observed any of these behaviors in any of your own patients?"

"I have seen great distress and fainting spells."

"Hallucinations? Have you seen the kind of hallucinations you seem to be implying might be present in this case?"

"I cannot say that I have."

Hill nodded his head, as if he were satisfied. "I have no more questions of this witness," he said and returned to his seat.

Ralph Carson rose and walked to the stand, facing Dr. Blake with a slight smile. "Dr. Blake, is it still your opinion, based on your academic studies, that a woman experiencing severe menstrual distress might believe she had been attacked?"

"Yes, it is."

Carson turned and walked back to the defense table, nodding at Will Fair, who looked up in appreciation. Sanders stood at his seat and addressed the judge. "Your Honor, the defense rests."

As the noise level in the room began to rise, Judge Gage pounded his gavel. "There will be a ten minute recess, and then we will hear the closing arguments."

———⊷———

When the court reconvened, Albert Hill strode purposefully to the jury box and stood quietly for a moment, facing the jurors.

"Gentlemen of the jury: as I said at the beginning of this trial this morning, this is a very simple case. You have heard a young woman describe to you very calmly and carefully how she was attacked in her own house by a Negro man, a man who assaulted her and gained carnal knowledge of her in a brutal way. She later identified that man in a lineup at the state penitentiary and has not wavered in her testimony in any way. We have proved that the man she identified, the defendant, Will Fair, was in the vicinity of the crime scene at the time of the crime. He, himself, admitted that he had seen her in the road near her house.

He, of course, claims he never went in the house, but she saw him there and declared, without any doubt, that he was her attacker. If you believe her story, then you have no choice but to deliver a verdict of guilty as charged. That is your duty, and you must do it."

The audience gave a low murmur of appreciation for the short and clear argument of the prosecutor. All watched with anticipation as Cotesworth Sanders took his place in front of the jury.

"Gentlemen. We are thankful for the very brief and artful argument given by my worthy opponent, Mr. Hill. He would have you believe that the case is very simple, that it really boils down to believing one person and not the other. Clearly, he is confident that the voice of a prominent young white woman will be heard and believed over that of a Negro laborer. But, it is the prosecution's duty to prove, beyond a reasonable doubt, that the defendant, Will Fair, went into the Potter home where he assaulted Mrs. Potter and is guilty of rape. In fact, there are two very big problems with the carrying out of this duty by the prosecution. First of all, they have offered not one iota of proof that Mr. Will Fair ever entered the Potter house. Secondly, there is no real proof that Mrs. Potter was physically assaulted.

We have shown you a variety of witnesses who validated Mr. Fair's good character and the account of his own actions. He missed the train from White Stone to Spartanburg, where he intended to make a connection to go to a job in Wellford. It was suggested that he go to Glendale to catch the electric streetcar that could get him to the railroad station in time to get to Wellford as planned. On the way to Glendale it was necessary to pass the home of Mrs. Potter. She saw him on the road as did others. He saw her, as he clearly testified. But he never went in the house and absolutely no one saw him do so.

Mr. Hill has made a strong point about the alleged victim's identification of Mr. Fair. We submit that this identification was based entirely on the fact that she saw the defendant pass by her on the road. She saw him clearly and described very precisely what he was wearing. It is important to note that his clothes that she described and that he had on when he was arrested were not torn, nor had any stains or signs of a struggle of any kind. Her description of the attack, that she saw only the attacker's feet, and how he grabbed her from behind and threw her down, make it hard to believe she could have had a good enough look at him to have described him as she did. Also, it should be remembered that she at first had identified a different man, before changing her mind.

On the second point, Dr. Lancaster could not affirm that there was any physical evidence of an assault on Mrs. Potter. We do know she was having distress because of her monthly period. Could this have been a reason for her to believe she had been raped? There is no way to know that for sure, but the testimony of two physicians casts some reasonable doubt. If there was a crime committed, there is absolutely no proof that the perpetrator was Will Fair.

You men of this jury have a solemn duty. We know that you want to do it and provide justice in this case. Remember that a guilty verdict means that the defendant has been proved guilty beyond a reasonable doubt. There are two very reasonable doubts in this case that you must keep in mind. The first is that there is not even a shred of evidence that Will Fair went into the Potter house. The second is that there is no physical proof that the alleged crime even happened. Based on these two facts, your verdict can only be 'Not Guilty!'

Thank you for your service."

# FIFTEEN

# The Verdict

Some quiet conversations broke out around the room. Howard Walters had closed his business early and, joined by Henry Fernandes, had managed to get into the courtroom during the recess.

"What do you think, Henry?" Howard whispered. "It may not be the easy win that Albert Hill promised us."

"They may get that damned nigger off," responded Fernandes. "We should've tried harder to get him strung up when we had the chance."

Sam McCravy nudged his friend Sam Nicholls. "That close by Cotesworth was pretty impressive, Sam. The defense team has done a nice job."

Nicholls' reply was interrupted by Judge Gage, who called the room to order. "Thank you for your fine cooperation throughout this trial," he told the audience. "I know of the intense interest in this trial, and your behavior has been exemplary. Now I ask for your patience for a few more minutes while I address the jury."

Complete silence descended on the courtroom. All eyes focused on the jurors as Judge Gage began his charge to them.

"Gentlemen of the jury: as I stated to the grand jury on Monday, so I state to you now that a case like this not only tries the prisoner at the bar but it even tries the very integrity of our institutions.

"Job cried out in his despair, 'Oh, that I had a day between Thee and me.' You, gentlemen of the jury, are the day that stands between the bar and the penalty of the law. You know what rape is—the carnal knowledge of a woman by force against her will.

"The defendant does not deny, or, I should say more properly, his counsel do not deny, that on the day named at the time of the assault, defendant was in that vicinity, but the contention is bold and strong that if there was any wrong done to her this defendant did not do it.

"The jury may take one of three views in this case: (a) That defendant did it. (b) That some other Negro did it. (c) That it was not done at all.

"The human mind is a wonderful thing. The most of us stand just on the border line between consciousness and unconsciousness, and sometimes just one step carries us beyond the veil from what we see and hear and know to that which we do not see, do not hear, do not know. We are wonderfully made, and woman is more wonderfully made than man.

"The object of this trial is not to ascertain who did this thing, or, if it was done at all. The object is to find whether this defendant did it, and the law requires that you must be satisfied beyond a reasonable doubt that he did it. The testimony ought to lead you to certain conviction, and stand your feet on the rock of truth, and cause them to be firmly fixed there. If the testimony so leads you, so declare. If the testimony leaves you uncertain—if it leaves you in doubt, then it is your duty to write a verdict of 'Not guilty.' Such a verdict, I will say, does not mean that this woman has falsified, it does not mean that she has sworn untruthfully—that, I say is not necessarily implied. I have tried cases like this before, more than one of them. It is not improper to state in this connection that I tried a case in Columbia against a very respectable doctor at the instance of a very respectable lady patient of his. She swore point-blank that he raped her while she was under his care as her physician. The testimony of the doctors, and the preponderating testimony in the case was that she thought she had been dealt with wrongfully, but had not been touched. She swore in absolutely good faith. I tell you now what I told the jury in that case. I told them if they believed the woman, and if they believed what she said was true, and believed that under all the circumstances she had the power to tell the truth, they should find a verdict of guilty. If it, on the other hand, left them in doubt, they ought not to convict. This is your case. It is not my case. It is not the case of counsel. It is not the case of the congregated and waiting public. It is the case of these twelve men, and in the sight of God and under your oaths it is your duty to write a verdict as you see the truth.

"The more I preside as judge, and the more I see of courts and witnesses, the more I feel like crying out and pleading 'guilty' myself. How often I feel like uncovering my head and saying, 'I am guilty' instead of passing on the guilt of my fellowmen. How solemn is this thing of passing judgment on one's fellowmen! It is a delicate power—a great power—and one that ought to be exercised in a spirit of devotion with uncovered heads.

"You may say, 'Guilty.' You may say, 'Guilty with recommendation to mercy.' You may say, 'Not guilty.' Take the record gentlemen and write your verdict."

---

It was 4:57 p.m. as the bailiff and another guard led the jury out to the jury room. Sheriff James White and three other officers led the defendant back to his cell. A few members of the audience left the room, but many, expecting a quick decision by the jury stayed behind. Albert Hill stepped up beside Cotesworth Sanders as the lawyers filed out.

"Very clever, Cotesworth," said Albert with a quiet chuckle. "How did you know about Blake?

"Pretty impressive, hey Albert. He came to see me on Wednesday and told us what he knew."

"Well, it's made this verdict a bit harder to predict."

"So, do you still think our client is guilty, Albert?" asked Ralph Carson.

"Ralph, what do you expect me to say to a question like that? I wouldn't have charged him if I didn't think he was guilty."

"Well, I suppose we all thought he was guilty in the beginning, but maybe things have changed."

Hill laughed. "You don't think I'm going to admit that you guys are that good, do you?"

Nothing more was said as the two teams of lawyers went their own way.

In the jury room, the 12 men had taken seats around a big center table. The bailiff had directed them to choose a foreman, and then set about reaching a verdict.

"I nominate Joseph Lee to be our foreman," said A. F. Burton.

"Who is Joseph Lee?" asked N. W. Bearden. When Lee identified himself, Bearden asked, "Where are you from?"

"I'm from Landrum and proud of it," asserted Lee.

"Hell," grunted D. L. Poole with a hearty laugh. "What good ever come out of Landrum?"

"Let's get this job over with," growled Donald Young. "I second the nomination."

After a bit more conversation, it was agreed that Lee should be the foreman.

"Thank you men," said Lee, who had actually hoped to be chosen. He suggested that each person give his name and hometown, and this was done.

"Let's get to it, then," said Young. "It ought to be easy enough. That nigger's bound to be guilty. Let's vote on it and get out of here."

"Hold on," said A. M. Sondley. "I don't think that is clear at all. We hold the defendant's life in our hands, and he deserves to be treated like any other human being."

"Don't lecture me," shouted Young. "I can't imagine any day when I would take the word of a brute like that over a young white woman."

"If that's how you feel," said Sondley, "you should have told the lawyers at the beginning, and the judge would have let you go home."

Before Young could respond, Joseph Lee spoke up. "Let's calm down here gentlemen. We all agreed that we could be fair in coming to a verdict. You heard what the judge said in his charge. Let's try to talk about the evidence we heard and recall the testimony."

Young was angry and wanted to continue the dispute, but he could see that the others didn't like what he had said. He decided to hold his tongue and wait for a better time to try to sway the others for a guilty verdict.

"They never proved that Fair went into that house," noted A. F. Burton. "I think that gives us more than a reasonable doubt."

"I was convinced at first, particularly after the woman's testimony," said S. E. Brian. "But the testimony of Dr. Lancaster shook me a bit. If the man hit her in the head with a lath, there would have to be a bruise on her head."

The conversations went on for some time before D. L. Poole brought up a topic that was on everyone's mind. "There's something that needs to be said, here, men. What happens if we were to find this man not guilty? There was a mob ready to hang him before. What will they do now?"

"We can't let that enter our thinking," exclaimed Sondley. "Public sentiment can't figure in this."

"That's great in theory, Mr. Sondley," answered Poole. "but not so great in practice. If we do the wrong thing, it could mean that Negro's life anyway."

Everyone started to talk at once, and Lee struggled to get some order. Nearly two hours expired before Lee suggested that a vote be held.

"I move that we vote 'not guilty'," proposed Sondley. "I'll vote yes on that motion."

"I second the motion," said Burton.

Joseph Lee was quick to go forward on this line, preferring that a yes vote be in favor of acquittal. No one objected and the vote was held. There were five yes votes and seven against the motion.

"We're a long way from a decision, folks," said Lee. "Perhaps it is time for us to have supper."

That suggestion met with unanimous approval, and Lee notified the bailiff.

"Let me check with the judge," was the reply.

There was still a sizable crowd in the courtroom and in the halls outside. Judge Gage was disappointed with the news.

"Are they even close?" he asked.

"They are pretty much split down the middle, far as I can tell," replied the bailiff.

"Inform the crowd that there will be no verdict this evening," said Gage with a sigh. "Take them to the jail dining room for supper, then over to the Gresham Hotel for the night. "I will have the arrangements made for them. The Huff-Hughes jury is in there, too."

———•———

Jake Potter had taken his wife home after she testified, and then asked his father to go back into town with him to watch more of the trial. The guard at the door knew the two men, and agreed that they should be allowed in, although he warned them that they would have to stand. They had arrived just after the dinner recess. Now, hearing the announcement that there would be no verdict this evening, they returned home. There was little conversation for several minutes. Finally, Jake broke the silence.

"What do you think, Dad? It isn't goin' quite the way I expected."

"That damned Blake," sputtered Tom Potter. "I've a mind to pay him a visit and tell him what I think of him and his hellish testimony."

Jake had been greatly shaken by Blake's testimony, but he was calmer than his father about such things. "It didn't help, but neither did Lancaster's." Although he didn't want to admit it to his father, Jake had his own doubts about his wife's story. "I'm glad Abigail didn't have to hear what Blake said," he added.

They were driving Tom Potter's Model T Ford, and as they drove into Jake Potter's front yard, Abigail and Charlotte Potter came out onto the front porch. Charlotte had been left at the house to keep her daughter-in-law company. Jake had not wanted to leave her alone.

"Did they find him guilty?" asked Charlotte expectantly as the men departed the car. Abigail stood beside her with a worried look.

"No verdict yet," explained Tom. "The jury's locked up for the night."

Charlotte was clearly a bit surprised. "I thought this was supposed to be an easy case," she said.

"Not so easy as we thought, Mom," said Jake just before kissing his wife on the cheek. "The defense put up a strong case."

"But how could they?" Charlotte persisted. "I thought there was no question they had the right man."

"Well, the prosecution could never prove decisively that the Negro went into the house." Jake thought he would emphasize that point, and not the testimony of the two doctors.

Abigail gave a short cry, and went back into the house. Charlotte watched her go in, before turning again to the two men. "She thought she gave strong testimony. Is that wrong?"

"She did a very good job," said Jake. "There was no problem with that."

"Then, I don't see how those men on the jury will not believe her," insisted Charlotte.

"Well, they probably will in the end. Let's not talk about it right now. Is there anything for supper? Dad and I are famished."

Sheriff White had seen to it that Will Fair was returned to his cell and some supper delivered to him there. White was looking forward to getting back to the residence, where he hoped Viola had his supper waiting. On the way there, he was intercepted by Robert Gantt.

"James, I need to talk to you about a couple of things."

"Yes, Robert, what is it?"

"The defense did quite a job, there, James. We need to plan for a situation in which the jury comes back with a 'not guilty' decision."

"You think that's really possible?" asked the sheriff. "When Mrs. Potter identified Fair at the pen down in Columbia, I pretty much thought it was all over."

"The point is, what do we do if he is acquitted? He wouldn't be safe."

"Sanders and Carson talked to me about that. They believe we have to get him out of town."

"I agree. How do we do that?"

Sheriff White stood quietly for a moment, before replying. "I'll check the train schedules, and my deputies and I will make sure he gets away safely."

"That's good. I'll be glad to help with the cost," said Gantt.

"The lawyers told me they are willing to help with that also," affirmed White. "What else is on your mind?"

"I'm worried about Will Fair's wife. I had promised I'd bring her to the trial, but decided it wasn't wise, as she might not be safe herself."

The sheriff smiled. "I should have known you would be concerned for her. You've been a real friend to her I must say."

"I wonder if it would be all right with you if I brought her in to see him yet tonight. Otherwise, if he is acquitted, she wouldn't see him at all, and maybe for a very long time."

"It's all right with me, but not the children, Robert. Just the wife."

"Thank you, James. I'm on my way out there right now."

Viola White was waiting for her husband, greeting him with a question as he entered the kitchen. "What was the verdict?"

"Nothing yet, sweetheart," answered James, giving her a quick kiss before going to the stove where he lifted the lid to the large pot.

"But didn't you think it would be over pretty quick?" asked Viola, following her husband to the stove.

"Well, we may have been wrong about that," said White. "I'm mighty hungry, and that chicken and noodles looks awfully good."

"Well, sit down honey, and I'll fix you up real quick. I fed the children earlier." She put two plates on the table along with knives and forks. "There's biscuits, too," she added.

There was silence between them for a few minutes before Viola returned to her inquiry. "They told me that the jury retired around five o'clock, so I thought they would have come back before you came home."

"Sanders and Carson made a strong defense," explained James, "and the jury is not even close was the word we got. The judge sent them to the Gresham for the night."

"James," exclaimed Viola. "Could there be trouble here? What if they don't convict him?"

"That question is on everyone's mind, Vi," answered White. "If that happens, we'll get him out of town."

"I'm worried, James. I heard the crowds were really big."

"They are, but we'll be ready."

"My god," replied Viola. "Sometimes I wish you'd lost that last election."

The sheriff laughed. "You'll probably get your wish at the next one."

———•———

The Gresham Hotel was just three years old, built in 1910. A convenient inn for rail travellers, it was located on Magnolia Street, not far from the Union Depot, and also not far from the courthouse. Its seven stories towered over neighboring buildings. The twelve jurors had been escorted to the hotel by two officers, and taken up to their quarters on the sixth floor. The single elevator was a source of interest and delight to several of the men who had never seen one in a hotel before. Two of them had slipped out of their room near midnight, intending to experience another elevator ride. They had not reckoned with the two officers left on guard in the hallway and who took a dim view of the jurors' intent. The two men were quickly ushered back into their room.

Morning found all twelve men on the way down to the New York Restaurant where breakfast was awaiting them. They were to be back in the jury room by 9:00 a. m. to continue their deliberations. Judge Gage watched them come in just as the waiter brought him his second cup of coffee. The Hughes-Huff jury had gone back to work earlier, and word had come that it had reached a verdict. That was good news for the judge, who was still hoping that both trials would be over in time for him to go home by the evening.

Over on Church Street, the Olympia Café was filled with customers. Howard Walters and Henry Fernandes were seated in their usual booth when joined by Jason Calo.

"Hello Jason," was the greeting from Walters. "Haven't seen you in a while."

"I have to work for a living," he growled as he took a seat. "What's goin' on with the big trial? I heard there was no verdict yet."

"You heard right," said Howard. "Deliberations start again at nine this morning, or so we've been told."

Calo looked at Fernandes, who shook his head. "I thought you said this case was a sure thing," said Jason, glaring at Walters.

"It's what Hill told me and I think he believed it," said Howard. "Those damned defense lawyers have muddied the waters quite a bit. It ain't clear what this jury might do."

"Hell, they're white men ain't they," snarled Jason. "They ought to know how to do their duty."

"The question is," interjected Fernandes, "what do we do if he gets off?"

"We find where he lives and get our justice," exclaimed Calo. "He won't have no sheriff and no deputies guardin' him there."

"My guess is they'll get the bastard out of town. It's what they did before," noted Walters.

"Then let's get a mob together and get down to the train station," said Calo. "We'll grab him when they bring him there and string him up, just like we meant to all along."

"I don't think so," said Howard. "The sheriff as much as promised that he'd arrest me if I was involved in something like that again. I think you'd have to kill him to do what you want, and they'd fry you for that."

"So, you think that bastard is goin' to get away with rapin' a white woman, and there's nothin' to be done?" asked Fernandes.

"Unless the jury finds him guilty," replied Walters. "The fact is, I'm not even sure myself that he did it."

"Hell, Howard you may as well turn in your Klan card," said Henry with disgust. "You can pay for my coffee," he added as he turned and walked out.

Calo threw a dollar on the table and walked away, saying nothing.

———·———

Back in the jury room, Joseph Lee tried to get the men focused on their task.

"Let's start off by having another vote on yesterday's motion by Mr. Sondley, to see if any minds have changed overnight," proposed Lee. "A yes vote means you are voting for a 'not guilty' verdict."

There was agreement to take another vote, and the result was a 6-6 tie.

"Ah," said Lee. "One vote has changed. Was that you Mr. Brian?"

"Yes," agreed Brian. "I believe if Will Fair had attacked that woman the way she described it, she would have had some bruises."

The discussions continued for more than an hour, with each juror expressing an opinion. Lee was trying to think of a way to gain some movement.

"Is there anyone here who truly believes that Will Fair attacked Mrs. Potter in her home?"

The room remained in complete silence for several moments. Finally, Donald Young spoke up. "Well I'm the one who insisted that we declare the man guilty and be done with it. I have to admit now that I have come to believe that there is some reasonable doubt. There is no way, however, that I could vote 'not guilty' and face that crowd out there."

This comment prompted Poole to speak again. "I agree with that last statement. What would happen if we acquit this man?"

"We're not supposed to consider such things," insisted Sondley as he had several times already.

W. W. Bearden, who had mostly been quiet, brought up a new idea. "Look, if we just remain undecided, the judge will declare a mistrial. Let another jury decide this case when the public is less agitated."

This suggestion brought excited agreement from four others. It was clear now to the foreman that none of the men actually thought Fair was guilty. That was his own feeling and his conviction had continued to strengthen.

"Men," exclaimed Joseph Lee. "If none of us think that Fair committed the alleged act, we must acquit him. There is no other way."

"I believe that Will Fair is not guilty," asserted Burnett Bright, "and I believe we need to end this right now and vote to acquit." Bright was from Wellford, and knew about the construction work that Fair had claimed was his destination.

G. P. Stephens announced that he was in favor of acquittal and R. H. Lethco sided with Bearden.

"What about you, Mr. Leonard," asked Lee. "We haven't heard much from you."

"I guess I'm the silent type," chuckled Leonard. "But I'm from Greer, and we Greer folks like to stick together. I go along with Young, there."

It was clear now to Lee where everyone stood, and two more votes at 6-6 bracketing some intense discussions convinced him that the jury was hopelessly deadlocked. This was communicated to Judge Gage.

The judge entered the courtroom and took his seat at the bench. He directed the bailiff to bring the jury in. The room was packed just as it had been the day before and the lawyers filed in to take their places at their respective tables. Will Fair was dressed as he had been on Friday, and the shackles were removed before the jurors entered. The noise level in the room was high, for the spectators assumed that a verdict had been reached.

"What do you think, Sam?" asked Sam Nicholls of Sam McCravy, the two lawyers at their usual spot at the back of the room.

"Not guilty," answered McCravy.

"Five dollars says you're wrong," challenged Nicholls.

"You're on," was the reply.

The judge's gavel banged the room into silence as the jurors filed in. When they had been seated, the judge asked them a question.

"Have you reached a verdict, Foreman Lee?"

"No, sir, we have not," said Lee. "We are hopelessly tied up, Your Honor."

"Is there anything I can say to you that will help you in arriving at a conclusion in this case?"

"I fear not," replied Lee. "We are hopelessly disagreed."

Judge Gage shook his head, then entered into a long soliloquy.

"I have had juries so often say that to me, and then go out and find a verdict within ten minutes. I tried a case in Charleston where the jury was out two nights and a day and said they could not agree, and that jury agreed in ten minutes after that.

"You cannot agree if you each make different points—if one man sets his head this way and another sets his head that way and another

another way. If the members of the jury get to combatting views, and especially, if they lose temper, and if they get up that thing called 'pride of opinion' they will never agree. But if they put everything under their feet, and go at it in the spirit of truth seeking, in the spirit of honesty--I mean, honesty with yourselves—let every man, every juror go down into the bottom of his own heart and uncover himself before his Maker and his Maker alone and enquire calmly and quietly what is the truth, and, when you do that, and see the truth in the small and silent chambers of your heart, and, if you do that and own it and proclaim it, you will all be of one mind.

"The court was called for the trial of this case and nothing else. It has been held at an enormous expense in money, in time and nerve. I have been on the bench now sixteen years and I have never held a court that caused me such nervous strain. It is too much to put on anybody again and too much to put on you.

"It is next to impossible for us in matters of this kind to put away all outside considerations—I speak from my own experience, and out of my own heart and my own knowledge. I was raised on a plantation with Negroes and I think I know them as well as any man knows them. I know their weakness and I know our own weakness. They are here by a strange providence, but they are here. How our final relationship with them is to be determined no man knows and no man need question himself. If we go to our duty day by day and do justly man by man the end will come, and the One who made us and who made them and who put us here together, will bring us all safely to some common end.

"I know that men are almost incapable of weighing a nice balance of truth where the contest is between one race and another race, especially where the one race is charged with the awful crime of rape. I know the awful anxiety and the awful peril our country women are subjected to. I was raised in the country, and I know its duties and beauties, its glories and its perils, its joys, and its sorrows and burdens, but the only question for you in this case is did this man assault this woman, and under all the testimony is it true beyond a reasonable doubt. It if is, it is your duty to so declare, it is your duty to say, 'guilty.' If it is not true as you see it, if it is not true beyond a reasonable doubt then to write a verdict of 'guilty' in answer to anybody's demand would be to crucify the law, to degrade our courts and to stultify you men. I know there is such a thing as public opinion that drives and whirls men like a sandstorm, but I tell you this: a wave of public opinion in times of excitement is sometimes the most uncertain thing in the world. The only certain thing is the knowledge which points to the truth and which never errs. If you follow it, you are in the sure path, and, if you leave it, you are in quagmires all the way.

"Now gentlemen, I do not mean to take from you the prerogative of deciding the truth. If you believe the charges in the indictment have been proved by the state beyond a reasonable doubt, it is your duty to say so, but, if you're left by the testimony in a state of uncertainty and your minds are unsettled, it is your duty to say so. I cannot reach your inner consciousness; these men cannot. You can, and the God who presides over you can.

"I am not going to say another word to you. I am done. But I don't want to leave this city with this case unsettled. The Supreme Court has directed me to sit at this court, and it has been ordered by the governor. It has been held at great expense. To order a mistrial would be to have all this furor and excitement continue and through another term of court. I will confidently wait upon you with the expectation that will find a verdict in this case. You may retire."

Relieved that this long statement had ended, Joseph Lee turned to his fellow jurors with a questioning look. Burton, who was next to him, leaned over and whispered something to Lee, who then addressed the judge.

"Your Honor, could we have your original charge read to us again?"

Judge Gage directed the court stenographer to read the charge. When he had finished, the jury filed out and returned to their deliberations in the jury room.

"That was quite a pronouncement," observed Cotesworth Sanders to his colleague, Ralph Carson. "Do you think it will help us or hurt us?"

"It won't hurt us, I think," remarked Carson, "but who knows whether it helps."

Will Fair watched his lawyers talk, wondering what it meant for him. He guessed it was good that the jury was having some trouble deciding he was guilty. Still, his pessimistic view about his chances would not go away. He had been unable to sleep the previous night, knowing that a decision was being made about whether his life was to be ended. Magistrate Gantt had been to see Rosa, and he had come in very late to tell Will that they had decided against bringing her in to the trial. Gantt thought it too risky for her sake, and Will agreed. He knew that he would only see her and his family if the verdict went against him. He had agreed with Gantt as well as with Sanders and Carson that he must leave town if he were acquitted.

In the jury room, Joseph Lee was determined to lead his fellow jurors to reach a decision. He wasn't optimistic, but perhaps the judge had helped to change some minds. He knew that no one really believed that Will Fair was guilty of rape.

"What do you think men?" he asked. "Have any minds been changed."

"Mr. Bearden," said A.M. Sondley. "I know that you are very concerned that a not guilty verdict may cause a riot that will bring great shame on all of us in Spartanburg County. I respect that concern, but you heard what Judge Gage said. We must trust our own minds and not public opinion. Still, I think all of us here realize that there is plenty of reasonable doubt in this case. Have you changed your mind?"

Bearden was annoyed at being put on the spot, but he could not deny the truth in what Sondley was saying. "I suppose you're right, Sondley," Bearden said after a short delay. "It isn't fair to put this burden on other men, even though it might be safer. We have to get this over with. I am ready to vote yes on the old motion."

I. J. Leonard was sitting next to Young and patted him on the shoulder. "I'm tired of all this," he announced. "I vote yes."

"All right," exclaimed the foreman. "That makes eight votes for acquittal. Who else wants to talk."

"It ain't just the worry about a riot," said Young. "I'm still grapplin' with how I explain to my neighbors that I took the word of a black man over that of a white woman."

"You don't have to look at it like that, Mr. Young," said Brian. "It's like the judge said in his charge. We don't have to think the lady was lyin', she was just confused, maybe, or like the doctor said, it was a result of her condition."

"The doubt is strong," added Burton. "They never proved he went into the house, and they never proved she had really been attacked. I believe she thought that she was, but she was just confused."

"There's plenty you can explain to your friends, Young," said Leonard, eager to change the mind of his friend now that he had come to his own conclusion.

Other men chipped in with similar comments until Young finally raised his right hand. "All right, all right, I give it up. I'll vote yes."

Lee could see that the dam was now broken. He immediately asked for a new vote. It was unanimous. They had a verdict. He sent word to the judge.

No one had left the courtroom, for it was no more than ten minutes since the jury had retired. Judge Gage asked for quiet.

"Ladies and gentlemen, please take your seats and be silent. The jury has reached a verdict and will soon be here to give its report."

"Hope you've got your money ready," murmured Sam Nicholls quietly to McCravy. He retrieved his watch from its pocket, noting that it was just past 12:10.

The spectators remained very quiet, but were on the edges of their seats as the jury took its place in the jury box. Mr. Bennett, the clerk, asked each man to identify himself, then asked whether the jurors had come to an agreement.

"Yes, we have," announced Foreman Lee. He handed the indictment to the clerk.

Bennett read from the document. "Indictment against Will Fair for rape. Not guilty. Joseph Lee, foreman."

The reaction from the audience was subdued, and there seemed to be little evidence that the people were surprised. Sam Nicholls produced five dollars rather quickly and handed it to Sam McCravy as the judge began to speak.

"Gentlemen of the jury: inasmuch as you have had the courage to do your duty in this matter, I ought to have the courage to commend you for it. Time will show that your verdict is right. There are many things that cannot be proven in evidence, but when you sift this thing to the bottom, you will find that your faces have been set in the right direction. I discharge you. This case is closed, and this court is adjourned."

———•———

Ralph Carson turned and offered his hand to Will Fair, who appeared to be stunned. Fair shook the proffered hand and shook it vigorously.

"I can't believe it," he said. "I never thought there was a chance."

Cotesworth Sanders walked around to the front of the table, where he could face the defendant. "Congratulations, Will, you are a free man."

"I guess so," responded Fair, still shaking his head. "A free man."

"Well, not completely free, Will, I'm afraid," said Sanders. "We are all agreed that you had best get out of town. It is being arranged. We'll buy you a train ticket, and give you some spending money."

"Will you tell Rosa, my wife? " asked Fair. "Or did she come to the trial?"

"No, Will. Mr. Gantt thought it best for her that she not be here, which could put her in harm's way," explained Sanders.

"Well, I knew that, but she don't always listen to what she's told."

Both Sanders and Carson laughed at that remark. "Well, that could be said of lots of wives, I suspect," said Carson.

"Magistrate Gantt will get word to her right away," said Sanders.

Albert Hill approached the defense table, extending his hand to Sanders. "Congratulations, Cotesworth, and you, too, Ralph. You men did an outstanding job, and I commend you."

"Thank you, Albert," replied Sanders. "You did a fine job as well, and you were always fair. We surely appreciate that."

Sheriff White appeared, flanked by two of his deputies. He addressed the two defense lawyers. "Mr. Fair is now in your custody, gentlemen. I have sent Officer Vernon to the train depot to buy a ticket for Mr. Fair. There is a train to Asheville that leaves about 3:40 this afternoon. I think it best if you take the prisoner, I mean, the former prisoner, over to the jail. That will be the safest place to wait until time for the train."

"The crowd seems quite passive," observed Carson.

"Yes," agreed Hill. "I don't think the verdict was that big of a surprise to them."

"Perhaps so," said the sheriff, "but moods can change in a hurry, and a dangerous mob could gather very quickly. Mr. Fair will not be completely safe until he is on that train."

The sheriff's advice was agreed upon, and, except for Albert Hill, the men made their way out the door at the front of the courtroom, and across the back courtyard to the jail. Hill was joined by his co-counsel, C. P. Sims, and, together, they walked out the main door at the back of the courtroom and into the hallway. A sizable number of people were still crowded into the hall, but a small path was opened for the prosecutors. A few condolences were offered, but mostly the crowd was quiet.

One man pushed his way close and cried out, "You failed us, Mr. Solicitor. You let that nigger off!" Others tried to force the man back and away from Hill and Sims.

Hill said nothing, but Sims could not resist. "A jury of your peers judged him not guilty. That is our justice system."

"It ain't no justice," shouted the man, but by now the two prosecutors were out the front door, down the steps and on the street. Nothing else was said and they returned to Hill's office.

At the jail, the party was met by the jailor, Mr. Wilson. "E. L.," said the sheriff. "Will you go and retrieve Mr. Fair's property from his cell? We will wait here until it is time for him to be put on the train."

Wilson nodded his assent and went on his assigned errand. The others found seats and prepared for a three hour wait.

"I'll have some food brought in," said Sheriff White, who left to have that arranged.

The time passed slowly. Officer Vernon came in with a train ticket in hand. Sanders and Carson had thought to leave, but the sheriff convinced them that their presence was important and might help to calm any observers who were contemplating some rash action at the train station.

Will Fair was going through a variety of emotions. The foremost thought was that he should just go home and take his chances. When he expressed that to Sanders, it was quickly pointed out that he would be putting his whole family at risk were he to do that. He gave it up finally when Magistrate Gantt came in around three o'clock.

"I've been to see Rosa," Gantt explained. "She was thrilled to hear the news, Will, and she said to tell you that they all loved you and thought it best that you go out of town, at least for a while. She and the children are going to her mother's place to stay until you can come back."

This report was soothing to Will, for it was what he had wanted for Rosa all along. "Thank you Mr. Gantt," he said with great feeling. "You've been so kind to my family."

Sheriff White had sent word to Chief Hayes to ask for some of the city police officers to help escort Will Fair to the rail station. "We need at least eight officers beside me," White said. "Also, Mr. Sanders and Mr. Carson should go with us."

Four city policemen had reported just before 3:30. White selected four of his own deputies. "It is time to go now," he announced.

Twelve men departed through the jail yard gate, out to Choice Street, and down to the Union Depot. There were people scattered about near the station, but nothing that appeared to be threatening. The party passed around the station house and to the trackside, where they could already see the train approaching from the west.

"It's the Number One Train, from Augusta to Asheville," said Officer Vernon, who still held the ticket. "Right on time."

Will Fair suddenly realized that he had never really said anything much to Sheriff White, who was standing just to his right. He turned to the sheriff and tugged on his left sleeve to get his attention.

"Sheriff White, I reckon I owe you my life. I've never thanked you, but I do now. Thank you so much."

"Just doin' my job Mr. Fair. No more, no less."

"But it saved me, you and these lawyers. I ain't able to do enough to thank you."

"Be a good citizen, Will. That's how to thank us."

The train came to a stop and the conductor stepped down. He was taken aback to see so many police officers. "What is it?" he asked. "What is going on?"

"Nothing special," replied Sheriff White. "We just want to see this man put safely on your train." White pointed to Will, as Vernon handed him the ticket.

"Is he a criminal," asked the conductor.

"Nope, he's a free man, same as you and me."

"So why the escort?

"Just for safety reasons," said White. "It's all you need to know."

Will Fair said his goodbyes and stepped up into the passenger car. The conductor helped the remaining passengers aboard, and climbed on himself. The sheriff watched Fair take a seat near a window, and as the train pulled away, gave a sigh of relief.

"You have to feel good," remarked Cotesworth Sanders. "You saved an innocent man's life. One of the greatest things anybody can ever do."

"I had help," replied White. "From my deputies, from you and Mr. Carson, and from Judge Gage, who I thought was mighty fair."

"True, but you're the hero, James."

S. J. Alverson, of the city police had stepped up to the sheriff's side. "I've been exonerated by the city council, Sheriff. Did you know that?"

Alverson had been charged with shooting three men during the mob attack on the jail back on August 18. "Yes, I heard that, and I'm very pleased," said James White. "You were a big help that night."

"You were a real hero, Sheriff. As brave a man as I've ever known, and you saved a life. You must feel it now."

"I do, Officer Alverson. I feel really good."

"There's a line somewhere in the Book of Proverbs that says something like this," said Alverson. "'By the blessing of the upright, the city is exalted.'[2] You have made Spartanburg shine!"

The End

---

[2] Proverbs 11:11

# NOTES AND ACKNOWLEDGEMENTS

This novel is based on an actual incident that happened in Spartanburg, South Carolina in August and September of 1913. It follows the newspaper accounts given in the city's two newspapers, *The Spartanburg Herald* and *The Spartanburg Journal*. William James White was the sheriff of Spartanburg County, and he is a true hero. A Negro laborer named Will Fair was accused of raping a woman and lodged in the county jail. The woman's name was never given in the newspapers, and the court records have been lost. The woman in our story has a fictional name. A good deal of fiction and fictional characters are introduced, but the principal events are basically true. Real names have been used for the principal characters, police officers, juries, and authorities, except for the alleged victim and her family. Conversations and attitudes of these people are my own constructions and not intended to represent those of the actual characters.

To realize what a striking anomaly the episode related in this novel really is, one should be informed about the actual conditions faced by African-Americans in the old South in 1913. An excellent source of such information can be found in "The Warmth of Other Suns" by Isabel Wilkerson. This treatise gives an exhaustive account of the effects of Jim Crow customs and laws in place in the southern states in the first half of the twentieth century.

The help of a number of people in the Spartanburg County Public Libraries was indispensable in the preparation of this novel. They guided me into finding microfilm, maps, books, and other helps. In addition, I received aid from a number of attorneys, including, the Honorable John R. McCravy, III, attorney, Greenwood, S. C., and member of the South Carolina House of Representatives, David Stumbo, Solicitor for South

Carolina 8th Circuit, Joe Barberi, attorney, Mt. Pleasant, Michigan, and Gordon Bloem, attorney, Mt. Pleasant, Michigan. The attorneys tried to keep me somewhat straight in regard to court proceedings, but any errors along those lines are purely that of the author. Thanks go also to Dr. Peter Koper, Emeritus Professor of English Language and Literature at Central Michigan University, Mt. Pleasant, Michigan. His editorial advice was invaluable.

Finally, I wish to thank my beautiful wife, Diane, who read every word while providing editing advice along with the encouragement that kept me going.

Richard J. Fleming

CPSIA information can be obtained
at www.ICGtesting.com
Printed in the USA
LVHW041148201119
637825LV00005B/342/P